my sister's only hope

BOOKS BY ALISON RAGSDALE

Her Last Chance
Someone Else's Child
The Child Between Us
An Impossible Choice
My Husband's Child

Dignity and Grace
The Liar and Other Stories
The Art of Remembering
A Life Unexpected
Finding Heather
The Father-Daughter Club
Tuesday's Socks

my sister's only hope

ALISON RAGSDALE

bookouture

Published by Bookouture in 2025

An imprint of Storyfire Ltd.
Carmelite House
50 Victoria Embankment
London EC4Y 0DZ

www.bookouture.com

The authorised representative in the EEA is Hachette Ireland
8 Castlecourt Centre
Dublin 15 D15 XTP3
Ireland
(email: info@hbgi.ie)

Copyright © Alison Ragsdale, 2025

Alison Ragsdale has asserted her right to be identified as the author of this work.

All rights reserved. No part of this publication may be reproduced, stored in any retrieval system, or transmitted, in any form or by any means, electronic, mechanical, photocopying, recording or otherwise, without the prior written permission of the publishers.

ISBN: 978-1-83525-653-4
eBook ISBN: 978-1-83525-652-7

This book is a work of fiction. Names, characters, businesses, organizations, places and events other than those clearly in the public domain, are either the product of the author's imagination or are used fictitiously. Any resemblance to actual persons, living or dead, events or locales is entirely coincidental.

For my beloved sisters. My forever friends.

Sisters are like stars, you may not always see them, but you know they're always there.

Unknown

PROLOGUE
JUNE – INVERLOCHY, SCOTLAND

There was nothing that could have prepared Kenzie Ford for the phone call that had come straight out of her nightmares, jolting her from sleep just moments ago and turning everything else around her to white noise.

Her mind still groggy from sleep, her heart pounding dangerously as dread filled her insides, Kenzie couldn't rationalise what her brother-in-law, Glenn, had just said, his voice tremulous and strangely muffled on the phone.

'I'll be there as soon as I can,' she croaked, rubbing her gritty eyes as she heard the call end abruptly.

Next to her in their bed, her husband Arran's hand was on her back, and he was talking to her, but his voice was muffled by the turmoil inside her head.

As Kenzie felt the room begin to spin, she pressed her eyes closed and shook her head, unwilling to give Glenn's words life by repeating them.

'Kenzie, love. You need to breathe.' Arran had sat up and his arms were around her, his touch bringing her back into her body. 'What's happened?'

Suddenly light-headed, Kenzie leaned back into him for a moment, feeling the rapid rise and fall of his chest. Letting the phone drop to her thigh, she swallowed hard.

'It was Glenn. There's been an accident on the mountain. Oh, Arran. It's Olivia...'

SPRING

1

APRIL – TWO MONTHS EARLIER

Kenzie sat in the stuffy doctor's office, twisting the strap of her canvas bag around her index finger. Her cotton T-shirt was stuck to her back, and her denim-clad knee was bouncing as she pushed out long slow breaths.

The window across the room was slightly ajar and the floral scent of the apple blossoms on the trees behind the building filtered in on the breeze, a welcome contrast to the smell of disinfectant.

This appointment had been a long time coming and Kenzie's need for a good outcome was all-consuming, her one desire to help grant her older sister Olivia's wish to have a child.

The results of these fertility tests could be the most significant in both Kenzie's and Olivia's lives, and as she waited for Doctor Kennedy to come back into the room, despite her best efforts to remain calm, Kenzie's heart was racing.

She checked her watch for the umpteenth time, then stared out of the window behind the deep, leather-topped desk, the afternoon sky dull, and dotted with ominous, purple-tinged clouds. Shifting in the hard chair, her insides jumped with excitement as she pictured telling Olivia that it was going to happen for her. After several years of disappointment, with Kenzie's help, Olivia was finally going to become a mother.

Her nerves winning out, lifting her from the chair, Kenzie walked to the far wall, to the left of the window, and stood in front of the small oval mirror that hung there, taking in her reflection. Her eyes were the same deep turquoise ovals as Olivia's, but where Kenzie's hair was long, wiry and a rusty red, Olivia's was a softer auburn and fell in gentle waves to her collarbones. They had the same long chins and narrow noses, but Olivia alone had inherited their mother's full mouth. When Olivia spoke, though her voice was soft compared to Kenzie's, people listened, as Kenzie had, all her life.

Lost in picturing her sister, and the longing behind her eyes when she talked about being a mother, Kenzie jumped when the door opened and Doctor Kennedy walked in, a slim folder in his hand.

James Kennedy had been recommended by a co-worker at the marine biology research centre, where Kenzie worked, in Oban. She had said she wanted the best fertility specialist in the region and her colleague had said there was none better than James Kennedy.

'Sorry to keep you, Kenzie.' A tall, lean man of approximately sixty, he smiled kindly at her and gestured towards the chair she'd been sitting in.

'No problem.' She returned to the seat, her legs trembling slightly until she gripped her knees with her fingers. 'So, how did I do?'

His grey eyes assessing her, Doctor Kennedy sat behind his desk and opened the folder, his long fingers lingering on the top sheet of a small stack of papers.

'Well, it's not *quite* what we were hoping for, but it's by no means bleak.' He met her eyes. 'Let me talk you through everything and then I'll answer any questions you have.'

Kenzie frowned. 'That doesn't sound good.' She shifted

forwards in the chair, straining to see the paper that was under his hand.

As he talked, Doctor Kennedy's voice was extraordinarily low, as if a chesty baritone with an Aberdonian accent was reading her a bedtime story. It was mellow, conciliatory, soothing in a way that made Kenzie feel slightly drugged as she listened to what he was saying, his tone conveying more than the words did themselves. His speech was practised, and formally positive, sending a trickle of anxiety through her.

Some of the terms he was using were familiar, but others were new, and as she focused on his close-cropped silver hair, noting the slight tan to his angular face, she forced a swallow.

'So, based on all that, how do you feel about everything?' He eyed her.

Kenzie blinked, realising that she had slipped into a semi-aware state, her mind reeling, trying to process what she was hearing.

'Honestly, I'm not sure.' She sucked in her bottom lip. 'Are you saying I *can't* donate eggs to Olivia?'

He shook his head. 'Not *can't*. Just that the situation isn't quite as clean-cut as we'd hoped.' He watched her lace her fingers tightly together in her lap, then release them. 'Take a look at this chart, Kenzie. It might help to illustrate what I'm talking about.' He handed her the top sheet of paper.

Kenzie stared at the report, scanning the confusing medical jargon at the top of the page. But below that, even as a layman, she could interpret the data points right in front of her, the descending line on the axis indicating her fertility, the sad trajectory of her ovarian reserve, the numbers nothing like what she'd been hoping for.

As she tried to refocus on what the doctor had just told her, she felt the prick of tears behind her eyes. The fact that with this seemingly simple mission that she had set her heart on accomplishing for her sister she was likely to fall at the first hurdle, was as heartbreaking as it was startling.

'Kenzie?' Doctor Kennedy leaned forward, the sleeves of his white coat riding up his wrists.

'Sorry. Just give me a second.' She nodded, then read the report again, processing that not only did she have advancing endometriosis, a condition that she'd been dealing with since she was in her teens, but that she also had what was considered to be a diminished ovarian reserve.

To add insult to injury, from what she could glean from the summary at the bottom of the page, her endometriosis had the ability to negatively affect the quality of the eggs she *did* have, making them less viable for donation, and it could also increase the risk of complications during the retrieval process.

She let the page drop to her knee, her heart pushing up painfully under her ribs, and as she took a moment to steady her breath, her sister's face materialised behind Kenzie's eyes.

Olivia had been unable to conceive naturally, after three years of trying, followed by five unsuccessful IVF cycles that had left her and her husband, Glenn Mackintosh, emotionally bruised. Unable to bear Olivia's pain any longer, Kenzie had decided to donate eggs to her sister, but if her eggs were few, *and* not good quality, the chances of granting Olivia's wish to have the child she had always longed for had just become significantly harder.

Kenzie had just turned thirty and, as fate would have it, had never wanted to become a mother so had accepted her situation and the consequences of her endometriosis. Before they had married, she and her husband, Arran, had agreed on not having children of their own, but now, seeing the sad reality of her situation reinforced in black and white, eroding her ability to do this for her sister, was devastating.

'I get the big picture. I mean, how could I not.' She lifted the paper from her knee. 'But what does all this mean, exactly?'

'It means that if you want to do this, I'd recommend that you only do one cycle. If we're lucky, we'd retrieve enough quality eggs to donate to your sister.' He paused. 'But because of your condition, the risks are higher that the hormonal stimulation could exacerbate your symptoms. Added to that, your own chances of conceiving down the line could be reduced, should you ever change your mind.' He surveyed her over his wire-framed glasses, the skin on his cheeks leathery and deeply creased around his eyes.

'There's no danger of that happening.' Kenzie's voice was raspy. 'I'm not doing the baby thing.'

His eyebrows lifted as he nodded. 'I understand, but I'd be remiss if I didn't give you all the pertinent information.' He tapped his pen on the desk, his coat startlingly white, highlighting the paleness of his silver hair.

'It's all about Olivia. This is all she's ever wanted.' Kenzie's throat began to narrow, but she refused to cry. It was galling enough to find out that, despite her promise, there was a possibility that she might let Olivia down, but blubbering in front of her fertility doctor was not an option.

'It's your decision, Kenzie. Take some time to think it all through and let me know if you want to go ahead.'

Kenzie stared out of the window, and as she took in the view over the car park, she recalled Arran's expression the last time they'd talked about her donating eggs to Olivia, the way his mouth had dipped as he stood at their kitchen window, his back to the scenic vista over the river Lochy. She pictured the tiny scar at his left cheekbone, the ash-brown hair slightly receding at the temples, the partial narrowing of his moss-green eyes as he'd shared his fears with her.

'I'm worried that it could get messy, Kenzie. Something as significant as this could create tension, long term. What if you feel connected to the baby somehow? Maybe have a hard time seeing Olivia with it later? Or what if the donation, or the pregnancy, don't work out? It might affect your relationship with her.' Arran had shrugged.

'That wouldn't happen, Arran. First, you know how I feel about kids. This is for Olivia. And she knows the risks, and the odds. She'd never hold me responsible if it doesn't work out. Besides, I am probably her last chance.'

He'd paced to the doorway, his hands bunched in the pockets of his jeans.

'Look, it's up to you. It's your body, and she's your sister; I just worry about the risks, and all the unknowns.'

Kenzie had tried to reassure him, make him understand that this was something she felt she had to do, but they'd left things open-ended, based on her finding out today what the results of her tests were. They'd agreed to talk again, and now she had the information they'd been waiting for.

Outside the clinic, Kenzie stood in the doorway, scanning the rows of vehicles, looking for the roof of her bright blue Volkswagen Beetle, just visible behind a sporty white car. As she pictured the test results again, the disappointing numbers and analysis of her fertility, something inside her shifted.

Kenzie had never wanted children, ever since she had decided to become a marine biologist at twelve. She'd told her mother this and Hazel Grey had simply nodded, her thick brown hair escaping from the comb that held it behind her ear.

'And that's OK, love. If you decide that when you're grown up, it's completely up to you.' Hazel had then smiled, her dimples deepening. 'But you might change your mind when you fall in love and get married, Kenzie.' Her mother had cupped her chin, Hazel's bright blue eyes glistening behind her tortoise-shell glasses.

'I'm not doing that either,' Kenzie had quipped. 'Boys are such a waste of time.'

Recalling the way her mother had laughed, grabbed her into a hug, then swung her in a circle inside the airy kitchen, that was now Kenzie's own kitchen, she felt the familiar tug of loss.

She missed her parents more than words could express, all the years they'd been gone not having softened their tragic and premature departure from her and Olivia's lives. Doing this for her sister not only felt right, it felt like something their mother would have been proud of, and that was a force that was propelling Kenzie towards a decision.

As fat raindrops began to patter onto the cars around her, she tented her leather jacket above her head and made a dash towards the Volkswagen, her thick red hair flying out behind her in the quickening breeze.

The clinic was on the Western edge of Fort William, the view of Loch Linnhe breathtaking, and as she reached her car, despite the rain now coming in from the side and stinging her face, Kenzie took a moment to soak in the familiar vista.

Across the water of the loch from Fort William, the impressive Ardgour hills towered behind a cluster of small, white stone houses, each sitting on the flat land close to the water's edge next to clumps of tightly packed firs and Scots pines. The deep green of the trees looked like thick swipes of paint on a canvas, separating the properties and the lush fields between each home. A stunning backdrop, the steep slopes were a mixture of swaths of mossy green and deep rust, slashes of grey-white granite clearly visible in some areas, the combination of colours creating a giant, moss-covered staircase that wound up towards the sky.

Kenzie had never tired of this view, her entire life, and she knew she never would, this place being the seat of all her happy memories and, she hoped, for the ones she hadn't made yet.

As she opened the door and slid into the car, she tossed her wet jacket onto the passenger seat and checked her face in the rear-view mirror, but her sister's face flashed into her mind again, the gentle turquoise eyes that held the same kindness as their mother's had.

Kenzie didn't relish the idea of delivering less than positive news to Olivia about the plan they'd been hatching for months. Olivia, though the older sister, was less outgoing than Kenzie, her tendency to take a step back and let Kenzie have the limelight having started when they were only four and eight. Kenzie would dance in the living room, spinning in circles until she made herself dizzy, but rather than join her, Olivia would sit with their parents on the sofa and clap when Kenzie was done.

Olivia had treated Kenzie like her pet, caring for her as a parent might, putting Kenzie's needs first, and now, finally, after everything Olivia had done for her, Kenzie was determined to do this one thing, this monumental thing, that Olivia wasn't able to do for herself.

As Kenzie backed the Volkswagen out of the space and turned towards home, her heart ached for her sister. If she couldn't do this for Olivia, she might never have the child she longed for, and everything Olivia had been through already, all the losses, pain and disappointment, would feel even crueller.

A flash of defiance made Kenzie shake her head. No. She was going to think positive and protect Olivia from as much as she could, tell her only the necessary information. That meant that the tougher conversation would be with Arran, and at this moment, Kenzie was pretty sure that would be her biggest challenge.

Whatever else happened, and whatever she'd have to do to persuade him, Kenzie's determination to do this for her sister was stronger than ever. She simply couldn't let Olivia down, no matter what the consequences.

2

When Kenzie got home later that afternoon, Arran's Audi was parked in their section of the drive at the left side of the old Victorian house.

Since they had subdivided the house, Kenzie and Arran lived on the ground floor and Olivia and Glenn on the first floor, both of their high-ceilinged flats overlooking the river Lochy. The river flowed directly into Loch Linnhe, one of the largest sea lochs on Scotland's west coast, and connected to the ocean via the Sound of Mull and Firth of Forth. Its presence was a constant that both Kenzie and Olivia had always loved, and appreciated. The enormity of the loch had made them feel small, but safe, as the statuesque hills around their home seemed to cradle and protect them from the outside world, which as children they'd imagined to be full of hazards – some real, some imaginary.

The living arrangements afforded each sister a piece of their family home and yet enough privacy not to be living in each other's pockets. Each time Kenzie came home, she felt grateful that they'd found a way to stay here, connected to their memories of their parents.

She was surprised to see Arran's car as he hadn't told her he'd planned on leaving work early. As she squinted up at the house, looking for movement at the windows, a knot of foreboding gathered in her chest, so she parked behind the Audi and turned off her engine.

Kenzie had texted him when she'd left work earlier, to go to see Doctor Kennedy, but Arran had not replied, which was unlike him. As an environmental biologist, he was often out in the field, but she knew he was based in the Oban lab for the next few weeks, before heading back to Wick, in Sutherland, Scotland's most north-easterly point. He was studying the peatland areas of UNESCO's Flow Country, the 35th World Heritage Site in the UK, and the first natural one in Scotland. He'd waited a year to get a spot on the research team and, while it sometimes meant him being away for a couple of weeks at a time, Kenzie had been over the moon for him when the placement had come up.

Arran had always been proud of her work as a marine biologist and, in turn, she admired his passion for the environment, and the world's best 'living laboratories', as he called them, all around them in the Scottish Highlands.

As she walked up the front path looking over at the drive on the opposite site of the house, where Glenn and Olivia parked their Land Rover, it was empty, as expected. Knowing that she had a little more time to refine the news she had to share with her sister was a relief.

Olivia was at the call centre where she worked in Human Resources, and Glenn was rarely home from the police station until after 6 p.m. Her brother-in-law was a sergeant in the Highlands and Islands Police force, a soft-spoken, wiry guy with giant hazel eyes and a mop of chestnut-coloured hair that flopped across his forehead. At five-feet-nine, he had the perfect build for a climber, scampering over rocks and jagged overhangs like the proverbial goat.

Olivia had already been a good climber when Glenn had moved back to Fort William from Darwin, in Australia, where his family had emigrated when he was six. He had recently been living near his mother, brother and sister-in-law while they shared the care of their ailing father. When their mother passed away peacefully shortly after their father, Glenn's homesickness for the mountains he loved had pulled him home to Scotland. When he had joined the local climbing club, Olivia's skills had improved from climbing with him, and their relationship had quickly blossomed from climbing partners to romantic partners. They'd been married for five years now and as Kenzie approached her front door, she mentally sifted through all the times Olivia had come to her crying over the past three years of them trying for a family; after her miscarriage, a false positive pregnancy result, or one of the many failed IVF cycles she and Glenn had been through.

Kenzie put her key in the lock, her throat tightening with sadness for her sister, the juxtaposition of their individual situations universally unfair.

Inside, she passed the huge gilt-framed mirror above the table in the hall where they tossed their keys, and she caught sight of her reflection. Her fiery red hair was as wild as ever, so she raked it away from her face and twisted it into a long spiral, which instantly bounced free across her back as she released it. Frowning slightly, she listened for the usual noises Arran made when clattering around in the kitchen, but there was only a disquieting silence.

'Arran?' She stood still for a moment, then when there was no answer, walked along the hall.

The room was dim, the tall window behind the kitchen sink framing the darkness of the hills behind the house, so she flipped the light on. Scanning the space, she noticed that the coffee press was half full, just as her husband walked into the room behind her.

My Sister's Only Hope

'Hi, you. Where were you?' She caught the distracted smile, his green eyes taking her in.

'I was in my office.' He hovered in the doorway, his hands in his pockets.

Kenzie saw the tension around his mouth, the way he raked his bottom lip with his teeth, and her stomach dipped. He always hugged her when she got home, so this new, distancing thing was puzzling.

'You're home early. It's only four.' She glanced at the clock on the wall by the back door, and then added, a little too brightly, 'Skiving?'

'Nope.' There was a dullness to his tone that sent another bolt of anxiety rushing through Kenzie. 'I'm due a few early days after that last stint in Sutherland. Plus, I wanted to be here when you got home.' He paused, then distractedly combed his fingers through his hair. 'Calvin is fine with it.'

At thirty-seven, Arran's boss was only three years older than him, and them being graduates of the same university meant that they had similar approaches to their work and a camaraderie that was good to observe.

Momentarily lost in thought, Kenzie took in Arran's chiselled face as he tipped his head to the side, his smile tentative.

'So, what happened with the doctor?'

Refocused on the task at hand, she walked to the old farmhouse table where they shared all their meals. She pulled out a chair, the significance of what she had to tell Arran once again filling her with trepidation.

Taking a moment, she sat, then beckoned to him. 'Come and sit down, love. I've got lots to tell you.'

His brow creased. 'Sounds ominous.'

'No, but after speaking to Doctor Kennedy today, I'm pretty sure I know what I want to do, but I'm not sure how you're going to feel about it.'

He scanned her face, his jaw ticking slightly. 'OK. Talk to me.'

She nodded and took his hand in hers. 'I love you, and I do respect your concerns about me donating eggs to Olivia, but this is bigger than just you and me, or our fears, Arran. This might be the most important thing I ever do, so I really need you to be on my side.'

He blinked several times, then sighed. 'Well, I think I know what you're going to say, but tell me anyway.'

'Please just hear me out first, then we can talk. You and I are a team, and if we can get on the same page, we can do this, Arran. For Olivia.'

Arran's eyes were locked on hers, his mouth twitching as he chewed the inside of his cheek.

Kenzie's heart was already aching, knowing that she was asking him to support her in something that deeply concerned him, but even with that knowledge, the need to do this for her sister was overwhelming, and as she continued to talk, Kenzie let his hand slip from hers, needing to root herself firmly in what she was saying, and in her resolve, without the distraction of his touch.

3

Arran sat at the kitchen table, leaning on his elbows. Kenzie was next to him, her cheeks beginning to feel warm. She kept her voice even as she told him about the test results, and her disappointment in what she'd learned, all the while his eyes were locked on hers, his mouth in a tight line.

When she stopped talking, he took her hand.

'So, it's *not* viable for you to donate?' He sounded confused, his frown deepening.

'No, I'm not saying that, just that if I do, it could be a bit riskier for me than for other people, because of my endo. Also, it'd be harder to conceive naturally, should I ever want to.'

He shook his head almost imperceptibly. 'But we don't want that, anyway. Right?'

'Right.' She nodded, suddenly transported back to a night, four years earlier.

When they'd first met, she had quizzed him about his position on children and his response had left her both impressed and emotional.

Arran had sat across from her in a pub in Fort William. It was their seventh date and Kenzie, true to form, had already decided he was the man for her. She'd sipped some of her whisky, sat back and locked eyes with him.

'So, you know why I don't want kids, mainly because of my endometriosis. But why don't you, exactly?'

Arran had given a half-smile, amused at her directness.

'Because my older brother died when I was twelve.' He'd dropped his gaze momentarily to the tabletop, then met her eyes again. 'And I saw what it did to my parents. They were never the same after that, and it eventually broke them.' His voice had grown thick.

Moved, Kenzie had reached across the table and touched his hand. 'I'm sorry, Arran. That's awful.'

'They divorced when I was fourteen, and it was gut-wrenching. My mum left me with my dad and moved to Glasgow. I saw her only rarely. The pain was too much for them. They couldn't move past it.' He'd shrugged. 'I don't want to go through that, Kenzie. So, no kids.' He'd eyed her as she'd blown her nose on a tissue, then stuffed it up the sleeve of her sweater.

'Right.' She'd nodded decisively. 'In that case, we're perfect for each other.'

Snapped back to the moment by him squeezing her fingers, Kenzie smiled at her husband.

'So, with that in mind, I'd like to go ahead with the donation. Do the stimulation cycle as soon as the doctor can get it set up, and however many eggs are any good, give them to Olivia, and Glenn. Then you and I can get back to our lives, and I'll know that I've done everything I possibly could to help.'

Arran looked down into the water glass in front of him, his back straightening as he leaned away from the table. It took him a few moments to meet her eyes.

'It's ultimately up to you, love. I know you want to do this for her, and I understand, and admire that.' He gave a crooked smile. 'You were going to do it, regardless.'

His last statement had a sting in the tail.

'Not without your support, Arran. I might be the one going through the physical procedure, but you'll be going through the experience, too.' She paused, seeing his eyes flick to the window and then back to her face. 'I won't feel right going ahead unless you are with me on this.'

'Look. It's fine. I support you, really. I'm just still a bit concerned about it all, especially the effect it might have on your health.'

Kenzie loved him for his concern, but she needed him to tell her this was all right, as adding guilt to the anxiety she already carried about the egg donation working out for her sister would be a heavy burden.

'The risks to me are manageable, love, and I know that if the roles were reversed, Olivia would do this for me, in an instant.' Kenzie covered their linked hands with her free one. 'Olivia gave up her dreams of going to university to take a job at the call centre in Fort William, just so that we could afford to stay in this house after our parents' accident. She became my legal guardian, and she helped me cope with my grief. I'd never have got through that time without her, Arran.' Kenzie gulped back a sob. 'She insisted I pursue my dream of becoming a marine biologist and I took that gift willingly. Then, when she met Glenn, she poured her heart and soul into their relationship believing that they'd build the family she dreamed of, together.' She shook her head sadly. 'It's not her fault the universe had other ideas.'

He stared at her, his jaw twitching, as Kenzie took a shaky breath, determined to get him to understand.

'I will take every precaution. Do exactly what the doctor tells me to do. I promise, everything will be all right.'

Arran's green eyes were intense, then they softened, as always happened when he looked at her, really saw her.

'All right, Kenzie. Tell me what you need and I'll help you any way I can. Olivia deserves to make her dreams come true, and there's no one better to make that happen than you.' He lifted her hand and kissed the back of it. 'You are a force of nature, Mrs Ford.'

Overcome with relief, Kenzie leaned in and kissed him, his lips warm and dry under hers. 'Thank you. You're the absolute best, Mr Ford. Thanks for understanding.'

He nodded, a flicker of something behind his eyes sending a trace of worry through Kenzie. He was doing this out of love for her, and it was a lot to ask of him. But her *not* doing this would leave Kenzie questioning herself, as a person and, more importantly, as a sister.

Kenzie waited until she saw Olivia's car pull into the driveway, her heart pattering under her breastbone. Typical of when he was processing something difficult, Arran had gone quiet after their conversation, then disappeared down the hall, past the living room and into the office that overlooked the back garden, so as Kenzie grabbed her keys from the hall table, she bellowed, 'She's back. I'm going over there.'

Arran sounded distracted as he called back, 'See you.'

Torn between her wish to reassure him and her excitement to share her news with Olivia, Kenzie considered running along the hall and into the tiny bedroom that they'd converted into an office, then planting a kiss on both of his eyelids – something that always made him smile. But she couldn't wait another second to see her sister's face when she told her the news, so she tugged her denim jacket on, walked out and closed the door behind her.

Olivia was unloading some shopping when Kenzie walked into the long kitchen that ran the length of the front of the house on the first floor, directly above Kenzie and Arran's. Olivia had wanted an open-plan layout, so the wall had been taken down between two former bedrooms to create the bright, airy space, with the original fireplace at one end.

Being on the upper floor, Olivia and Glenn's flat was slightly brighter than Kenzie and Arran's, but, in return, being on the ground floor meant that they were able to walk out of the French doors at the back of their living room and sit on the patio, in the shadow of Ben Nevis.

The mountain had been a part of their lives since the day the girls were born, but Kenzie had not set foot on its slopes since her parents' deaths, and while she admired Olivia's determination to conquer the granite beast, Kenzie had no interest in it now, other than to watch the seasons and the weather change at the summit, the way the clouds would gather at the top, then seem to descend like a mystical blanket, obscuring the highest peaks.

As Kenzie tossed her keys onto the marble-topped island, Olivia jumped and spun around.

'Dammit, Kenzie,' she half-shouted. 'Stop creeping up on me like that.' She widened her eyes at her younger sister, then a smile tugged at her mouth, as Kenzie pulled a face.

'Well, who else would it be?' She pulled a stool out and sat at the island, then shrugged her jacket off. 'What's for dinner?'

'Trout, or pasta, depending on what his lordship is in the mood for.' Olivia's glossy hair was in a tight French roll, the style one that their mother used to wear when she was going somewhere nice. It accentuated Olivia's long, elegant neck – another feature that Kenzie had not been blessed with – and as Olivia put away her shopping, moving gracefully between the fridge and the deep pantry at the left side of the stove, Kenzie took in her sister's profile.

As a child, she'd been jealous of Olivia's looks. While Kenzie had been told she was pretty, Olivia had always been the true beauty. She also had a goodness about her, a wholesome, gentle energy that drew people in, while Kenzie had grown up believing that she, in contrast, was something of an acquired taste.

Olivia was a natural with children, too, having babysat for various families in the neighbourhood since she was thirteen, where Kenzie felt awkward around children, afraid that she'd break the tiny ones, or say or do the wrong thing, irreparably damaging them in some way.

Ever since their parents had died, Olivia had talked about her wish to continue the family line, not to let the name of Grey fade to grey, as she put it. She'd kept her own name when she'd married Glenn, but for Olivia, it was far more than the moniker, or even her desire to be a mother. Kenzie was sure that it was all about Olivia's refusal to let her and Kenzie be the last link to two people whom they had both adored.

Kenzie understood that and had felt bad that she had no such desire. Her and Arran's decision to remain childless had felt entirely right, at the time, but knowing the struggles Olivia had faced with infertility, it now left Kenzie feeling like a bit of an ingrate, and a let-down, to her sister.

Hoping to keep the mood light, and not let anything spoil her news, Kenzie sat up straighter and spread her palms on the cool marble.

'Come and sit. I need to talk to you.'

Olivia neatly folded the two reusable shopping bags she'd emptied and stuffed them into the bottom drawer next to the fridge.

'OK. Fancy a cuppa?' She nodded at the kettle, but Kenzie shook her head.

'No, thanks. Just sit.' She patted the stool next to her, then swivelled around to face her sister.

Olivia tossed her cotton jacket over the back of the leather sofa that split the room in two, then sat down.

'So, I didn't tell you because I didn't want you to stress out, but I saw Doctor Kennedy again today. He had the results of the tests.'

'Oh, my God. Tell me. What did he say?' Olivia's hands curled into tight fists in her lap, her eyes widening.

Kenzie took in the anxious expression, and the trademark move Olivia had of licking her bottom lip whenever she was nervous. All Kenzie wanted to do was see Olivia smile, the way she had when they were young, so she took her sister's hand in hers.

'It's good news, Liv.' She smiled, then began sharing what she'd learned, while editing out the elements of the report that she had decided to omit.

As soon as Kenzie stopped talking, Olivia's eyes were instantly full, her chin beginning to tremble as she squeezed Kenzie's fingers.

'Are you sure? I mean totally sure you still want to do this? And is Arran OK with it?'

Kenzie nodded. 'He fully supports me. He wants this for you, too, Liv. He's seen everything you two have been through, and he knows how much it means to you.' She looked at her sister. 'So, is that a yes, then?'

Olivia held her gaze, their two identical sets of turquoise eyes locked on each other, and their hands still linked.

'Yes, yes, triple yes!' she shouted, her face a picture of joy. 'I'll never be able to thank you enough, Kenz. I mean it.' Olivia's voice caught in her throat, as Kenzie stood up and wrapped her arms around her sister.

'You don't have to thank me. You have given me so much, for years. This is just redressing the balance.' Kenzie felt her throat narrow, so she stepped back. 'These eggs might not be organic, or super top-notch, but they're all yours.' She laid her palms flat on her stomach.

Olivia laughed softly. 'Well, they might not be organic, but they're certainly grain fed.'

Kenzie took a moment, then caught on to the reference to her penchant for an overly large whisky now and then. 'Ha ha, very funny.' She pulled a face. 'There will be no more whisky for me until after the egg retrieval, apparently.' She pouted. 'The things I do for you.'

Olivia stood up and hugged Kenzie again. 'You're the best, little sister. Thank you.' Her voice cracked, so Kenzie leaned back and scanned her face.

'No blubbering. This is a good thing. And when I get all hyped and hormonal from the injections, and am calling you a cow for making me do this, just remember to ignore me.' She grinned. 'Because if all goes well, I'm going to be an auntie.'

Olivia smiled as a single tear crept down her cheek. 'Can you imagine?'

Kenzie shook her head, released Olivia and rounded the island. 'No, I can't, and yet, I can.' She opened the cupboard next to the extractor hood and pulled out two wine glasses. 'Sod the tea, let's celebrate.'

Olivia laughed, her cheeks pinking as she wiped her nose on a tissue. 'There's a bottle of Pinot Noir in the pantry.' She nodded at the still open door. 'Grab the crisps too. Let's make it a party.'

Kenzie walked into the pantry, spotted the wine, grabbed a giant bag of salt and vinegar crisps and a box of Maltesers. 'This could be our last sister wine blow-out for a long while. Let's go nuts.' She shook the box of chocolates, as Olivia took the wine from her and began opening it.

She watched Olivia pour two large glasses of wine, accepted one, then tapped it against Olivia's.

'Here's to you, and Glenn, and to the future of the Grey slash Mackintosh family.'

Olivia took a second, her eyes seeming to mist over, then she nodded.

'To the Greys, and to you, Kenzie. I love you more than chocolate.'

Kenzie took a sip of wine, the warmth of the liquid easing the knot in her throat at the affectionate saying they'd coined as children.

As she followed Olivia into the living area and sat in the rocking chair next to the tiled fireplace, her mind was suddenly filled with the contents of the disappointing piece of paper she had held in her hands a few hours earlier. This had to work, because if it didn't, Olivia might forever carry the weight of sadness that Kenzie had seen grow in her over the past few years, and the thought of that was unbearable.

If Kenzie achieved nothing more in her life, she'd do whatever she could to make this happen. This was the first step towards giving Olivia what she craved and deserved, and for Kenzie, there was nothing more important right now.

4

A month later, on a crisp, mid-May morning, Kenzie arrived at Doctor Kennedy's office before 8 a.m. She had started the hormone injections ten days earlier and was already feeling the effects, her breasts swollen and painful, her stomach bloated and her moods a little erratic. The doctor had told her that she'd need to take the hormones for between eight to fourteen days, and she was counting them down.

Her ultrasound was scheduled for eight o'clock and she planned to go straight to work afterwards, as Anders Nilsen, a visiting biologist from the Institute of Marine Research in Norway, was coming in to meet with her and her boss, Harry Mitchell. They were discussing the institute's recent study on brown crabs that had been identified as carrying heavy metal isotopes, presumably from the disposal of mining waste into the fjord ecosystems. The findings were disturbing and the study something that Kenzie was extremely interested in being involved with, so she didn't want to miss the meeting.

After the technician completed the scan, Doctor Kennedy was in a good mood as he came into the office.

'How are you today, Kenzie?'

'Good. Fine.' Kenzie nodded politely, trying to be gracious, but, niceties not high on her agenda, she then blurted, 'So, how does everything look?'

Doctor Kennedy sat, then glanced at the monitor on his desk.

'Well, everything looks good, so we're on track to do the retrieval in three days, this coming Friday.'

Kenzie nodded, a flutter of nerves making her palms clammy, so she shoved her hands into the folds of her cotton skirt. 'Right, good. And then it's over to you.' She gave a nervous laugh.

'Indeed.' He smiled. 'Any more questions?'

'Yes. How many eggs are we expecting? Pardon the pun.' She grimaced.

'Well, we won't know until the day, but I'm hoping for around fifteen.'

'Why fifteen?' She frowned, having a number to meet or a standard to be judged against suddenly daunting.

'It's become something of a magic number in IVF. Too many can lead to poorer quality eggs, and too few eggs can mean fewer high quality. It's different with every individual, of course.' He paused. 'Remember to fast for eight hours before the procedure, because you'll be sedated. Then, after a short recovery period, you'll be free to eat and drink.'

'Will I be in pain afterwards?' She laid her palm on her middle, the bloating making the skin across her abdomen feel taut.

'You shouldn't be. Perhaps some mild discomfort.'

Relieved, she nodded. 'All right then.'

Kenzie waited for him to say something more, but he kept his face impassive, his grey eyes on the monitor. Was he avoiding looking at her?

'Is there anything else I should know, or ask?'

He shook his head. 'Just take it easy for the next couple of days and we'll get you set up for early Friday. The eight o'clock appointment again. Oh, and no driving that day, so you'll need someone to bring you in and take you home.'

She nodded again, lingering nerves tugging at her core. 'OK. You're the boss.'

She saw him smile then, the slightly distant look in his eyes clearing.

He stood up. 'See you Friday for the fun part.'

Outside, the sky was bright and mostly clear of clouds, and the brisk breeze instantly swept her hair from her shoulders, wrapping her cotton T-shirt tightly around her middle. As Kenzie scanned the half-empty car park, hearing a dog barking in the distance, the anxiety that had been simmering turned to a gentle buzz of excitement.

Three more days and her part would be done, and the need to share that with Arran felt critical. The end was in sight, and she knew how relieved he'd be.

Sitting inside the Volkswagen, she texted him, her fingers trembling a little.

All good. Retrieval is Friday morning 8 am. No driving, so are you able to take me? :)

She started the engine, watching him typing a reply. It seemed to take forever, but then his answer sent her stomach into knots.

Any idea how long it'll take? Got a meeting at Glenfinnan at 1.

She felt stung, having hoped for something a little more upbeat. Perhaps a thumbs-up emoji, or a *Good to know*. And yet, she understood. He had gone along with this whole donation idea to support her, but his concern for her wellbeing and the potential for complications had been clearly etched on his face every time he'd had to help her with an injection.

While obviously distressed by the changes in her moods, he'd been a prince when she'd burst into tears at the slightest mishap or misunderstanding. He'd made her endless cups of ginger tea for the nausea she'd been experiencing since starting the hormone injections. He had even occasionally stood awkwardly in the bathroom with her, when she sat on the floor thinking she might throw up. He'd done his part, and more, and now she wanted them to get back to how they'd been before. To have this somewhat tense, monosyllabic version of her husband gone, and their life back in balance.

She took a moment for the hurt to abate, lingering a little longer inside his perspective, and then she replied.

A couple of hours max. So you could make it out there by 1. If not though, I'll get Olivia to pick me up after. No worries :)

She watched the dot-filled bubble, then it disappeared, and just as she was about to ask him what was going on, his reply bloomed.

No. I'll be there. X

Relieved, blinking away the press of tears behind her eyes, she typed a quick thank you, then turned the car towards the road.

As Kenzie drove towards Oban, the road tracing the edge of Loch Linnhe, the huge body of water was choppy, topped with row after row of white crests as the wind came in from the west, plucking at the surface. Across the loch, the hills were a brighter green than over recent weeks, the highest peaks lusher, and shrouded in fluffy clouds that looked as if they'd been stencilled over the clear blue of the sky.

The air was laced with the tang of the loch and Kenzie cracked her window open a little, to breathe it in as she drove, the clean, sharp smell helping the nausea.

Despite the year-round, bitterly cold water, she'd passed a

few swimmers, diehard locals who swore by their daily dip, convinced it was more beneficial to their health than any other kind of tonic. Kenzie thought they were mad, but also admired their grit, their wetsuits not standing a chance against the power of the frigid loch.

Shaking her head as she passed two more swimmers, their heads bobbing on the surface in tight vinyl swim hats and goggles, Kenzie replayed the conversation she'd just had with Doctor Kennedy in her mind. Olivia would be excited to know it was all systems go, so checking the time and seeing that her sister would have arrived at work already, Kenzie said out loud, 'Call Big Sister.'

Olivia answered within a few seconds.

'Everything go OK?'

Kenzie took a ginger lozenge from her bag and put it in her mouth.

'Yes. All shipshape. Friday is D-Day.'

'Oh, Kenz. It's happening. Thank you, thank you. I mean...' Her voice faltered. 'I'll never be able to thank you enough for this incredible gift. I love you sooo much more than chocolate.'

Kenzie laughed softly. 'You better, because I love you even more than *that*.'

She swallowed hard, picturing Olivia wiping her eyes, her sister's voice giving away that she was having a little weep.

'I'll phone you when I get home and we can chat more. Got to get my head into crabs now.'

It took a moment, then Olivia echoed Kenzie's laughter, the sisters united in this precious moment of joy that would undoubtedly make it into the hall of fame of good memories.

As Kenzie approached the outskirts of Oban, she spotted the familiar outline of McCaig's Tower in the distance, the prominent landmark built in 1897 by a local banker called John Stuart McCaig. It stood on Battery Hill, above the town, and resembled a Roman coliseum. The elegant monument to the

McCaig family was simple in its design, as far as Kenzie was concerned, made more attractive because the sole purpose of building it had been to provide work for local stonemasons.

The tower also overlooked the gentle curve of the harbour below, and there were wooden benches at the centre of the structure where visitors could sit and look out to sea through the tall, open stone arches. Kenzie and Arran liked to walk up there and have lunch on warmer days, the climb taxing but the view always worth the effort.

He was also working at the marine science centre today, and as she turned her car towards Ardmucknish Bay, she could see the steep slopes of the Garbh Àrd point ahead, their outlines like old friends who needed no special greeting.

Pulling the car into the car park at the science centre, Kenzie felt another surge of nausea. Closing her eyes against it, she opened the car door and sucked in some fresh air.

'Three more days and I'll never have to feel like this again,' she muttered as she got out of the car, the breeze sharp against her cheek. The smell of seaweed filled her head, and she leaned against the car, willing herself not to be sick.

As she gradually felt the nausea begin to subside, she shoved the mass of windblown hair away from her eyes and walked towards the building where she worked, the sight of the distinctive roof with its two half arcs, much like waves, reminding her that it was time to get back into work mode.

It was alarming how hard she was finding it to concentrate these days, and as she pushed the heavy door open and walked through reception and into the long corridor that led to her office, fear tingled in her chest.

Olivia's voice had been filled with such hope and excitement. This had to work. It just had to.

5

At home that evening, Kenzie hadn't been hungry, so Arran had made himself a plate of pasta with pesto sauce. They were sitting across from each other at the kitchen table while he ate and Kenzie dipped a lemon and ginger teabag into a mug of steaming water.

'Three more days and I'll be done.' She mashed the teabag with a teaspoon and dropped it on the table.

'Kenz, really?' Arran sighed, getting up and putting a saucer in front of her.

'Sorry.' She gave a half-smile and put the soggy teabag on the saucer. 'I'm so ready to be done with this nausea.' She shuddered, then took a sip of tea.

Arran was chewing, so just nodded, his thick, ashy hair looking windblown, sitting up from the top of his head. That he was totally unaware of how handsome he was was a huge attraction for Kenzie. She'd often find herself staring at him as he dressed in the morning, walking across their light-filled bedroom in his boxers, his leg muscles long and lean and his regular gym sessions delivering a delicious six-pack of abs that she liked to run her fingers over when he held her in his arms at night.

When she looked up, Arran was staring at her, his eyes full of affection.

'What?' Kenzie tipped her head to the side.

'You look so pretty.' He smiled, the dimples deepening in his smooth cheeks.

'Do I?' She frowned. 'I feel like poo.'

He laughed softly. 'Well, you don't look like it. Maybe this is the glow they talk about when women are pregnant.' As he said it, his expression changed, the light leaving his eyes.

His words made her pause, the notion that this was what pregnancy might feel like startling. She hadn't truly considered that, but she also knew how the concept frightened him, and she wanted to defuse that fear immediately.

'If I'm glowing it's because I keep having these weird surges in my body temperature. I go between feeling young and vibrant, to sickly and gross.' She gave a sharp laugh. 'If this is what it feels like, I'm surprised anyone ever has kids.' She pulled a face as he stood up and put his plate in the sink.

When he turned to face her, his eyes were glistening.

Her heart contracting, Kenzie stood up and walked to his side.

'What is it, love?' She found his hand and wove her fingers through his.

He kissed the back of her hand, reverently. 'You are remarkable. And you don't have to do that, you know. Try to downplay what you're doing for Olivia, for my sake. I am really proud of you, you know.'

Kenzie was caught off guard, his spot-on assessment of precisely how she'd felt compounding her love for him.

'It's not what we want for ourselves, but I think what you are doing, putting yourself through this for your sister, is the single most heroic act I've ever witnessed.'

Kenzie was touched by the heartfelt compliment, but as always happened when anyone said anything remotely kind or flattering, she deflected.

'I wouldn't say that. I mean, if I was giving her a kidney, or a limb or something, then maybe.' Her laugh was slightly forced, and Arran sighed.

'Why can't you just say thank you, and let the truth in.' He eyed her, her face suddenly feeling as if it was on fire.

'You know me, Arran. I find that stuff hard.' She shrugged, seeing his eyes take on a distant look. Wanting to bring him back, to let him know that his words actually meant the world, she put her palms on either side of his face and leaned in. 'Thank you, my love, really. It was a lovely thing to say.'

He took a second, then smiled, the warmth returning to his eyes. 'You're a royal pain in my arse.'

She poked the tip of her tongue between her teeth. 'And you in mine.' She let her forehead touch his chest. 'We're a match made in heaven.'

Arran pulled her close, his arms circling her back. 'So, talk me through the rest of the process. I know you've told me but tell me again.'

Kenzie talked quietly, her cheek pressed to his woollen sweater. She reminded him that, due to Glenn's own challenges, the sperm was coming from a donor and was frozen until twenty-four hours before the fertilisation, which would take place the day after the eggs were retrieved.

He listened to her voice, his cool breath occasionally tickling her forehead.

'And how many eggs will fertilise?' He leaned his hips against the sink, so Kenzie straightened up and met his gaze.

'Doctor Kennedy said approximately eighty per cent on day one, but only thirty to fifty per cent of those will make it to the next stage.' She watched him nod slowly, processing the information she had told him at least twice before. It was as if he was resisting letting it sink in, its relevance to their own lives not weighty enough to warrant permanent space in his mind.

'And then, how long to the embryo stage?' He frowned.

'About ten to twelve days.' She nodded to herself.

'And what's the average percentage of loss?' He blinked repeatedly, as if taking mental pictures of his own thoughts.

'Apparently, between ten and forty per cent, under normal circumstances. But it can be as high as sixty per cent.'

He looked startled. 'Damn, that sounds high.' He shook his head. 'What if you go through all this and only get a handful, then none make it all the way?'

Kenzie stepped back from him, her hands sliding into the pockets of her denim skirt. This wasn't easy to accept, but she had had to take it all in when Doctor Kennedy had shared the statistics with her. Even with her disappointing reserve, she had to believe that there would be enough decent eggs to give Olivia a fighting chance at being a mother. 'I know. It's hard to think about, but, Arran, it's better than not trying.' Her throat began to knot, so she coughed it clear.

'I suppose so.' He reached for her and drew her close again. 'Knowing you, you'll will it into reality, but it's hard to see you go through this with no guarantees.'

She leaned back from him, her vision beginning to blur. 'I know, and I'm sorry. But I had to do it, Arran.'

His eyebrows jumped. 'You *chose* to, and I get that. I supported that. I just want it over, Kenzie.' He dropped his arms, then stepped away from her.

Kenzie felt the separation like a bolt of electricity, her breath catching. His feelings weren't a surprise, but he'd never been so voluble about his frustration.

'It's just a few more days.' She tried to catch his eye, but he was staring at the floor. 'Arran?'

He looked up at her, his expression pained. She took in his face, the gentle green eyes, the strong chin and jawline, his high forehead, and her heart pinched. This man represented the love that she had always hoped for, the kind that she and Olivia had talked about, dreamed about as girls. That he was all Kenzie's was still as baffling at times as it had been the day he'd proposed, and while knowing that he was proud of what she was doing filled her with such joy that her chest felt as if it might explode, the knowledge that she had taken this course despite his concerns eroded that joy, and Kenzie carried that on her back like an anvil.

'I'm sorry I've worried you this much, Arran. I just need you to hang on for a few more days. I promise we'll get back to us. Our lives as normal.'

He scanned her face and nodded, his disconnected look making her throat knot.

'I've got some work to do. Let's talk more later, love.'

'OK.' Kenzie frowned, her need to fix things between them, to get them back to the safety of their lives before they'd found themselves on opposite sides of this decision, like a tourniquet around her heart.

As he walked into the hall, she pushed out a long breath, fear creeping up the back of her throat. What if what she'd done had created a rift between them that had changed their relationship more than for just a few weeks?

6

Three days later, Kenzie lay in the recovery room at the clinic, the tall window to her left coated with rain. She was slightly groggy, and as Arran handed her a glass of water, she noticed that his hand was shaking.

'How are you feeling, love?' He helped her sip some water, then set the glass on the cabinet next to the bed.

'A bit wobbly, but otherwise OK.' She smiled at him. 'How many eggs did they get?'

Arran walked to the window and leaned his hips against the sill. His face was strained, but he tried to smile at her. 'Doctor Kennedy said he'd come in. I'll go and tell someone you're awake.'

Kenzie nodded, shifting up higher in the bed. Her feet were cold, the room feeling icy and smelling of disinfectant. She could have killed for a cup of tea, the thought of wrapping her hands around a warm mug as soon as she got home making her lick her dry lips.

A few minutes later, Arran came back in, followed by the doctor. He was still wearing scrubs and his hair was covered by a green surgical cap, an electronic tablet in his hand.

'How are you, Kenzie? Feeling any dizziness or nausea?' He lifted her right wrist and pressed two fingers against her skin, feeling for her pulse.

'Fine. A little loopy, but no more than usual.' She gave him a smile as Arran walked over to the window again, his hands now in the pockets of his jeans. Her husband's shoulders were slumped forward, and his pale-green eyes were flicking to the door rather than looking at her, which sent a jolt of concern through her. But turning her focus to the doctor, she said, 'So, how did I do? Did we get more than the magic number?'

She watched as he released her wrist, then glanced at the tablet.

'We got eight. Not as many as we'd hoped for, Kenzie, but the eggs we retrieved look good.' He nodded decisively, but she caught his slight frown as a swoop of disappointment sucked at her chest.

'Oh, only eight?'

'Yes, but, as I said, they look to be of good quality.' He glanced over at Arran, who was now staring down at his shoes, his ash-brown hair looking muddy under the harsh, fluorescent light. 'So, have a quiet weekend. Drink lots of fluids and stick to light food. And no exercise, at least for a couple of days. Then, from Monday, you can go about life as normal again.'

She nodded, picturing eight microscopic eggs in a Petri dish, heading for the lab. As she tried to think through the statistics that she and Arran had discussed a few days earlier, calculating the average percentage of loss based on such a small number of eggs, her mouth felt impossibly dry.

'Remember to use protection until your next period.' He glanced over at Arran, who was still staring at the floor, his toe tapping nervously as he avoided making eye contact. 'And phone the clinic if you have any problems, like bleeding, bloating or abdominal pain.' He smiled at her. 'You did really well, Kenzie. I understand that, after fertilisation, Olivia wants to freeze any viable embryos for a few weeks, until she's ready for the implantation.'

Kenzie nodded. 'Yes, she's got to sort things out at work so that she can take a few days off after the transfer.' Kenzie looked over at Arran again, just as he walked to the end of the bed. Him coming nearer was reassuring, as if he was re-entering the conversation. His closer proximity directly affected her body chemistry, her concern over his odd behaviour abating a little. 'She wants to make sure she's able to take it easy after, like you advised.'

Doctor Kennedy nodded approvingly. 'Good. We want to ensure we give her every chance of a successful pregnancy.'

Arran walked to the opposite side of the bed and lifted Kenzie's hand in his, his fingers warm against her chilled skin. She gripped his thumb tightly, her message a thank you for sticking with her, which she hoped he'd received.

'You've done a good thing, Kenzie. Now, can I take her home, Doc?' Arran looked at the doctor.

'You certainly can. I'll get the discharge paperwork underway, and you'll be off within the hour.'

'Thanks for taking good care of her.' Arran released Kenzie's hand and once again dug his into his pockets.

'My pleasure. Bye, you two.' Doctor Kennedy dipped his chin in farewell, then turned and walked out into the corridor.

Kenzie beckoned Arran closer as he seemed reluctant to stay near her side for more than a few moments, which fed Kenzie's concern. 'Sit with me.' Needing his touch, she patted the bed at her hip. 'Just for a minute.'

He hesitated, then perched awkwardly on the edge of the bed. He looked tired, his eyes shadowed and his cheeks a little sunken.

'Are you all right?' She gently stroked his jaw. 'You look done in.'

'I'm fine. Just didn't sleep well last night.' He paused. 'I'm glad it's over and we can get back to normal.'

'Yes, agreed. No more puky, grumpy wife to deal with.' She poked his firm shoulder, his faded rugby shirt feeling rough under her finger. Seeing his mouth twitch, the shadow of stubble making his chin seem more prominent, she smiled.

'That will be a relief.' He squinted at her, then stood up. 'Right, do you feel OK to get up?'

Kenzie threw the covers off and swung her legs out of the bed, a little surge of pain in her lower abdomen making her pause. She breathed slowly and deeply until it passed, then stood up.

'There. I've got my sea legs back already.' She repeatedly transferred her weight from one foot to the other as Arran pulled her clothes out of the plastic bag the nurse had given her when they'd arrived two hours earlier.

'Don't be a pillock. Just take it easy.' He shook his head at her, his mouth reluctantly curving into a gentle smile.

Kenzie let him help her dress, his gentle ministrations easing her anxiety, and making her feel so loved and cared for that her eyes filled.

Arran caught sight of her expression and pulled her into a hug. 'Are you getting all mushy now?'

Kenzie wiped her nose with her palm and then huffed, 'No chance. I'm just still jacked up on hormones.' She shook the hair out of her eyes and reached for her jacket that lay on the bed. 'Take me home, kind sir. I am in dire need of a cuppa and a sandwich the size of a doorstep.'

Arran laughed softly now, sounding more like himself, as he lifted her bag from the chair next to the bed. 'I'll go and see if we can leave. Just hang tight, OK?'

She nodded, feeling a little light-headed. 'I'll be here.'

While Arran went to check what was happening, Kenzie lowered herself onto the plastic chair at the bedside and took her phone out of her bag. She was desperate to tell Olivia that the procedure was over and that she was fine, knowing that her sister would be anxiously waiting for news, but a flash of concern over the small number of eggs made Kenzie hesitate. Eight wasn't going to leave much margin for loss, and breaking the news to Olivia might be difficult.

All they could do was think positively, hope that the next stages went smoothly and leave the rest to the universe. This was not something Kenzie was usually comfortable with, her need for control at the forefront of much of what she did, but in this instance, there was nothing more that she could do.

That evening, Olivia and Glenn sat in Kenzie and Arran's living room. The sunset had been spectacular over the river and now there was a golden light that had seeped into the room, gilding the wooden floorboards.

The four of them had spent many a fun evening together, either here, or upstairs in Olivia and Glenn's place, but the mood this evening was different. Kenzie was slightly puzzled, as there was almost a solemnity to the atmosphere, and as she saw Glenn settle in an armchair by the fireplace rather than sit next to Olivia on the sofa, Kenzie frowned.

'Who died, you lot?' She lifted the glass of wine that Arran had poured for her, the first in over a month. 'There might not be a shedload of eggs, but I just know that everything is going to work out fine. So, let's celebrate.'

Glenn looked startled, then glanced at Olivia, whose smile was slightly strained.

'Right. Yes. We know.' He lifted his glass into the air. 'Here's to you, Kenzie, and to a great outcome.'

Olivia nodded, 'Yes. Absolutely.' Her face was rather pale and there was an odd quality to her voice, as if her throat was raw from crying. Kenzie knew that tone well, and hearing it sent a shiver of worry straight to her core.

Suddenly uneasy and concerned that Olivia wasn't being honest about her disappointment in the number of eggs, Kenzie stared at her sister, looking for signs of that around her eyes.

'Liv, don't worry. It's going to be all right.' She glanced at Glenn, who was staring out of the window, his jaw pulsing as if he were chewing something. There was a disturbing, palpable force field of tension between him and Olivia, but just as Kenzie was about to ask what was going on, Arran brought in a large wooden board and set it on the coffee table.

'Hungry, anyone?' He nodded at the selection of glossy serrano ham, peppered salami, dark-green olives and tiny cherry tomatoes, all surrounding a large chunk of Manchego cheese that he'd bought at the farmers' market the previous weekend. 'Dig in while I get the bread.' He seemed more at ease now that they were home, and Kenzie smiled at him, relief tasting sweet on her tongue.

'Thanks, love.' She watched him walk back into the hall, heading for the kitchen, then she turned her attention back to her sister. 'Is everything OK with you two?'

Olivia looked startled again, as if she'd been caught with her fingers in the jam pot, then she gave another strained laugh.

'Of course. It's just a lot to take in. I mean, it suddenly all feels real.' She looked over at Glenn, who just nodded, his tousled tawny hair flopping over his left eye. 'Fertilisation is tomorrow, and then it's a waiting game, I suppose.'

Olivia sipped some wine, a little colour returning to her face, but even with her reassurance, Kenzie was sure that there was something Olivia was holding back, which niggled at Kenzie like a hangnail that had to be bitten.

'But at least it's not too long to wait.' She took a big swallow of wine, savouring the rich, berry flavour on her tongue. 'Just think. In a few weeks, you could be pregnant.' She watched as Olivia's eyebrows lifted.

'That's right.' She blinked several times, then smiled warmly at Kenzie, a more genuine smile that eased the knot of concern that had gathered at Kenzie's core. 'You are a rock star.'

Glenn stood up and refilled his glass. 'Agreed. We owe you so much.'

His statement sounded somewhat perfunctory and uncharacteristically restrained. Puzzled, Kenzie frowned as she met her brother-in-law's eyes, the hazel irises looking almost amber in the shadow of the heavy chandelier that hung above them all.

'We have to agree that you both need to stop thanking me. Honestly, it's going to get annoying.' Kenzie lifted her chin, determined to inject some light into the conversation. 'Let's think positive, and eat. I'm starving over here.'

As she filled the small plate Arran had given her, Glenn followed suit, then rather than return to the armchair, he sat next to Olivia. Kenzie expected her to lean into him as she would have normally, but, instead, Olivia sat still, her back rigid, as if she were standing to attention, and her eyes were fixed on the board of food on the table.

Seeing the bizarre body language filled Kenzie's heart with angst again, but rather than call them out on it, and embarrass Olivia, she swallowed her next question. Couples who had been through everything they had in their struggle to have a child were bound to have their share of tension crop up between them. Their battle with infertility had been heartbreaking and exhausting, testing them to within an inch of despair, and Kenzie knew that some couples didn't survive that. It was natural for Olivia and Glenn to be gun-shy, nervous and remain cautious even now, afraid to allow themselves to believe that finally, after so many disappointments, they might become parents. But as Kenzie bit into a piece of cheese and took in her sister's face, there was a persistent voice deep within Kenzie.

The way that Olivia was turning her body slightly away from Glenn, her legs crossed away from him too, was unsettling. What was Olivia not saying?

As she popped an olive into her mouth, Kenzie shook her head almost imperceptibly. No. There had never been any secrets between them, because Olivia was incapable of keeping things to herself, or hiding her true feelings. Kenzie had always been able to read her sister like a book, and nothing had changed in that regard, but as Kenzie swallowed the briny olive and looked over at Olivia, who was still avoiding Kenzie's eye, she wondered if on that particular score she could be wrong this time.

7

Two weeks later, as May drew to a close, Doctor Kennedy had phoned Olivia to let her know that only one of the six embryos had reached the blastocyte stage. She immediately texted Kenzie, and now, Olivia was standing outside Kenzie's front door, rain pelting down, making Olivia's auburn hair stick to her face and her long, floral dress cling to her slender frame.

'Come inside, you daft bat,' Kenzie beckoned to her. 'Quick.'

Olivia dashed in the door and shook her head like a dog, droplets of rain speckling the mirror above the hall table.

Kenzie opened her arms and hugged her sister, catching the jasmine scent of her perfume lingering at her neck.

'Cats and dogs out there.' Olivia stepped back and dragged her damp hair into a twist behind her neck, then slipped off her wet clogs.

'I'll put the kettle on.' Kenzie walked along the hall and into the kitchen, her leather flip-flops making a clipping sound on the wood floor, as Olivia followed her. 'So, Doc Kennedy was happy with it?'

Olivia sat at the table while Kenzie filled the kettle.

'Yes, he said it seems good, and Kenz, it's a boy.'

'Oh wow! I forgot you'd done the PG testing.' Kenzie spun around, Olivia not having shared this information with her yet. As she scanned her sister's face for an indication of whether this was good news or not, Olivia seemed impassive which was puzzling. 'So, is that good or bad?' Kenzie put the kettle on the stove and sat next to her sister.

'No, it's fine. I mean, I didn't have a preference. Though, if I'd had to choose, I'd have said a boy anyway.' She shrugged, a half-smile twisting her mouth and her eyes seeming a little vacant. This wishy-washy demeanour wasn't like Olivia, especially when talking about this particular subject, and Kenzie felt the tug of concern again that had been coming and going this past couple of weeks, each time she'd seen her sister.

Frustrated, and determined to get to the bottom of whatever was going on, she took the arms of Olivia's chair and jerked her around so that they were face to face. 'Right. What's going on? You look like your dog just died, not that you have a very good chance at being a mother.'

Olivia looked like a deer in the headlights, her eyes wide and her hand nervously going to her mouth. 'No. It's not that. I'm fine. Happy.' She nodded vigorously, then took Kenzie's hand in hers. 'It's just nerves. I'm scared that I won't know what to do, when it's here. That I'll be a terrible mother. It's exciting and terrifying, and I'm just trying to process it all.' She dropped Kenzie's hand. 'I'm sorry if I'm being weird.'

Kenzie took in the pinched expression, the dull eyes, and suddenly remembered the evening when Glenn had sat away from Olivia, them both seeming tense around each other.

'Is everything OK with you and Glenn?'

Olivia's head snapped up, and she frowned. 'Yes, why?'

'That night when you were here, when I got back from the

hospital, the atmosphere was distinctly weird. You two seemed off with each other.' Kenzie didn't mince her words. She knew that Glenn could sometimes get so focused on his work that Olivia felt a little abandoned, and if he was doing that now, when they needed to be in lockstep over the next few weeks, Kenzie was quite prepared to give him a talking-to.

'We're fine. Honestly. It's just nerves.'

Kenzie frowned, unconvinced, then got up and turned off the stove. She made tea in two giant café-au-lait cups that her co-workers had given her on her last birthday, then set one in front of her sister.

'If there's something else you're worrying about, you can tell me.' Kenzie eyed her. 'This is supposed to be a happy time for you, and Glenn. You should be excited, not afraid. You are going to be the best parents in the world.' She sipped some tea, then baulked. 'Ouch, that's hot.'

Olivia's face softened. 'Kenzie, we are OK. I'm sorry if we're not giving that impression. You need to stop worrying about us. You've done the most amazing thing, and we are truly grateful.'

Kenzie mock glowered. 'We had a deal. No more thank yous. Just try to let the worry go. I know we're not at the finish line quite yet, but I have such a good feeling, Olivia. This is going to work out.'

Olivia's eyes filled, her chin dipping. 'You are always so confident, and strong. I wish I was more like you.'

Kenzie huffed, 'And I want to be more like you, so where does that leave us?'

The sisters laughed together, the deep affection between them dissolving the momentary tension that had filled the room, as it always did.

Three days later, on the first Monday morning of June, Kenzie was walking to her car just as Glenn was backing his motorbike out of the driveway. She waved at him, unsure whether he'd seen her through the visor of his helmet, but then he stopped, turned off the bike and planted his feet in the gravel of the drive.

She crossed the shared front lawn and waited as Glenn raised his visor.

'What's up?' His eyes were hooded and his voice oddly gruff.

'Nothing. Just wanted to say have a good day.' Kenzie frowned, as Glenn nodded.

'Thanks. You too.' He made to close the visor, but something in Kenzie made her reach out and stop him.

'If there was anything wrong, you'd tell me, right?' Her stomach was suddenly flip-flopping as a series of bizarre images of Glenn changing his mind about being a father, packing up and leaving Olivia bereft, flickered behind her eyes.

He held her gaze, his eyes seeming to clear. 'It's nothing for you to worry about, Kenz. So stop, OK? It's getting annoying.' His tone had returned to that of a teasing big brother, the one that he adopted whenever he thought she was fussing unnecessarily or was being exasperating.

Relieved, Kenzie pursed her lips comically. 'Kiss my backside, Mackintosh.' She widened her eyes at him. 'Not too long from now, you'll have your own annoying little bundle to take my place in the annoying Olympics.' She laughed softly as Glenn rolled his eyes, then closed the visor, obscuring his expression.

'You'll be hard to beat on that score.' His voice was muffled, but she heard the gentle jibe, before he restarted the bike.

As she mocked kicking the front tyre, he raised a gloved hand and slowly backed out of the drive and onto the road.

Watching him go, Kenzie frowned. Despite his attempt to joke, there was something odd in his voice, a quality that she couldn't quite place. As he turned right at the end of the road and disappeared, she checked her watch to see if she had time to check on Olivia, before she left for work.

Glancing back at the house, she looked up at the top floor, scanning the wide bay window. A shadow moved behind the glass, so Kenzie walked over to the right side of the house, dashed up the external staircase and rang the doorbell.

Olivia looked alarmed to see her, instantly checking her watch and frowning. She was obviously about to leave for work, her giant leather handbag sitting just inside the front door and her white denim jacket open, over a silky shirt. Her hair was loose, and a touch of soft brown eyeliner was making her eyes piercingly blue. 'Is everything OK?' She grabbed her keys from the narrow hall table and switched off the overhead light. 'I've got to go.'

Before Kenzie could edit her thoughts, the bizarre scene she'd just imagined about Glenn took over, and she blurted, 'Have you decided on a date for the implantation?'

Olivia looked taken aback. 'Not precisely, but we're thinking around the end of this month.' She lifted her handbag and moved forward, causing Kenzie to have to step back out into the hall. 'Sorry, but I've really got to go, Kenz.' She closed the door behind her and, without meeting Kenzie's eyes, headed for the staircase.

Kenzie followed her down the stairs, then waited as Olivia opened the car door and tossed her bag onto the passenger seat. Something in her manner was setting off alarm bells again, so Kenzie reached out and touched her sister's arm.

'Glenn seemed a bit off, just now.' She motioned towards the road. 'Are you sure you two are OK?'

Olivia turned to face her, her cheeks pinking slightly. 'Yes, he's just a bit ticked off at me because I said I wanted to do that two-day climb up Five Finger Gully with a group from the club. It's planned for mid-June, so a couple of weeks before we'd do the implantation.' She shrugged, then swept her hair over her shoulder. 'It's like a last hurrah, if you will, before everything changes for us.' She scanned Kenzie's face, fine lines bracketing Olivia's full mouth.

'Did you tell me about that?' Kenzie frowned. 'I don't remember.'

Olivia nodded. 'I think so. It's one weekend, that's all, but he's making a big thing about it. So, I said, it's not like I'll already be pregnant or anything.' Olivia's mouth dipped at the edges. 'He's just a bit uptight about everything at the moment.' She dropped her eyes to the ground and shoved at the gravel with the toe of her shoe. 'We both are.'

Kenzie hesitated, unsure what to say when her gut reaction was to agree with Glenn. With everything that was about to happen, was it wise for Olivia to tackle the most hazardous face of Ben Nevis?

Kenzie's silence must have spoken volumes because Olivia closed her eyes briefly.

'It'll be fine. We're all advanced climbers who've all done the gulley before, and if the conditions are good, it'll be the perfect way to end the season.' She checked her watch again. 'Sorry Kenz, but I'm really going to be late.'

'Right, right. Go. We can talk later.' Kenzie stepped back from the car. 'Text when you get home.'

Olivia nodded. 'Have a good day.'

Kenzie watched her sister reverse down the long drive, waving until the Land Rover disappeared at the corner. As anxiety filled her chest, Kenzie forced a swallow. Her instincts were seldom wrong, and right now, they were telling her that there was more to this odd behaviour, and slightly subdued energy, than her sister and brother-in-law simply disagreeing about a climb.

As she turned and walked back to her car, Kenzie sucked in the briny mist coming off the river, leaving a salty coating on her tongue. The undefined timing on the transfer of the embryo was worrying, and the way Olivia had said *last hurrah* had left Kenzie feeling unsettled. After everything that she and Glenn had been through, wouldn't they want that date fixed, a huge, significant day in their journey to parenthood, noted in big, bold letters on their calendar?

SUMMER

8

Twelve days later, Olivia and Glenn were prepared for the Five Finger Gulley climb. While Glenn was finishing his last shift before the weekend, Kenzie sat at the island in Olivia's kitchen, watching her closing the same battered backpack she had been using ever since their parents had taken them both climbing on the lower slopes of the Grampians, as teenagers.

'Got everything?' Kenzie shoved a twist of wiry hair behind her shoulder and leaned forward on her elbows. Her white cotton T-shirt was tucked into the waist of her pale-blue capris, her stomach flat again as the effects of the hormone injections had finally passed.

'Think so.' Olivia hefted the backpack across the kitchen and propped it against the wall by the pantry. 'There's no room for anything else, anyway. So, I'd better have.' She shrugged, a broad smile transforming her face, and light filling her eyes.

'Right.' Kenzie was both relieved and delighted to see her sister genuinely smiling again. It felt like weeks since she'd seen this look in her eyes.

'I'm so excited. I really need this climb.' Olivia pulled out a stool and sat next to Kenzie. 'It'll be great to blow away the cobwebs.' She gathered her glossy hair behind her neck and twisted it around her finger. 'I can't wait to get up there.' She gestured behind her. 'The gulley can be a pig, but this group of climbers is really strong. Even Glenn thinks so.' She pulled a comical face.

'And remind me why you're not doing it in a day?' Kenzie tried to keep her tone light.

'The group wanted to camp overnight, so we can rest. We'll get a clearer view on the descent, too. Not hurrying to get back before dark.'

'So, you'll be back on Sunday, around lunchtime, right?' Kenzie lifted her phone and opened the calendar.

'Yep. I'll text you when we're heading back down, as always.' She eyed Kenzie. 'You need to stop worrying, you know.'

'Who's worried?' Kenzie put her phone down and shook her head slightly.

'Everything will be fine, and we'll be back before you know it.' Olivia reached over and squeezed Kenzie's hand.

An image of their parents flashed behind Kenzie's eyes: their mother's gentle smile, the blue eyes, warm behind her glasses, their father's thatch of red hair, his legacy to Kenzie, and the way his hazel eyes almost closed completely when he smiled. They had left for the same mountain that day, fourteen years earlier, saying the same thing, 'We'll be back before you know it,' unaware that this would be the last time they would see their daughters.

As Kenzie tried to put the memory out of her mind, Olivia nudged her leg. 'Oi. Stop it. Do you hear me?'

Kenzie met her sister's gaze. 'You're sure about doing this climb?'

Olivia rolled her eyes. 'Yes. One hundred per cent. The weather is perfect, and Glenn, and the other three guys, will be with me all the time. We'll be fine.' She patted Kenzie's knee. 'The last hurrah, remember?'

'*Fine.*' Kenzie pulled a face, then halted, realising that, aside from Glenn, she had no idea who was going, but before she could ask that, or edit herself, she blurted, 'Are you feeling better about everything now? Moving on with the transfer?' She couldn't help herself, as they still hadn't told her exactly when they planned on implanting the embryo.

Olivia sighed, then nodded. 'As soon as we get back, we'll figure things out.' She twisted towards the window, her shoulders seeming to sag a little, then she turned to face Kenzie again. 'I do have something to tell you, but it can wait until after the climb.'

The statement like a gut punch, Kenzie frowned. 'What do you mean? Why can't you tell me now?'

Olivia shook her head. 'No, after is better.' Seeing Kenzie's shocked expression, Olivia sighed. 'Please, Kenz. Just let me have this weekend, and then we'll talk about everything. OK?'

Feeling as if something precious was beginning to slip from her grasp, Kenzie gripped Olivia's stool and turned her back to face her.

'Once you and Glenn hold your child in your arms, all your anxiety about parenthood will fade away. You will be great at it.'

Olivia's eyes were bright as she leaned forward and hugged Kenzie tightly. 'I love you, little sister. More than chocolate.'

Clearly, Olivia wasn't ready to tell her whatever it was she was keeping to herself, and anger replaced Kenzie's anxiety.

'All right then,' she snapped. 'Go and climb that bloody mountain. Get it out of your system, and don't forget to tell it to eff off from me while you're up there.' Kenzie flicked an angry V sign in the direction of the window as Olivia's face softened.

'I will, on both counts. And don't be angry, Kenzie. Everything will be all right.'

Kenzie stood up and shoved her stool back in. 'I'm not

angry,' she huffed. 'Oh, and tell that husband of yours that it's his turn to cook for us all when you get back. It's been weeks since he took a turn.' She wanted to stay angry, but when she saw her sister's expression, the familiar, patient, half-smile, Kenzie knew that she was beaten. She would find a way to wait until Olivia was ready. What other option did she have? 'I love you, more than chocolate, too. You big pain.'

Olivia smiled, warmth radiating from her eyes. 'See you Sunday.'

Kenzie nodded, turned and walked along the hall and out the front door. As she closed it behind her, the claws of foreboding snagged at her throat. Shaking her head, trying to banish the nerves that she always battled whenever Olivia was on the mountain, Kenzie blinked her vision clear and ran down the stairs.

Two days later, Kenzie's phone rang in the dark bedroom bringing her bolt upright in bed, her pulse instantly thumping at her temple. Their room was dim, the outline of the window a grey rectangle against the mauve of the pre-dawn sky.

Trying to figure out what day it was, and what time it was, she raked a hank of hair away from her face, and twisted to look at Arran, who leaned over and turned on his bedside light as Kenzie listened to her brother-in-law, his voice fractured with distress.

The phone pressed to her ear, Kenzie's stomach went into free fall, Glenn's words nightmarish and surreal, as she nodded, struck dumb with shock, until she was finally able to assure him she'd get to him as soon as she could.

Arran was saying something, but Kenzie couldn't focus on him, her sister's beautiful face filling her mind.

Still disorientated, she shoved the duvet away and stood up, her mind reeling and adrenaline coursing through her like lava.

As Glenn hung up, she turned to her husband. 'Oh, Arran. It's Olivia.'

'What's happened?' Arran's voice was thick with sleep, but panicked.

Kenzie's chest clamped tight, making it hard to breathe.

'Something happened up on the gulley, and she fell – slid over an arret.' Saying the words punched the final breath from Kenzie, her insides contracting into an agonising knot.

'What? I mean... Is she OK?'

She shook her head, disbelieving, as she repeated Glenn's words. 'He says she's unconscious, and they've taken her to the Belford.' Kenzie's voice was little more than a whisper, her mind instantly teeming with devastating memories and garish images that brought her chin to her chest as she began to hyperventilate.

'Oh, my God!' Arran leapt from the bed.

Even mentioning the hospital in Fort William, where local trauma patients were taken, especially after mountain accidents, made Kenzie nauseous, her hand going to her mouth.

After the avalanche that had swept their parents into a deep glen on the north side of the mountain, partially burying their father, and breaking their mother's neck, Hazel and Jack Grey had been taken to the Belford too, before they'd died. That place had been where her worst nightmare had come to fruition, and hearing the name again catapulted Kenzie back to that night, the night her world had imploded.

Overcome by those memories, Arran's voice brought her back to the moment.

'We have to go, love.' He beckoned to her.

As she sifted through another series of horrifying images, Kenzie closed her eyes, her legs trembling and her insides heaving as if she'd just run a marathon. She would wake up now. She would wake and see the light creeping in behind the curtains, this Sunday morning as welcome and untainted as any other. But then, as she opened her eyes and took in Arran's expression, Kenzie thought she might vomit.

She looked at Arran as he held his hand out to her, but Kenzie wasn't sure if she could move, terror and dread paralysing her.

This had to be a terrible mistake because Olivia was an expert climber, as was Glenn. Perhaps Glenn was in shock, confused, and the woman they had brought down from Five Finger Gully was someone else?

Kenzie closed her eyes again and tried to feel her sister, divine the tacit connection that had kept them inseparable since their parents had died on the mountain fourteen years earlier, but all Kenzie felt was numb.

'What if she dies?' Her voice cracked, locking her eyes on Arran's, the pale-green irises seeming luminous as he shook his head.

'She won't. This is Olivia. There's no way she's going anywhere. She'd never leave you.' He gently rocked her stiff body, his ash-blonde hair tousled from sleep and his chin darkly shadowed.

Kenzie's face was numb, her mouth slack. All of their lives, Ben Nevis had loomed behind the house like a giant granite pyramid, its very presence a challenge that Olivia had never been able to resist – despite what had happened to their parents. As Kenzie pictured it now, her heart forced its way up the back of her throat.

This could not be happening, again. Surely the universe couldn't be this cruel. But what if it was? What if the mountain had finally won, and was tearing her last remaining family member from her, leaving her alone, as she'd always feared?

When they arrived at the hospital, Kenzie sprinted down the trauma care corridor to where Glenn stood, his expression tortured, and his eyes glistening. He opened his arms to her, saying her name, but she pushed past him, going straight into Olivia's room.

The sight of her sister in the bed made Kenzie clamp her hand over her mouth and pant into her palm. Approaching the bed, as she gently lifted Olivia's hand, Glenn told her what had happened.

He said that the dawn light had been dim on the mountain, the wind picking up as a bank of cloud encased the summit. Olivia and another climber had insisted that it was safe to begin their descent, but then it had started to rain. Heavy, battering rain that had made everything underfoot slippery.

As Kenzie leaned in and kissed Olivia's forehead, hot tears tracking down Kenzie's face, he described the fall. The way Olivia had been passing another climber and lost her footing, grabbing for the rock behind her before sliding over the edge of the ledge.

Kenzie listened, but closed her eyes, banishing the visual of her sister disappearing from view, as her fellow climbers, and her husband, watched, helpless to stop her.

Kenzie sat at the side of the bed, holding Olivia's hand, Kenzie's face streaked with tears. Olivia had been intubated, the right side of her beautiful face masked by long, concertina tubes that distorted her mouth, making her look alien and machine-like. Her left cheek, below where her helmet would have been, was crushed, the bones around her eye having collapsed into a terrifying mask of livid flesh that the heavy bandages could not hide, and that was hard to look at.

Her heart fit to shatter, Kenzie was trying to focus on the parts of Olivia's face she could recognise, the horror of the injury to the other side beyond her comprehension. Since she had arrived, the trauma doctor and three different nurses had come in and out of Olivia's room at regular intervals, and each time, Glenn had stood at the door and talked quietly to them, his face drawn and his hair matted and plastered to his head.

Struggling to breathe, Kenzie gently stroked Olivia's hand, feeling the skin cool, and papery under her fingertips, as, across the room, Arran was talking to Glenn in the open doorway.

'So, what's the situation? Are there internal injuries?'

'There's damage and swelling in the brain. She's comatose.' Glenn's voice cracked, and Arran grabbed his shoulder. 'They keep checking for reflexes, but...' Glenn stopped, and Kenzie's heart threatened to stop too as the word *reflexes* seemed to swell inside her head.

'What does that mean?' She stood up, her legs like jelly. 'Glenn, what does that mean?'

As she staggered across the room, Arran stepped forward and slid his arm around her.

'Kenzie...' Glenn choked out her name. 'If there are no brainstem reflexes, and she can't breathe on her own...'

Kenzie curled her hands into tight fists, then a low, animalistic moan floated from her. 'No. It can't be true.' She gagged, her empty stomach heaving. 'She'll wake up. She has to.'

As Kenzie's worst nightmare began to take physical form, something that she'd battled since the loss of her parents and her sister becoming her entire world, she felt Arran's arm tighten around her side. She had to stop this. Find a way to slow time, to turn back the clock, to shake Olivia until her eyes opened, her sister coming back to her and, in turn, the universe becoming whole again.

Arran spoke quietly to Glenn, but she couldn't hear him, only the urgent slamming of her own heart in her ears, so she pressed her eyes closed and shouted, 'Do something. She can't leave me. She can't leave me alone.'

When she looked back at him, Glenn's face was mucky, tear tracks running from his hazel eyes down to his lower jaw, clean, white lines that seemed to slice into his mottled flesh.

'I don't know what to do.' He shook his head, his chin dropping to his chest. 'I just don't know.'

Arran led Kenzie to a chair near the window and helped her sit down. She couldn't feel the ground under her feet as she walked or the seat beneath her, and as she looked down at her legs and grabbed her thighs, her striped pyjama bottoms looked brash and ridiculous under her fingers.

The men talked quietly again, then Arran led Glenn out into the corridor, glancing at Kenzie on the way out and nodding at her. His message, *I'll be back in a minute*, Kenzie was numb to, unable to respond, her whole body trembling as if she were naked and buried under a fresh fall of snow.

Olivia was motionless, her slim body shrouded by a light blanket and her arms lifeless at her sides. Seeing her there, alone, was more than Kenzie could bear, so she stood up, taking a moment to steady herself, then walked to the bed.

Moving to the right, undamaged side of Olivia's body, Kenzie eased herself onto the bed and carefully reached across her sister's chest, enclosing her in a hug. As Kenzie listened to the suck and hiss of the ventilator, and the beep of the heart monitor, she closed her eyes and prayed, begged God and the universe, and every force of nature that had any power to bear on what was happening here, to help her. Not to take her sister. She asked her parents for help, for a sign of what she should do, but even as Kenzie's heart was splintering into a thousand pieces, every cell in her body screaming for a miracle, deep inside, she knew that this was goodbye.

9

Olivia lived for three more days before her heart stopped.

Kenzie had gone home to have a shower and change her clothes, but Glenn had been at Olivia's bedside when it happened, and when his call had come in a few minutes ago, Kenzie had been unable to speak. She had handed the phone to Arran, then walked out onto the back patio, her chest constricted and her breathing jagged.

In the garden, the June afternoon was bright and warm, the beauty and majesty of the mountain in front of her appalling in the face of her unbearable pain. As tears dribbled down her cheeks, Kenzie hugged herself, the pressure of her own arms all that was keeping her from folding over and melting into the warm stones beneath her bare feet.

Olivia was gone, the foundation of Kenzie's life ripped from under her, and now she was the last bastion of her family, the last Grey standing at the foot of the mountain that had stripped her of almost everyone she loved. Her greatest fear realised, her family was gone.

As she stared at the sharp outline of Ben Nevis, through a fog of tears, agony turned to anger as she screamed, 'You win!'

just as Arran walked up behind her and circled her with his arms, right as her legs gave way.

'I'm so sorry, Kenzie love.' He supported her weight until she could steady herself, then she turned around and buried her face in his neck, her throat on fire.

'I don't know what to do, Arran,' she hiccupped. 'How to live, or breathe. Nothing makes sense without her.'

Arran held her tightly, stroking her back. 'I know, my love.'

'I can't stay here, looking up at that every day.' Her words were lost in a sob as she jabbed a thumb over her shoulder. 'I hate that mountain. I hate this place, now. It's poisoned everything.' She felt her legs judder again, and they began to give way, so Arran scooped her up like a doll, his arm supporting her under her thighs.

'Let's go inside. I'll make us a drink.' He carried her through into the living room, then, laying her gently on the sofa, he covered her with a light blanket. 'I'll be back in a minute.'

Not wanting to see the mountain out of the tall bay window across the room, Kenzie rolled over to face the back of the sofa, her face pressed into a soft cushion. As she took in the slightly musky scent of the fabric, the lingering tang of the winter's wood smoke, she imagined pressing her face in a bit harder. Closing her eyes and letting her breaths become farther apart, her lungs barely inflating as she slipped towards silence, a place where there was no pain, loss or emptiness. Far away from a world without Olivia.

Startling her, Arran gently rolled her onto her back.

'Here. Drink some of this.' He cupped a brandy glass in his palm. 'Just a sip or two.' He helped her sit up, then carefully placed the glass in her hand.

She was trembling so much, the amber liquid sloshed around inside the wafer-thin bowl of the glass.

Wrapping his hands around hers, he guided the glass to her lips. 'Just a little.'

Kenzie took a moment, then sipped some brandy, the burn on her tongue making her gag. 'I can't, Arran.' She pushed the glass towards him. 'Take it away.'

He took the glass and set it on the coffee table, an old, Arab door that they had had made into a table, with a glass top. Kenzie had seen the door in an antique shop in Oban and Arran had asked a friend who made custom cabinetry to craft the table for them. It sat in front of the L-shaped leather sofa by the fireplace and was where they'd play board games with Olivia and Glenn. Where the four of them had eaten many a takeout, and where they'd planned the hiking trip that they'd taken to Spain two years earlier to walk the El Camino trail, until Kenzie had twisted her ankle and they'd had to leave early.

She stared at the table, as all the hours they'd spent around it wove themselves into a picture show of memories, a rich tapestry made up of laughter, camaraderie, of the whispered wishes and secrets of sisterhood, and even the occasional spirited disagreement, all the components of a shared life, and the reality of Olivia's loss was so overwhelming that Kenzie could barely breathe.

Arran was hovering next to the sofa, his fingers running through his hair. His eyes were glistening, the green of the irises iridescent in the afternoon light.

'What can I do, love?' He knelt at her side and took her hand in his. 'Tell me how to help you.' His voice caught.

'I want to lie down...' She gulped. 'Close my eyes and not wake up.'

He looked startled. 'Don't say that, Kenzie.' He helped her stand up. 'Olivia wouldn't want to hear that, either.'

She leaned on his arm, the strength of him all that was keeping her upright. Even through her pain, she'd heard his distress at her statement, so she leaned her head on his shoulder as he walked her along the hall and into their bedroom, then pulled back the duvet on her side.

She lay down, drawing the quilt up to her chin as she began to shiver.

'Stay with me.' She swiped at her wet cheeks, then closed her eyes as Arran lay next to her and drew her into his side.

'I'm here. I'll never leave you,' he whispered, as she hiccupped against his shoulder.

'Olivia said that, too.' Kenzie sucked in her bottom lip, picturing her sister's face when she'd broken the news of their parents' deaths to Kenzie. *I'll never leave you, Kenzie. You'll always have me.*

As she shook her head against Arran's shoulder, another wave of pain choked her, tears continuing to soak Arran's T-shirt.

If she'd only tried a little harder to dissuade her, could Kenzie have stopped Olivia from going on that climb? And what was it that she was going to tell Kenzie? The thing that was so hard to share that she wanted to wait until she'd done one more climb. With Olivia gone, how would Kenzie ever find out?

There was nothing other than silence to answer Kenzie, but she knew that these questions could be the most significant of her life.

It took almost ten days to make all the funeral arrangements and, during that time, to Kenzie's distress, they had hardly seen Glenn at all. She missed his presence and lay awake at night worrying about him, the sudden emptiness of the space he'd occupied in her life for years foreign, and compounding her loss.

Kenzie had taken a week off work and each morning as she made coffee, she'd hear the rumble of Glenn's bike as he left the house, but even if she went out into the drive and waved at him, he'd just raise a hand and ride away, leaving her hurting at his seeming lack of need, or desire, to be around her and Arran. His isolating himself like this was unprecedented, and Kenzie had no idea how to navigate it. Him avoiding her was hurtful, but more than that, she was worried for him. Worried that he might slide into such a dark place that neither she nor Arran would be able to reach him, or help him if he needed it.

This morning, the day before the funeral, she'd tried to catch his eye again, but he hadn't seen her, and, disappointed, as she had walked back inside and closed the door, Arran was in the hallway.

'Why is he avoiding us like this?' Kenzie shook her head, her chest aching. 'I thought he'd need us more than ever now, or at least you.'

Arran shrugged. 'We all grieve differently, love. Perhaps it's too painful to be around us.' He ran his thumb down her cheek. 'Too many memories.'

Touched by his compassion, Kenzie turned Arran's hand over and kissed his palm.

'Maybe. It's making me sadder, though. It's as if we've lost him, too.' Her throat knotted tightly as fresh tears pressed in behind her eyes. She had cried so much this past ten days that the skin around her eyes was pink and raw. 'Can you talk to him, maybe?'

Arran gave a sad smile. 'I can try, but you know us men don't handle emotional stuff like you girls do.' As soon as he'd said it, Arran's eyes widened, the reference to Kenzie as part of a twosome seeming to brand itself in the air between them. 'Sorry...'

She shook her head. 'It's OK. We *must* talk about her, Arran. I *need* to talk about her. Say her name. If we don't, it's like pretending that she was never here.' She swept her hand in a trembling arc in front of her. 'She was the bigger part of me, the better part of me, honestly.'

He drew her into a hug. 'Not better. Just the yin to your yang.'

Kenzie wiped her eyes with a soggy tissue, then pushed it into her pocket. 'It feels as if my insides are empty. Like they've been scooped out with a spoon.' She mimed the action. 'She gave me so much strength. The belief that I could do anything came from her.' She swallowed hard and met his eyes. 'You are the love of my life, but *she* made me who I am.'

Arran nodded. 'I understand, Kenz. I really do.' He paused. 'I was only twelve when Danny died, but I remember that feeling of being rudderless. Sort of cut loose in a storm at sea. I was so angry at the world. At everyone who got to live when my big brother didn't.' He paused as she took in the hurt glowing in his eyes, his pain exactly reflecting her own.

'I'm so sorry, Arran. I've been so caught up in my own pain...' She looped her arms around his neck. 'You've been right where I am.'

He kissed her cheek. 'It was a long time ago, and I still had my parents back then, but Danny and Olivia will never become invisible, or forgotten. They left indelible fingerprints on our lives, and our hearts.'

Kenzie nodded, swallowing a sob. 'Exactly.' She shoved a hank of hair away from her face. 'Do you think Glenn feels that way, too? Or perhaps he wants to try to forget her. To move on.'

Arran shook his head. 'He adored Olivia. This is his way of dealing with the loss and we should probably try to respect it.'

'I know that. But we could help him. Help each other. I just wish he'd let us in.'

'I'll talk to him tonight. See if he wants to walk down to the pub for a pint. Tomorrow is going to be a hard day for us all, so try to cut him some slack.'

'Of course I will. I'm just missing him, Arran. He's been a brother to me for almost a decade. That kind of connection doesn't just go away, even if Olivia is gone.' Her vision blurred as she fished out the tissue and dabbed at her eyes again. 'Please try.'

'I will. I promise.'

'Thank you. I love you.' Kenzie rose onto tiptoe and kissed his full mouth. 'If you ever leave me, I will hunt you down.' She gave a half-smile as he laughed softly.

'Not likely to happen. At least not by choice.'

She took in the gentle eyes that had mesmerised her from the first time she'd met him over four years ago. He had become a good part of her world, but within that world, her sister had been the other pillar. Without Olivia, could she and Arran find their balance? Stay solid? As she laid her palm on his smooth cheek, Kenzie could only hope so.

10

The podium at the crematorium was decorated with white calla lilies, their long fluted petals pristine in a simple glass vase, next to a photograph of Olivia, smiling, her climbing helmet on as she waved from the summit of Ben Nevis. Glenn had chosen it, and Kenzie had wept at her sister's joyful expression when he'd emailed it to her.

The previous night, he'd told Arran that he didn't feel like a pint, but that he was sorry he had been distant. He'd promised to drop by soon and that he'd send Kenzie the photograph he'd chosen for the ceremony.

Arran had assured him that he mustn't feel bad for going through his own process of grief, but when Arran had come home and told Kenzie about the conversation, she couldn't help but be disappointed.

'It kills me to think of him going through this alone, when we are right here.' She'd frowned in the mirror above the sink as she and Arran had brushed their teeth together. 'Olivia wouldn't have wanted him to, either.' She'd spat foam into the sink, then wiped her mouth on a flannel. 'Do you honestly think this is the right thing, though, Arran? To just leave him be.'

My Sister's Only Hope 71

She'd frowned, the ever-present knot in her throat tightening. 'It feels like there's something else going on. They were kind of off with each other the last couple of times I saw them together, and then Olivia told me she had something important to talk to me about, after the climb.' She'd shaken her head as a grotesque image of Olivia, sliding over the arret, had snatched at her breath. 'Do you think there could be something else bothering Glenn?'

Arran had shaken his head. 'I think you're overthinking it. Like I said, this is probably the only way he knows how to cope with losing her.'

Kenzie winced, hearing him say that, the reminder that the next day, they were about to go to her sister's funeral paralysing, and gut-wrenching as any nightmare come true.

She desperately wanted to reach Glenn, but Arran was probably right, and if space was what her brother-in-law needed, she'd try to respect that.

'It still doesn't feel right, but I'll give him the space he needs, and hopefully he'll come back to us, at some point.' She'd swiped away a single tear as Arran had nodded.

'I'm sure he will, love.'

At the funeral reception, amongst a small gathering of climbers from the club, a few of Olivia's work colleagues from the call centre, several police officers from Glenn's station, Sally Childs from the village store, and some other neighbours from the street who had known their parents and the girls since they were young, Kenzie sat at the back of the room nursing a coffee. As she scanned the group of people who'd come to pay their respects to her sister, and to her, milling about with teacups and small plates of sandwiches, it struck her, not for the first time, how insular she and Olivia had become after their parents' deaths.

They had withdrawn into their own world, healing, and relying on one another for everything, for a long time. Kenzie's morbid fear of being alone had been born at that time, the idea that Olivia, her best friend and anchor, her one remaining family member, might be taken away from her enough to have Kenzie regularly wake up in the night crying.

Olivia had moved Kenzie into her room, the sisters sleeping together in Olivia's double bed, and always with a night light on, until Kenzie had felt able to return to her own bedroom. It had been months until that had happened, but even as time had helped their wounds heal, they had kept their microcosm closed, all but excluding other people, until Glenn and then Arran had come into their worlds.

Olivia had made some casual friends through work, and then when Glenn had joined the climbing club, that circle had grown, but Olivia had remained Kenzie's best friend, and having her had meant that Kenzie hadn't felt the need for other girlfriends. As she contemplated what her world would be like now, without her sister, the one constant in her life, Kenzie closed her eyes, the landscape ahead dull, and cold, and a persistent longing tugging at her core.

Letting the hum of the voices around her fade to white noise, Kenzie heard Glenn's voice, rising above the others. He sounded agitated, not his usual, controlled self, so her eyes shot open, and she scanned the room for him.

He had given a beautiful eulogy, his touching words about his wife making Kenzie cry so much that she had barely been able to recite the Robert Burns poem that she'd chosen to read at the end of the service. She'd had to stop twice, and only by locking eyes with Arran in the front row had she been able to collect herself enough to finish.

Glenn had barely spoken to her, or Arran, since they'd arrived at the reception, and now he was at the far side of the room, talking to a man Kenzie did not recognise. He was a head taller than Glenn, fair-haired with a chiselled, Nordic look to his distinct features. He was wearing a tweed jacket and dark trousers, and his eyes were a piercing blue that, even from across the room, were remarkable.

Glenn's sleek black suit looked formal by comparison, his normally messy hair combed flat and his face pale. He leaned in towards the other man and dipped his chin, Kenzie guessed to whisper whatever it was he had to say next. The taller man stepped back, then raised his hands, as if surrendering to an arrest, and said something that obviously made Glenn angry. He closed the gap between the two of them and stuck his chin out threateningly, the set of his jaw speaking volumes.

Alarmed, Kenzie stood up and focused on Glenn's mouth, trying to lip-read. What she thought she saw him say was, *you're not welcome here*, which made her anxiety flare. Glenn was a calm, metered man, so for him to say something like that, especially in this way, was not only out of character but was also alarming. If she was right about what she'd seen, he meant business, and whoever this other man was, Glenn's message was clear. He wanted the man to leave.

Just as she was about to cross the room, Glenn pointed to the exit and the taller man said something more, then turned and walked out of the door. As she watched him go, she saw Arran approach Glenn, Arran's broad back in his dark-grey jacket making Glenn seem even slighter than usual. The two of them spoke quietly to each other as Kenzie made her way towards them, then, when she reached them, she put her hand on Glenn's arm.

'Are you OK?' He looked beyond her, at the door, then, after a moment, he nodded.

'Yeah. Just doing a little crowd control.' His voice was hoarse, as if from lack of use.

'What do you mean? Who was that guy?' Kenzie nodded at the door.

'Never mind. It's all fine now.' Glenn tried to smile, but instead his face looked oddly contorted. 'I need a drink. Anyone else?'

Arran shook his head. 'No, thanks. I'm driving.'

'Me neither.' Kenzie slid her hand through Arran's arm. 'Why don't you come over for some food tonight, Glenn?'

Glenn surveyed her face, his eyes hooded and his mouth dipping at the edges.

'I can't tonight. I'm taking a shift at the station to cover for someone.' He nervously smoothed his hair, then seemed to pick up on her disappointment. 'Let's do it soon, though. OK?'

Kenzie was about to ask when, but Arran said, 'Sure, mate. Just let us know.'

She watched as Glenn walked away from them, his gait somewhat unsteady and his hands clenched into fists. His distancing himself from them, and this odd, aggressive behaviour with the tall stranger, was now even more concerning, and Kenzie's gut was screaming at her that aside from being devastated at losing his wife, there was something deeper going on here, and regardless of what Arran said about giving Glenn space, she intended on finding out what it was.

Kenzie's questions were multiplying. What had Olivia been holding back from her, and how did Glenn know the tall stranger? Who was he, to Glenn?

The next two weeks seemed to slither by, and it had been the wettest start to July Kenzie could remember, for years. The rain was relentless, day after day, sheets of it masking the view of the river and the mountains, and as she'd stand at her back window and look out at the murky sky, part of her was grateful that she couldn't see Ben Nevis clearly, as the sight of it was still like pressing a livid bruise.

She had been back at work for over a week and while being

involved in the Norwegian study on the brown crabs was fascinating, she was struggling to stay focused. Her mind would drift back to Olivia, her gentle laugh, the way she'd scold Kenzie with a smile tugging at her lips, how she would always know when Kenzie was worried about something even if she'd done her best to hide it, then Kenzie would dissolve into tears and hide out in the ladies' room for a while until her pink eyes calmed down and she could control her voice again.

As the reality of Olivia being gone had begun to sink in, Kenzie's mind was constantly being drawn to the embryo that had been frozen, pending her sister being ready for the transfer. Kenzie had had a nightmare the previous week about the freezers at the fertility centre failing, and it perishing, then she'd woken up bathed in sweat, Olivia's voice in her head saying, *I'm sorry, Kenzie,* over and over.

The previous day, her boss, Harry, a rotund, sandy-haired man in his mid-fifties who was a keen curler, and whose wife, Celia, who had been an Olympic kayaker, had taken her into his office, his pale eyes concerned behind his thick glasses.

'Are you sure you're OK, Kenzie? Do you need some more time off?'

Kenzie had tried to smile. 'No, Harry. But thanks. I'm fine. I need to stay busy. I'm just trying to come to terms with everything, and adjust to...' Her voice had failed her then, and he had kindly handed her a tissue.

'If you're sure?' He'd paused, then glanced at his phone on the desk next to him. 'I need to go to a meeting, but let me know if you change your mind. You could easily work from home for a few days. The field study is still over a week away.' He'd slid the phone into the pocket of his too-tight khaki trousers. 'Do you still want to go?'

Kenzie had nodded. 'Of course. I told Anders I would.' She'd tried to picture packing a bag and travelling to the research institute in Bergen, where she'd be part of the team analysing the effects of the tainted fjord water on this species of crab. The idea of getting away had initially seemed attractive, but now that her departure date was getting closer, the thought of distancing herself from home, from the place where she and Olivia had been bound together for Kenzie's entire life, was unsettling.

When she had assured him again that she was fine, Harry had left her to her thoughts, and as she'd packed up her desk for the day and headed home, Kenzie had resolved to go to Norway and see the research through. After everything Olivia had done to allow Kenzie to pursue her dream career, she owed Olivia this, at least.

The following week, the night before she was leaving, Arran had cooked them a meal. While she rinsed the dishes and put them in the dishwasher, he was sitting on the window seat in the bay window, nursing a brandy. Behind him, the evening sky was dim, but the phase of persistent rain had ended, and the river was visible again, a dark smudge at the base of the tall hills across the water.

'Will you check on Glenn while I'm away?' Kenzie wiped her hands on a tea towel. 'I can't believe we have hardly seen him since the funeral. I'm worried he's become a total hermit.'

Glenn had continued to be as elusive as a ghost, sometimes leaving the house before dawn, and Kenzie, who was having trouble sleeping these days, would stand at the window and watch him silently wheel his bike to the road before starting it and riding away. She had phoned and left him voicemails, texted a couple of times, and even popped a note through the letter box upstairs, but he hadn't responded to any of her attempts to reach him. Her concern for her brother-in-law was growing and Arran continuing to tell her to keep her distance was beginning to grate.

'He's going to be OK, Kenz.' Arran sipped some brandy. 'I'm in Sutherland from Tuesday to Thursday, but I'll be home Friday, probably before you get back.' He smiled at her. 'I'm glad you decided to go to Bergen. This will be good for you.'

Kenzie sat opposite him, then gathered her mane of fiery hair into her fists behind her neck.

'I hope so. Anders is good to work with, and maybe the change of scenery...' She shrugged, releasing her springy hair down her back. 'I don't know.'

Arran reached across the table and took her hand. 'Just focus on the work. Let yourself enjoy it. It's OK to keep doing the things you love, Kenz. Olivia wanted that for you, more than anything in the world.'

She knew he was right, but carrying on with her life, living her dream, waking up each day to a man she loved deeply, and being in her home, the safe place that she and her sister had created together, when Olivia had been denied all those things, still felt like a betrayal.

'I know she did. I just hate that it was all ripped away from her.' Kenzie's throat knotted. 'She deserved her life.'

Arran nodded, then sat back, his hand dropping into his lap.

'So do you, Kenzie. We both do.' He sounded tired, the flat tone of his voice making Kenzie frown.

'I'm sorry. I know I'm all over the place at the moment.' She watched as he shook his head. 'No, I am. One minute trying to be positive, the next a mess.' She shrugged. 'I'll get there, Arran, but thanks. You're always there when I need you.' Her eyes filled as he leaned forward on his elbows.

'I'll always be here, and don't apologise. I just wish I could do more to help you.'

'You do exactly what I need you to.' She smiled, her mind going back to the niggling concern she'd been dreaming about. 'One thing *I* need to do when I get home is talk to Glenn about the embryo. It's worrying me.'

Arran frowned. 'What do you mean?'

Kenzie stood up and pushed her chair in. 'I need to know what he wants to do with it. It meant so much to Olivia. He must have a plan, right?'

Arran leaned back, his hands clasping the back of his neck and his jaw twitching as it did when he was agitated. 'To be honest, with everything that's been going on, I'd kind of forgotten about that.' He looked out of the window, then reached over and lowered the blinds. 'What are you thinking?'

'I don't know, but at some point, a decision will have to be made.' She sucked in her bottom lip, Olivia's face materialising behind her eyes. 'I'll have to talk to him about it.'

'Yeah. I suppose so.' Arran nodded, then stood up, stretching his arms above his head, his T-shirt separating from the waist of his jeans, revealing a strip of firm muscle. 'Ready for bed?' He yawned, his head tipping back slightly.

'Very.' Kenzie was surprised by a dip of disappointment in his quick diversion of the topic, but pushing it down, she switched off the overhead light, then walked into the hall. His wanting to move away from the subject of the embryo wasn't entirely surprising, but what *was* surprising was how much Kenzie had been thinking about this question, and when she did, the feelings it engendered within her now were unsettling.

This was obviously not the time to talk about it further, so she walked along the hall, turning off lights as she went, Arran close behind her, his hands on her hips. A decision would have to be made about the fate of the embryo soon, and the fact was that she was the only one with any genetic connection to it. This was something which just a few weeks ago had not fazed her, but now, the more she thought about it, the more uneasy it left her.

This child had been both Olivia and Glenn's dream, and Kenzie doubted that once he began to heal, he'd be able to turn his back on that. But as she pulled off her clothes, slipped an old

T-shirt of Arran's on and cleaned her teeth next to him, Kenzie stared at herself in the mirror.

In her own turquoise eyes, she saw a reflection of Olivia's. In the same long chin as their mother, and the trademark high cheekbones, she saw her sister, too. As Olivia stared back at Kenzie from the mirror, she was suddenly, and alarmingly, certain that whatever Glenn was thinking, *she* couldn't turn her back on her sister's dream, even if he might.

11

Kenzie arrived back from Norway on the following Friday morning, to find a single red rose in a vase, and a note from Arran to say that he'd gone to the gym and would be back by 1 p.m.

Smiling to herself, and realising that she was starving, she opened the fridge, then sighed to see it practically empty. That Arran would go out and get her a rose but not think to grab some basic provisions was frustrating, and yet, as she put the scarlet petals to her nose and breathed in their light perfume, she instantly forgave him.

After dumping her dirty clothes into the laundry basket, stowing her suitcase in the cupboard under the stairs and taking a long, hot shower, Kenzie pulled on some light cotton trousers and her favourite white linen blouse, then grabbed her keys.

Outside, the morning sky was clear, the late July sun warm on her skin as she caught the familiar tang of the river. She loved to travel, but there was nothing like the sights and smells of home.

Glancing at Olivia and Glenn's empty driveway, then up at the house, Kenzie's throat contracted. The sense that she might see her sister at the window or waving from the old Land Rover as she headed off to work, while Kenzie knew that she wouldn't, ever again, was soul-destroying.

Blinking away tears, she walked to her car and got inside. Fort William felt like a better option, rather than going to the local shop for her groceries. Sally Childs, who ran the village store in Inverlochy, just a few minutes' walk from the house, was a friendly chatterbox with a smoker's cough and a wicked sense of humour. Kenzie and Olivia used to giggle about her habit of patting her tight grey perm and saying, *you know, sort of thing*, after everything she talked about, using the phrase as verbal parentheses around her every observation about the locals, tourists, the weather, the news or any morsel of gossip that she had gleaned from her regulars.

Today, Kenzie wasn't up to handling Sally's mischief, so the relative anonymity of the big supermarket on An Aird Road was preferrable.

The drive took only ten minutes, but Kenzie was on autopilot, not registering the backdrop of the lush and layered hills on her left or paying attention to the curve of the road as she passed the remains of the Old Fort of Fort William's wall, or the small canon that sat on the bank of the river that her father had made up outlandish stories about, involving Jacobites and Highlanders.

Soon, she was walking across the car park, hoping that her sunglasses would hide the bags under her eyes, and the fact that she had scrubbed her face of make-up when she'd showered.

Fifteen minutes later, with a trolley half full, she made her way to the checkout, but as she approached, she spotted a familiar figure in the line ahead of her. The tousled hair, the curve of the wiry shoulders and the trademark faded Triumph T-shirt gave Glenn away, and Kenzie's heart lifted as she moved in closer and tapped him on the shoulder.

He spun around looking startled, then when he saw it was her, he gave a half-smile. 'Hello, you.'

'Hi, stranger. How are you? You never called me back. I've been worried about you. Where have you been?' Kenzie scanned his face, his jaw seeming more prominent now, and his eyes slightly sunken.

'Trucking along. You know.' He shrugged, swiped his credit card through the machine and began packing a bag with his purchases. He seemed to be avoiding her eyes, so Kenzie cleared her throat, more loudly than she'd intended.

He glanced back at her, his face colouring slightly.

'Where are you going now? Straight home?' She began putting her shopping on the belt but locked her eyes on him, daring him to look away.

Glenn lifted his bag out of the way. 'Not necessarily.'

Before he could find an excuse to escape and hoping that talking to her in a neutral environment might be easier for him, Kenzie pointed to the far side of the store where there was a small café, with a handful of tables against the wall of windows facing the river. 'Can we grab a coffee then?'

He followed her finger with his eyes and hesitated, then looked back at her.

'Sure. We do need to talk.'

The phrase brought with it a spark of anxiety; those words seldom associated with anything good.

'OK. Grab a table and I'll meet you over there.'

He nodded, then walked away from her, his shoulders stooped under an invisible weight.

A few minutes later, with two mugs of coffee on the table between them, Glenn spoke quietly.

'I'm sorry I've not been around, much.' He stretched his neck to the left, a nervous tic that Olivia had told her about.

'Or at all.' Kenzie lifted her eyebrows, but sensed this was not the way to get him to open up now that she finally had his attention. 'Sorry. It's just that we miss you. You've literally disappeared lately, and I'm worried about you.'

He nodded, then sipped some coffee. 'I'm OK, Kenz. Just working through everything the best I can.'

'I understand that, Glenn. But isolating yourself like this. It's not...' She stopped herself, afraid she might cry, and unsure how to proceed without having him shut down again.

'I know, and I've been meaning to come over. It's not that I'm intentionally shutting you out, more that I needed to get my head straight, about various things, before we talked.'

She took in his pinched expression, the way he was frowning then shaking his head almost imperceptibly, as if having a silent debate with himself about something.

'So, are you getting any closer?' She took a sip of acrid coffee, and shuddered.

He sat back, his eyes seeming to clear of the fog she'd seen there recently.

'Yes, and it's time I told you what's going on.'

'OK. I'm all ears.' She pushed her cup away and folded her arms.

'This has taken a lot of thought, and it's not been an easy decision, but you deserve to know.' He paused, as Kenzie's chest began to feel weighted.

'Whatever it is, Glenn, it's all right. You can tell me.'

He took a moment, then said, 'Since Olivia died, I've been thinking about making some changes. To be honest, being in that house is just too hard.' He ran a hand through his hair, then clasped the back of his neck. 'But it's not just the house. I feel like I'm living a life that no longer fits. Does that make any sense?' He stared at her, his hand dropping to his lap.

'What do you mean, doesn't fit?' Kenzie leaned forward on her elbows, alarm bells ringing inside her. Surely he couldn't mean what she thought he did?

'I mean the flat was Olivia's. I just moved in when we got

married. Plus, she left it to you, so I'm now just a sitting tenant, so to speak.'

Kenzie's mouth went slack.

Seeing her expression, he frowned. 'Didn't you know that?'

'No. I didn't. I didn't even know she had a will.' She shook her head, letting the information permeate. Why had Olivia never mentioned any of this to her?

'She told me a few years ago, and I was totally fine with it, because it made sense. She wanted to know that if anything ever happened to her, you would be OK.'

'But I'm fine, Glenn. I don't need the flat. It's your home. You belong there.' She sat back and took in his expression, a palpable distance seeming to open back up between them.

'No, it's not mine. And without her, even more so. I think I need a change, Kenzie, so I've been thinking about applying for a transfer. Maybe move to a different force. A fresh start, so to speak.'

Kenzie's throat knotted as her fears materialised, and she tried to imagine Glenn not living upstairs. Not seeing his bike coming and going, or having him drop in for meals, or to talk about his job, watch football with Arran, or play board games. As the images gathered momentum, Olivia began to slip even further away, and Kenzie couldn't contemplate feeling any more lost than she already did. Glenn was a critical connection to her sister that Kenzie didn't know if she could bear losing, however selfish she knew that to be.

'But where would you go?'

'There are thirteen Scottish police divisions, Kenzie, I could transfer to Fife or Strathclyde or something.' He shrugged. 'I even looked at what's involved in re-applying in Australia. My brother keeps saying I should go back there now. Be near them again.'

At this, Kenzie gasped.

'I understand him feeling that way, Glenn. But surely you

wouldn't go that far away? *We're* still family, too. Don't you want to...' Her voice cracked, and she pressed her lips closed. She shouldn't use that to guilt him into staying, but hearing all this was driving a painful dart through her, loss piling on top of loss until she thought she might suffocate under the weight of it.

Desperate to find something to anchor him to them, to stay in their lives, she suddenly remembered the embryo. The last chance of the child that her sister had so longed for, and that Glenn had wanted too, and before she could stop herself, she blurted, 'What about the baby?'

He looked startled for a moment, then he dipped his chin before meeting her eyes again.

'I should've said something sooner, but it's taken me a while to be sure about what to do, and then I didn't know how to tell you, after everything you went through, for us.' He halted, then sighed. 'Kenzie, I can't do it without Olivia. There's just no way.'

Hearing him say this was a blow, a slam to the gut that Kenzie hadn't expected. As disappointment sucked at her, Kenzie realised that somewhere, deep inside, part of her had secretly been hoping that Glenn might want to go ahead, the child they had planned together providing a link to Olivia, however tenuous, even though the practicalities of that were impossibly complex.

A single man – no, a widower, trying to have a child, needing to use a surrogate, and him not even being genetically connected to the baby was the stuff of novels, and Kenzie knew that, but underneath it all, the crux of the matter was that it had been Olivia's dream, and her dream *with* Glenn. Walking away from that felt like yet another layer of devastating loss, which, considering everything Glenn had just told her about leaving, could be enough to crush her completely.

Glenn took a few moments, and when Kenzie stayed silent,

he continued, 'Please don't be upset, but I have to be completely honest with you.'

Unable to trust her voice, she simply nodded.

'I was only going ahead with the IVF, and the baby, for Olivia. I feel terrible admitting that after everything you did, but it's too important not to tell you the truth.'

Kenzie's breath caught. This was the last thing she expected to hear from him, as all she had ever believed to be true, based on what her sister had told her, was that both she *and* Glenn wanted to be parents. As Kenzie tried to wrap her head around this new twist, she couldn't help but wonder which of them had been less than honest about that, either with her, or each other.

Thinking about Olivia being anything other than truthful was impossible, leaving only Glenn as potentially holding back his true feelings, to support his wife's dream. And yet, the more she thought about it, the more she recalled his excitement, his joy when they discovered that there was a chance, albeit only one, that they could have a child, so this revelation felt hollow, and less than genuine.

'But you were so happy about it. At least I thought you were.' She locked her eyes on his, looking for any signs of deception, but all she saw was raw sadness. 'Is there anything that you're not telling me?' The old suspicion she'd been harbouring in the last weeks before Olivia's death, that something was amiss between her and Glenn, resurfaced, and then, bizarrely, Kenzie pictured the tall man at the funeral whom Glenn had told to leave.

He leaned forward. 'Look, the reading of the will is next week. Let's talk more after that. I'm going away for a couple of days, but I'll see you at the solicitor's office next Thursday. OK?'

Kenzie frowned, her anxiety and confusion growing. 'What's this got to do with the will?'

Glenn stood up, then carefully pushed his chair in close to the table. 'We'll talk more after that, I promise.'

'Why are we involving a solicitor anyway?' She squinted at him. 'It's pretty straightforward, isn't it?'

'I want it done formally so we all know where we stand.' He smiled at her, but his eyes were devoid of joy. 'I've got to go, but say hi to Arran. I love you two.' He surveyed her face, then walked to her side, leaned down and kissed her cheek. 'Don't worry, little bean. Everything will be all right.'

Hearing the nickname he'd given her when he'd first started dating Olivia jolted Kenzie out of her momentary daze. She had always hated green beans, but Olivia would insist she eat at least one each time Olivia made them. It had become a standing joke, and Kenzie had played into the fun, dramatically eating one bean, the smallest she could find, then gagging theatrically while Glenn and Olivia laughed.

As she let the images come, they made her sad, and nostalgic for simpler times gone by. If only she had known to lock them in her heart, to take mental pictures that she could look back on when she needed comfort. Surely all of those happy moments they'd shared, the years of fun, laughter and precious memories meant as much to him as they did to her? Wasn't any of that important enough to keep them bound together, to stop him from leaving?

Then, as she looked up at her brother-in-law, the strain in his face apparent, another wave of confusion engulfed her. Was a fresh start truly the only reason he wanted to leave? To leave his home, and now the baby he and Olivia had hoped for, too.

They had both said they had things to tell Kenzie, which was as puzzling as it was frustrating, but now, overshadowing her sadness at the sight of him walking away was her certainty that there was more to this situation than Kenzie was being told. Much more.

12

A few hours later, Arran had drawn the curtains in the living room, and when Kenzie walked in with a fragile brandy glass in each palm, he lit the big cathedral candle that sat on the coffee table.

He dimmed the overhead light and turned on the two Chinese lamps that flanked the sofa as Kenzie smiled at him.

'Nice. I need everything that's soothing.' She held a glass out to him, then tapped the rim gently against his. 'Here's to us. Wha's like us?' They nodded to each other at the beginning lines of her father's favourite toast, then they each took a sip of their drink.

'So, tell me what happened when you saw Glenn.' Arran sat at the end of the sofa nearest the window, then patted the cushion next to him.

Kenzie sat down, shifting in close to his side. As she took another sip and began to talk, the warmth of the brandy helped ease the words, and her worries, into the room.

A few moments later, Arran's jaw dropped. 'Really? He said that?'

Irritated at having to repeat herself, Kenzie closed her eyes for a second before replying. It wasn't Arran's fault that Glenn had ripped the rug from under her, in more ways than one, so she controlled her tone. 'Yes. He said he was going along with the IVF just for Olivia and that he was thinking of leaving, transferring somewhere new. Maybe even back to Australia.'

Arran frowned. 'It doesn't sound like him. I know he wanted a family, and he always told me how much he loved living here, in this house, and so close to the mountain. I know his brother is over there, but he loves his job here, and his team, too.' He shook his head. 'It's a bad move, if you ask me, making all these drastic changes so soon. I know he's grieving, but he needs to slow down.'

Kenzie nodded. 'Do you think if I transferred ownership of the flat to him, it'd make a difference?'

Arran shrugged. 'No idea. But maybe you should talk to him about it.'

'Right. I told him I don't need it, that it's his home, but I still think there's more to all this. My gut is gnawing at me, Arran, and you know it's never wrong.'

He slid his arm around her shoulder and pulled her closer, then kissed the top of her head. 'What's it telling you? I know better than to question it.' He leaned forward and put his glass on the table.

'That he's hiding something, or not being completely honest about his reasons for leaving.' She shrugged, feeling the warmth of Arran's leg through her cotton trousers.

'Maybe. But remember, I've said this before. Perhaps this is just his process.'

Kenzie leaned away, locking eyes with her husband. 'It's more than that. I'm telling you.' She put her glass next to Arran's. 'There are things that don't add up. It's driving me crazy that Olivia had something important to tell me, that I might never find out about now. And who was that guy at the funeral, the tall fair-haired guy Glenn practically threw out?

I'm going to ask him outright. He can't lie to me, Arran. I know him too well.'

Arran nodded. 'Ask, but just be gentle with him, OK?'

She scraped the hair away from her forehead.

'No promises.' She smiled sadly. 'I can't let him walk away from this family without a fight. Olivia would never forgive me.'

Arran stood up. 'I hear you.'

Kenzie's eyes were burning, the ever-present tears of the past few weeks pressing in behind her eyes.

'I owe her that, at least.'

That night, she dreamt about Olivia again. She sat in the window seat of her flat, her bare feet crossed under her. Her hair was glossy, coating her shoulders, and she wore boyfriend jeans and her favourite sweater, a pale-green cashmere V-neck that Glenn had bought her in St Andrews for her thirtieth birthday. She spoke to Kenzie, her voice soft but firm.

'We can't let the line end with us, Kenzie. We need to do it for Mum and Dad. Please. It's our last chance.'

Kenzie woke with a start, her heart racing. Next to her, Arran was snoring softly, his left arm curved above his head and his feet sticking out from under the end of the duvet, as always.

She took a moment, waiting for her rapid pulse to steady, then she rolled towards her husband and curled into his side.

'What's up?' he murmured, his right hand seeking hers.

'Nothing. Just had a weird dream,' she whispered. 'Go back to sleep.'

'K.' He squeezed her fingers, then turned to face the window, so Kenzie shifted in close to him and slipped her arm under his and around his chest, spooning his broad back. Suddenly, she tried to imagine life without Arran, a desolate chill instantly roiling in the pit of her stomach.

Everyone she loved had left her, one way or another. What

was to say Arran wouldn't go too, at some point? Kenzie still lived with her cloying fear, buried so deep that she hadn't shared it with anyone, not even her sister, that one day she would be entirely alone. That the void her loved ones had left would eventually swallow her whole and she would disappear into a sad and solitary existence, unreachable and isolated from the world.

She tightened her grip around Arran's chest, then gently kissed his back. 'I love you,' she whispered. 'More than life itself.'

She eventually heard his breathing return to the gentle rhythmic hiss that meant he was sleeping deeply, so she closed her eyes and tried to clear her mind of the dream, but Olivia's words played on a loop in her ear. *This is our last chance.* The more Kenzie heard it, the more awake she became, a question rising to the surface of her consciousness. If this remaining embryo was the last chance to continue the Grey family line, and Glenn wasn't willing, or able, to proceed with a pregnancy without Olivia, what would happen to it?

She recognised the softening of Arran's back when he entered deep sleep, and sighing, Kenzie considered the limited options. As she thought about what could very likely be her last good egg, frozen in both time and history, a stinging sadness filled her chest. *This is our last chance.* Could Glenn really walk away from that? Discarding Olivia's most fervent wish, without guilt, or regret?

Kenzie's stomach twisting into a knot, she rolled away from Arran, carefully slipped out of bed, lifted her robe from the padded bench at the foot of the bed and crept down the hall to the kitchen. She sat at the table and opened her laptop, and her hands were trembling as she typed in *what happens to unwanted embryos,* then she held her breath as the screen populated with line after line of text, each one feeling incendiary as the cursor hovered over them.

While she didn't want to think about this yet, knowledge was power, and until she understood the ramifications of what Glenn was considering, all she could do was try to learn, then she'd present the options to him, hopefully before he made any final decisions.

The following week, their meeting with the solicitor in Fort William had been both brief and surprising. Elizabeth Hampton, a soft-spoken woman, in her mid-forties, with a shoulder-length blonde bob and a simple, navy cotton dress on, had ushered them into a conference room. In the centre had been a collection of mismatched chairs around a long wooden table, hosting a bottle of still water and four stubby glasses on a tray. The walls were bare of decoration and the window overlooking the town centre was smudged with fingerprints, and, on the outside, tracks of the recent rain streaked the grubby glass.

As Elizabeth had condoled with them on their loss, then read the three-page document, Glenn had stared out of the window, his formal shirt and linen jacket incongruous over his faded jeans.

Arran had sat across from Kenzie, his eyes locked on hers as they'd listened to Olivia's final wishes, Kenzie's vision blurring as she let the words permeate. Olivia had indeed left the upstairs flat to Kenzie, along with all her personal possessions, and her few pieces of jewellery, barring her engagement ring which she'd wanted Glenn to keep.

As Kenzie had listened, the formality of the wording of the will had felt disjointed, boilerplate prose rather than personal to her sister's voice, and when Elizabeth had told them that Kenzie had been named the executor of Olivia's will, Kenzie had snapped her eyes to Glenn, who'd seemed frozen, his stare fixed on the window, showing no sign of surprise or concern at this revelation.

'Why would she do that?' Kenzie had frowned, nervous that this would be another hurt for Glenn to stomach. 'Surely, as her husband, Glenn should be the executor?'

Elizabeth had kept her voice low. 'These are her instructions, Mrs Ford. It's clearly stated here.' She'd pointed at the page in front of her, the sight of her long, scarlet fingernail jarring, like a droplet of blood-red wax, sealing the agreement.

Twenty minutes later, at Arran's suggestion, rather than go straight home they had walked down the street to the King George, and now they sat in a corner of the crowded pub, three glasses of whisky on the small, round table in front of them.

The ceiling was heavily beamed and the long wooden bar, with tarnished brass edging, ran the length of the far wall, then curved like a hook, a row of worn leather stools lined up along the front of it.

Kenzie was feeling slightly queasy, so she just sniffed the whisky and set the glass back on the table.

'So, what now?' Arran swirled the liquid in his glass. 'You're not seriously going to leave, are you, mate?'

Kenzie kept her head down as Glenn shrugged off his jacket and draped it over the back of his chair.

'I went to Perth earlier this week, met with the CI there, and there's a position coming up.' He nodded to himself. 'I'm going to take it. It's a promotion, and the right move for me, now. I need a fresh start.'

Kenzie's jaw tightened. While this was better than him moving to the other side of the planet, the statement still felt like a slap to her face.

'What about us?' She knew she sounded petulant, but at this point she was hurt, and beyond caring. 'We are your family, too. We lost her, too. Doesn't that count for something? Shouldn't we be sticking together. Helping each other through this?' She gulped back a sob. 'She was *my* sister, Glenn. My life will never be the same without her, but do I have to lose you too?' A tear broke over her lower lid and she mashed it away with her fingertip.

Arran pressed his knee against hers, a gentle and yet distinct message that she should try to stop this emotionally charged attack, but, unwilling to edit herself with Glenn any longer, Kenzie pulled her leg away and stared at her brother-in-law.

'Kenzie, I know this probably feels like a knee-jerk reaction to losing Olivia, and that I've not taken you and Arran into consideration, but it's not like that.' His angular face was pale.

'Then tell me what it *is* like.' She sat back, aware that she was talking too loudly, as Arran gently laid his palm on her knee.

The couple at the table next to them were both looking over their shoulders at her. Eyeing the grey-haired, tweed blazer-wearing man, approximately in his sixties, Kenzie shook her head slightly, as if asking him what he was looking at. When his face coloured, and he turned back to face his partner, a rail-thin redhead in a long floral dress, Kenzie turned her attention back to Glenn.

'There are things that you don't understand, but before you lambast me again, let me just say this.' He held his palm up to stop her jumping in. 'You will always be my family, and me being in a different town won't change that. Please just try to understand that staying here is too painful, Kenzie. Everywhere I look, walk, sit, eat, sleep, she is there.' He swallowed hard. 'I loved her so much, and I love you, but I need to give myself a fighting chance at survival, and I think Olivia would have understood that.' He held Kenzie's gaze as she pressed her lips together, her desire to disagree with him, to beg him to stay, like molten lava pushing up into her throat. 'You have always been there for me, and I will never forget that. You were as much Olivia's rock as she was yours. I think you know that.'

Kenzie nodded, wiping away another tear.

'When we talked last week, I told you that I'd agreed to the

IVF for *her*.' He waited until she nodded again. 'That wasn't strictly true. I *did* want a family, too. Not as much as Olivia did, but I was happy, and so grateful when you did that incredible thing for us.' He held a hand out to Kenzie and, unable to help herself, she gripped his fingers briefly, until he pulled his hand back. 'But without her, none of it makes sense anymore, so I've asked Elizabeth Hampton to write up a document that gives you full legal rights over the embryo. You can decide what to do with it as I can't be involved anymore. I'm sorry.'

Stunned, Kenzie looked over at Arran, who's face visibly drained of colour as he said quietly, 'Are you sure about that, Glenn? That's a monumental decision to make when everything is still so raw.'

Kenzie looked back at Glenn, who was shaking his head.

'It's not truly mine to make any decisions over, Arran. Think about it.'

'I know that genetically it's not, but it was about your and Olivia's future. Your family.'

Glenn shook his head. 'That's what I'm saying. That's not a future that I recognise any more, because she's gone. I know this might sound harsh, but I'm sure it's the right thing to do.' He met Kenzie's eyes again. 'I'm so sorry, little bean. You were an angel to do what you did for us, and I will never forget it.' His eyes filled, then he slipped his jacket back on and stood up. 'Thanks for the drink.' He nodded at Arran. 'I've got to get back to work.'

Kenzie was muted by shock, drenched in the realisation that she was losing her last connection to her sister, despite all her efforts to make him stay. Panic setting in, as she watched Glenn walk towards the door, she grabbed Arran's hand.

'Stop him, Arran.' She blinked away fresh tears. 'I can't let him go and leave me with this decision. Please.' She swallowed over a knot, her throat on fire. 'I don't know what to do.'

Arran covered her hand with his free one, then smiled

sadly. 'He's obviously given it a lot of thought, and he's made his mind up, Kenz. All we can do now is accept that and help him as much as we can. Olivia would've wanted us to.'

Kenzie's heart was thumping in her chest, her face feeling warm as tears tracked down her cheeks while the moss-green eyes she knew so well took her in. As she drew in some deep breaths, feeling her pulse balance out, she closed her eyes. She knew he was right. Olivia would have wanted what was best for Glenn, but Kenzie still couldn't believe that leaving behind the only family he had left in Scotland, that connected him to Olivia, *was* the best thing.

Aside from that, the disturbing realisation that, soon, she would have to make a decision about the fate of the embryo, the child that her sister had longed for, was terrifying. How could she possibly make that call, and if she destroyed Olivia's dream, would she be able to live with herself?

13

Three days later, while at the research centre in Oban, lost in reviewing the latest environmental management curriculum for a group of Masters students, Kenzie jumped when her phone rang.

She felt groggy, as she had hardly slept the night before, restless for hours and twisting the duvet into a massive cocoon of cotton around her. At dawn, she'd got out of bed, stood at their bedroom window and watched Glenn, walking his motorbike down the driveway, both sides of the classic Triumph loaded with a large saddlebag.

He'd told Arran that he was going to spend a week in Perth, to shadow the police officer whose position he would be taking over, and while he spotted the movement at the window and waved to her, his not saying goodbye properly had been another shot of hurt that had been hard to swallow.

As she lifted the phone from the desk, Kenzie hoped it was him, so seeing Doctor Kennedy's name on the screen was disappointing. Puzzled, she took a few moments to answer.

'Hello?'

'Hello, Mrs Ford. It's Doctor Kennedy's office.' The receptionist, Frances, a kind woman of approximately fifty who had checked Kenzie in for all her appointments and procedures, sounded oddly nasal, as if she had a bad cold.

'Hi Frances, how are you?' Kenzie spun her chair around and looked out of the window, the early afternoon bright, and the sky clear blue above the steep slopes of the Garbh Àrd point and the familiar peak of Glenn Lora.

'A bit of a cold, but otherwise fine.' Frances sniffed. 'Doctor Kennedy would like a chat if you've a few minutes.'

Kenzie frowned, a pop of concern bringing her to her feet. 'Um, sure. Now?'

'Yes, I'll put him through, just hang on.'

A few moments passed as she paced along the front of her work area, then the doctor came on the line.

'Afternoon, Kenzie. How are you?'

'Fine, thanks.' Kenzie walked to the window, to her left the water of Ardmucknish Bay sparkling in the early August afternoon.

'I wanted to say how awfully sorry I am about your sister. I had no idea until I saw it in the obits.'

Kenzie winced, the mere mention of Olivia like a needle piercing her bruised heart.

'Thank you.'

'I know this might not be a good time, but we do need to talk in person at some point.'

Kenzie frowned, suddenly knowing about what, but wishing to delay this conversation for a little longer. 'Right.'

'Could you possibly come in next week? It shouldn't take long.'

She mentally sifted through the events of the following week, involving conducting a seminar at the research centre on the marine carbon cycle in the Arctic, a dive class she was instructing in Oban, and some more lab work on the Norwegian crab study. As she pictured the days ahead, only the

Thursday, the fifteenth of the month, seemed like a possibility.

'I think I could do Thursday, if it's your first appointment, as I do have to get down here to Oban by noon.'

'We can make that work. I'll get Frances to book it in and send you a confirmation.' He paused. 'Again, I'm extremely sorry about your sister.'

Kenzie nodded, her eyes locked on the water of the bay. 'I appreciate that. See you next week.'

She slid the phone into the pocket of her lab coat and sat at the long worktable, scanning the rows of testing equipment, a variety of underwater cameras and hi-tech sonar gear.

Behind her, a tall free-standing rack held various wet suits, dive masks, regulators and sets of fins, all hanging on large hooks. Under the rack, a row of scuba tanks with the research centre's logo on them stood shoulder to shoulder, all filled and ready for her class the coming week.

She could almost taste the ever-present salty scent of the dive equipment, as she closed her eyes. Getting into the water again, for the first time since Olivia had died, would be a release.

Oban's setting was picturesque, occupying a spot on the Firth of Lorn. The bay formed a near perfect horseshoe, and was protected by the island of Kerrera; overlooking the islands of Mull and Lismore.

The firth – a body of water that connected directly to the open ocean – while bitterly cold even in the summer, was a special area of conservation and supported a large variety of marine species. In her years of diving there, and taking research trips out on boats, Kenzie had been fortunate to see dolphins, porpoises, minke whales and seals. Once, the year before, she had even seen a basking shark, and hoped one day to spot an orca, as one of her colleagues had done in the past.

Trying to imagine herself in her wetsuit, her hair held tight to her head under the neoprene hood as she paddled underwater, she sighed. The sky above the surface of the water was a guide that she would check regularly while under, as an indicator of any changes in the weather conditions, and that sense of freedom, of isolation and protection from the harshness of the world above her was like a tonic that she now craved.

She had often tried to persuade Olivia to take a diving course so that she too could experience the great silence, the feeling of being so minuscule in an underwater wonderland that had so many hidden treasures to behold, but Olivia had always laughed and shaken her head. 'The day you get me in a smelly old wetsuit, deep underwater, will be the day pigs fly.' She'd shudder. 'Terrifying.'

Kenzie would tut, then say, 'I know. You go high, and I go low, and never the twain shall meet.'

They'd smiled at each other then, accepting that their choices of environment to escape to were as different from one another as they could possibly be.

Picturing her sister's face, Kenzie's throat narrowed, her mind going back to the phone call she'd just taken. She knew what the conversation with Doctor Kennedy would involve, and glancing at the August calendar page on the wall, showing a stunning shot of an orca arcing out of the water in the bay, she counted that she had just six days to get her head straight. To make a decision that she'd never planned on making about the fate of the embryo, and the responsibility of that was intimidating.

That night, Kenzie made a light dinner and had a catch-up with Arran about his day out at Glenfinnan, near the iconic viaduct that the Harry Potter films had made world-famous. Arran was working on a pilot project, set up by Network Rail Scotland and Forestry and Land Scotland, to enhance and create biodiverse habitats over a huge section of the Mallaig Line. She loved how animated he became when he talked about his work and letting him have the floor that evening had been enjoyable. His deep voice had eased the tension out of her back and at the same time had allowed her to avoid talking about what was troubling her.

Now, while he watched the late-night news, she lay in the old, claw-foot bath, her hair tied up in a messy topknot, her head propped on a rolled-up towel and the stingingly hot water lapping around her thighs and stomach. Arran had brought her a glass of wine that sat on the wooden caddy that straddled the tub, so she sipped some, then carefully balanced the glass between the soap and a small, natural loofah that neither of them had ever used.

When she and Olivia lived together in the house, after their parents died and before they had subdivided it into the two flats, Olivia would rap on the bathroom door and say, 'For God's sake, you've been in there for forty-five minutes. You'll dissolve soon.'

Kenzie would shout back, 'Oh, bog off. This is the only place I get any peace.'

Sometimes Olivia would come into the bathroom, fill a tooth mug with cold water and, as Kenzie dared her, toss it at her face. They'd had many a water fight start that way, often with Kenzie squealing, and Olivia laughing until she cried, as they both slipped around on the white ceramic tile floor, until they'd end up panting and grabbing towels from the rail to mop up the mess they'd made.

Missing her sister so much that it robbed her of breath, Kenzie twisted out a cotton washcloth, watching the sudsy trail dribble into the bathwater, then unrolled it and laid it across her stomach. She pressed her palms onto the cloth, feeling her taut abdominal muscles, then, without thinking, she pushed her stomach out, the small mound under her fingertips sending a spark of something that she'd never felt before straight to her core.

As she inhaled and repeated the exercise, Kenzie closed her eyes, letting the feeling reveal itself, and as it solidified, she recognised that it was longing – a sense of housing a void that she wanted to fill. When she opened her eyes, she spotted Arran standing in the open doorway.

'What're you doing?' A deep frown was puckering his forehead.

Thinking quickly, she said, 'Nothing. Just doing that yoga breathing thing, where you're supposed to push the air into your stomach, to relax.' She pushed her tummy out as far as she could, then grimaced. 'Lot of rubbish, probably.'

He leaned his shoulder against the door frame, and scanned her face, his jaw taut.

'Are you OK?'

She nodded, feeling the towel slip lower behind her neck. 'Yeah, just... you know.' She sat up and began soaping the washcloth. 'Thinking about Olivia.'

He nodded, took the cloth from her, knelt at the side of the bath and began washing her back, moving the warm cloth in small circles.

'That feels lovely.' She sighed, leaning into the welcome pressure of his hand. 'Don't stop.'

'K.' He wiped down her side to her hip, his hand slipping under the water.

Kenzie dropped her chin to her chest. They hadn't made love since Olivia had died, the thought of feeling that alive and connected to Arran when her sister was reduced to ash in a crematorium impossible to reconcile. But now, she ached for him, to feel his weight, his arms around her, gentle but insistent, grounding her like an anchor.

She put her hand over his and guided him to her breast, then their eyes locked.

'Want to get out now?' His voice was husky as he dropped the washcloth, stood and handed her a towel.

Kenzie stood up, letting the cooling water trickle down her body.

'Thanks.' She wrapped the towel around herself and tucked it in under her arms, as Arran leaned in and scooped her out of the bath, his strong forearm under her thighs. 'Woah cowboy,' she laughed, but seeing his earnest expression, she cupped his face in her palms. 'I love you, Arran.'

'I love you bigger.' He smiled into her eyes, then walked into the hall and headed for their bedroom.

Kenzie woke at 4 a.m. feeling cold. They'd fallen asleep before she'd put on her pyjamas and now, albeit summer, the room was cool. Arran was snoring softly next to her, so she slipped from the bed and gingerly opened a drawer in the big chest under the bay window. As she pulled out her favourite pyjamas, she hesitated, catching the shadowy outline of her reflection in the mirror on top of the chest.

Turning to the side, she placed her hands on her stomach and pushed it out again, feeling the unaccustomed tautness of the skin across her front. As she stood there in the darkness, staring at her bizarre shape, tears pressed in behind her eyes. What if she were pregnant? What if *she* had this baby, this little boy that her sister had longed for? As she blinked her vision clear, Olivia's words came back to her from the dream. *This is our last chance.*

Shaking her head at the crazy notion, Kenzie slipped her pyjamas on and tiptoed back to the bed. She got in, careful not to move too quickly, then lay on her back, her hands once again going to her stomach. What if it wasn't crazy? What if she actually did this – this terrifying, life-altering and yet amazing thing? Would it be insane if she went ahead with it, as a final act of love that would honour her sister's wishes?

14

The following week, with only one day left until her meeting with Doctor Kennedy, Kenzie's nerves were in shreds. She couldn't stop thinking about the embryo, and how she could even be considering making this startling U-turn when it came to having a child. As she battled with her conflict around it, finding this new longing confusing, her biggest fear was telling Arran how she'd been feeling.

Today, they were both working in Oban, so she had texted him and asked him to walk up to McCaig's Tower with her, for lunch. She'd grabbed some bacon rolls from the bakery in the main street, and they'd climbed the hill, the mid-August sky azure, and strewn with patches of lacy clouds.

The wooden bench at the centre of the tower was warm beneath them and the westerly breeze cool, but gentle on their skin. The town and harbour below looked like a postcard, the water in the horseshoe of the bay glittering as the afternoon sun gilded the army of ripples that curved in towards the sea wall. Two small fishing boats moved slowly into the harbour, one behind the other, and to the left a large ferry was moored next to the dock.

The air was heavy with the earthy scent of the violet-coloured Meadow Cranesbill, a tiny variety of geranium that grew on the slope of the hill, and as she handed Arran his roll, Kenzie let the herbal smell fill her head.

'So, when are you going to tell me what's really going on with you?' He took the roll from her and unwrapped it from the paper.

Taken aback, and yet not completely surprised that he'd picked up on her slightly odd mood this past few days, she laughed softly. 'Can't get anything by you, Sherlock.'

'I know you, and that you'd talk to me when you're ready, so...' He smiled, then took a massive bite of his roll. 'C'mon. Out with it.' He spoke around his mouthful.

Kenzie shook her head at him, then bit into her own roll, even a few more seconds of delay feeling like a life raft. As she chewed, the pleasant, smoky salt of the bacon and the crisp outer layer of the roll took her back to childhood breakfasts at the kitchen table in the house, images of them when they'd been a proper family glittering behind her eyes. Then, Olivia's face materialised, the creamy complexion, the turquoise eyes, and the high cheekbones, the full mouth that Kenzie had always envied, all seeming to glow as she whispered, *This is our last chance*.

Stuffing the remains of her roll back into the paper bag, Kenzie shifted to face Arran.

'You're going to think I'm nuts, but please hear me out, OK?' She dipped her chin and locked her eyes on his, giving him her best *I mean it* look.

'All right.' His eyebrows jumped. 'Go on.'

Kenzie tucked one foot under her, her hands in her lap.

'I've been having some thoughts about the embryo, now that it's my decision what happens to it.' She paused, seeing his brow pucker and his eyes narrow, as if he hadn't heard her right. 'You know I never wanted children, and with my endometriosis, it was even less of a possibility...' She stopped, as his jaw visibly tightened, but the necessity to get this out forced her on. 'This past couple of weeks, I've been feeling conflicted. Trying to get my head around the options, and to reconcile how I'll feel about each of them.' She eyed him as he let his roll fall to his thigh, leaned back, propping one ankle on the opposite knee.

'Right.' He nodded slowly. 'And?'

There was no easy way to table this, so, true to form, Kenzie leapt in.

'I've been thinking about the possibility of having the baby myself.' The words out, they took on a heady reality. 'It was Olivia's dearest wish that our family line didn't end with us, and now, that's down to me. I'm the last Grey standing, and this is the last opportunity to make her wish come true.'

She waited as Arran uncrossed his leg and shifted to face her.

'But you don't want kids, Kenzie. We agreed.' His frown deepened, his voice low and fractured. 'You surely can't be considering having a child for your sister, now she's gone. That makes no sense at all.' He sighed. 'I thought we were done with all this.'

Fear at what she had just unleashed swirled inside Kenzie. What was she thinking? She knew Arran was dead set against children, so even by suggesting this, she was taking a huge risk. He was her everything. Could she truly let this new, unexpected sensation she'd experienced get in between them?

'I know it sounds crazy, Arran, but I can't stop thinking about that little boy. It's a boy, by the way. Did I tell you that?' Her throat began to tighten, so she twisted the lid off the bottle of water she'd brought and took a few gulps. 'Olivia asked for preimplantation genetic testing, so they'd know.'

'No, you didn't tell me.' Arran shook his head. 'But hang on.

Because you know it's a boy that somehow makes a difference? Changes your mind about something so... life-altering' He sounded genuinely confused, but she caught the taint of anger in his question. 'Something we talked about, and agreed we didn't want, years ago.'

'It's not so much knowing the gender as realising that this is the *last* chance I have to keep my family alive. To keep Olivia's dream alive.' To her annoyance, her eyes filled. She wanted to keep emotion out of this so that he'd know she was thinking clearly, and rationally.

'I thought *I* was your family.' He sounded hurt, his eyes glittering.

'Of course you are, love. But you know what I'm saying.' She gulped over a lump of sadness and grabbed his hand. 'This is more than about me, or us, now. It's about Olivia, and Mum and Dad, and even Glenn, because I know he wanted this child, too.' Bizarrely, she put her free hand on her stomach, and as Arran's eyes widened and he took a sharp breath, so did she. 'Look, I know this is completely out of the blue, and I'm sorry, but all I'm asking is for you to keep an open mind.' She leaned forward and took his hand. 'I'm not a lunatic, I promise. Just trying to work through all the thoughts in my head.'

Arran withdrew his hand, his deliberate separation sending a shiver of fear through her.

'You know how I feel about kids, Kenzie. You've always known. I understand that this is hard for you, and with Olivia gone you feel like the last vanguard in trying to keep her alive, but this is bigger than that. Bigger than honouring her wishes, or her memory. This is about changing *our* lives completely.' He drew a line in the air between them. 'In a way that we always said we *never* wanted.' The repetition of their long-held agreement was not lost on her.

She nodded miserably. 'I know, Arran, and I'm so sorry. I don't know where this has come from, truly. I'm as surprised as you are, but I'm just being honest about how I feel. Olivia would have moved heaven and earth for my happiness, and I'm not sure if I could live with myself if I just walk away from this.' She shook her head. 'It's a way of honouring Olivia's legacy – and our family.' She took in his ashen face, the way his mouth was pulsing as he clenched his jaw. 'We always said no secrets between us, right?'

He scrubbed a hand over the top of his head. 'Yes, and I appreciate you telling me how you feel, but you have to understand how *I* feel. I am one hundred per cent blindsided, Kenz. You couldn't have shocked me more.' He scanned her face as if looking for something familiar to hang on to. 'You understand, right? Why I can't just say, sure, cool, let's give it a whirl, because the consequences will last a lifetime, for you and me.' He dropped his hand to his knee as his words cut Kenzie deeply, their implication hinting at the very thing she feared the most. That this decision could drive a wedge between them that could permanently damage their marriage, or maybe even worse.

The following day, Kenzie sat in Doctor Kennedy's office, a tepid, paper cup of tea in front of her, and his shocked expression making her squirm.

'So, what are you saying?' He sat back, linking his fingers in his lap.

'That I want a little time to consider whether to do this, myself.'

His eyes narrowed. 'Right. But given that you told me that you and your husband were not intending to have children, you'll understand my concern that...' He halted.

'That I'm doing it for the right reasons?' A pulse of irritation was throbbing under her breastbone. It was enough to have to justify herself to Arran. 'I know, and based on what I told you before, that's fair, I suppose.'

'Don't mistake me, Kenzie, I will help you in any way I can if you really want to do this.' He leaned forward and laid his palm flat on the desk. 'And with your endometriosis, it's not going to be an easy path. In fact, based on your last scan, frankly, I'm concerned.'

Kenzie felt his words like a slap to the face. 'What do you mean?'

He took a breath. 'In your case, with the endometrial tissue on the outside of the uterus, I'd be particularly concerned about placenta previa. That could raise your risk and increase the odds of you needing a caesarean section.'

Kenzie pictured her insides, the condition that she had been coping with for years, potentially sabotaging this huge step she wanted to take.

'So, are you saying there's a time limit to me doing this?' She eyed him, her heart ticking insistently under her breastbone.

'I'd say that if you are going to go ahead, it needs to be now. The sooner, the better.' He sat back and linked his long fingers in his lap. 'We'll do everything we can, Kenzie, but you need to be aware that a pregnancy, for you, brings certain baggage, shall we say.'

She stared at him, letting this information sink in, and as she tried to imagine backing away from having this child because of fear, she couldn't reconcile that.

'I'll give it more thought, and make a decision soon, then.' She nodded decisively.

'Good. I just want to make sure you're certain.'

'I know. Believe me.'

Arran's words floated back to her, *the consequences will last a lifetime,* and as she stood and shook Doctor Kennedy's hand, that statement encapsulated the one immutable fact in this whole mess.

As she walked out of the building and headed for her car, somewhere deep inside, Kenzie wondered if her and Arran's relationship would weather the storm that suddenly felt like an inevitable force, surging towards them. Could she risk everything that was left to her that she held dear, to make Olivia's dream a reality?

AUTUMN

15

By the first week of September, there was a distinct chill building between Kenzie and Arran. After a couple more strained conversations, the subject of the baby had become taboo, and Kenzie had stepped back from bringing it up, to give him time to process.

Arran had grown quiet, gradually withdrawing from her when he'd come back from work, taking his laptop into his office and sometimes not coming to bed until after she was asleep.

Saying that the project was becoming more difficult to manage remotely, he was now spending more time in Sutherland, mostly returning at weekends, but not always. In response, Kenzie was also burying herself in work, sometimes not getting back from Oban until after 8 p.m., the empty flat feeling unhomely, and depressing.

Kenzie's inner turmoil had robbed her of her appetite and was keeping her up at night, making it hard to concentrate on work, and even Harry had noticed her general malaise.

'Are you sure you're OK?' He'd stood at her workbench that afternoon, his ample stomach straining the waistline of his white lab coat, and his kind eyes taking her in. 'You're not yourself, Kenzie. The team has noticed, too.'

'I'm fine, Harry. Just tired. Probably need a holiday, or a new mattress.' She'd tried to laugh, then turned back to look through the microscope she'd been using.

As groups of tiny oval cells had clarified themselves on the glass slide under the lens, Kenzie had pictured the looks of concern her co-workers were now giving her. Them tiptoeing around her these days, rather than poking fun, or making jokes as usual, felt like an indictment of her not coping, something that had turned her initial gratitude towards them into frustration.

'Why don't you take some time off? And more than a day or two, this time.' Harry had stood his ground until she'd straightened up and turned back to face him. 'I'm serious, Kenzie.'

'I'll think about it. But please stop worrying about me. You know me, Harry. I've got everything under control, despite appearances.'

He locked eyes with her for a few moments.

'If you say so. I'll see you on Monday, then.' He'd hesitated, then left the room, Kenzie turning to face the window before the tears that were blinding her gave her away.

As soon as she'd got in the car to drive home, she'd checked her messages, her heart lifting to see a text from Arran. But when she'd read it, disappointment had clogged her throat.

Something's come up. Going to stay in Sutherland this weekend. Sorry. X

After letting the initial hurt pass, she had replied, her hands shaking.

I understand. I really miss you. See you Monday x

As she'd tossed her phone into her bag and started the engine, tears had filled her eyes again, and she'd whispered, 'Enough now, for God's sake, stop crying.' Then she'd taken a few moments to gather herself before leaving the car park.

Now, sitting at the table in her kitchen, a glass of wine in front of her and the blinds drawn on the pink-tinged twilight, even the sight of the river – the body of water that had always brought her comfort – falling short today, Kenzie heard her phone chirp. Dragging it out of her bag next to her, she glanced at the screen, hoping it was Arran, so seeing Glenn's name made her eyebrows lift.

Home. Are you two around?

Kenzie stood up and walked to the sink, typing as she went.

I'm here. Arran is up north this weekend. Come over.

She noticed that he was typing as she opened the fridge, scanning the shelves to check if she could throw something together for them to eat. Seeing the meagre contents, she sighed, then slammed the door closed.

Half an hour? I'm grabbing a curry up the street. Want something?

Kenzie laughed softly, then typed, *You are my saviour. Tikka masala please :)*

Twenty minutes later, she had cleared the kitchen table of papers and various well-thumbed copies of *Marine World* magazine, put two plates in the oven to warm and had set out some napkins and glasses.

When the doorbell rang, she smiled to herself at the prospect of seeing her brother-in-law, then, as she passed, she checked her reflection in the hall mirror. Her fiery hair was wild, not having seen a comb since first thing that morning, and her complexion was as milky as Olivia's had been, her turquoise eyes cupped by dark shadows. As she shoved her hair away from her cheek, a dip of loss tugging at her core, she heard Glenn on the front step.

'Open sesame. I come bearing gifts.'

Kenzie opened the door and before he could say anything, or even step over the threshold, she grabbed him into a hug, her arms tight around his neck.

'Woah, there. Let a bloke in.' He laughed momentarily, but stayed still, perhaps sensing how much she needed the contact. 'What's up, little bean?' He pulled back from her, catching her swiping at her raw eyes. 'Have you been crying?'

Kenzie gave a huffing sound, then shook her hair back over her shoulder.

'It's all I seem to do these days.' She gave a short, unhappy laugh, but could clearly see the concern in Glenn's eyes. 'Come in. I'm bloody starving.' She found a smile, then took the heavy plastic bag he was carrying, catching the smoky scent of cardamom as she carried it into the kitchen, Glenn close on her heels.

As she unpacked the food, he opened the fridge.

'Not even a beer. Is this a dry hoos noo?' He closed the door and looked over at her as she spooned rice and a golden-coloured curry onto a plate.

'There's wine there. Stop moaning,' she quipped, happy to see a glimmer of the man she recognised as her cheeky brother-in-law.

'When's Arran back?' He took the half-full bottle of wine to the table, lifted the tumblers she'd set out and filled them with water at the sink.

'Monday, hopefully.' Kenzie carried the plates to the table and set them down.

'Hopefully?' Glenn pulled a chair out and sat opposite her.

'Yeah, things are a bit off between us at the moment.' She felt her throat begin to knot, so she tore a piece of naan bread off and stuffed it in her mouth. She was damned if she would cry thrice in one day.

'What do you mean, off?' Glenn frowned, his fork dangling from his hand.

'Tense.' Kenzie spoke around her mouthful.

He scooped up some food. 'What's going on?'

Kenzie swallowed the fluffy bread, then began to talk,

weeks of worry, conflict, pain and confusion flooding out of her as if a dam had burst.

Glenn, his eyes glued to hers, listened, ate a little, then put his fork down, giving her the space she needed to share her burdens, her worry about the family line ending, letting Olivia down, her conflict over the fate of the embryo, until she finally stopped, feeling spent but lighter than she had in a long time. As she sat back, the final thing she had to tell him pressing into her heart, she hesitated.

'What?' Glenn frowned at her. 'Tell me.'

She took a moment, and said quietly, 'I'm thinking about having the baby, Glenn.'

He was silent for a moment, then exhaled slowly.

'Really?' He shook his head almost imperceptibly. 'You're seriously considering having it yourself?'

'I don't know for sure. It depends on a ton of things, and of course on you.'

He looked freshly taken aback. 'What do you mean?'

'I mean on whether you are absolutely *sure* that you don't want...' She stopped herself as he pushed his chair back, stood up and walked to the window. 'The thing is, the doctor has told me that I need to decide now. As in soon.'

'I told you, Kenzie. It makes no sense anymore. I'm out of the equation.' His mouth was strained as he raked his chestnut hair away from his forehead.

'All right, I hear you. I just needed to ask one more time.' She shrugged, regretting having irritated him when their reconnection still felt fragile. 'Sorry.'

His face softened as he came back to the table. 'Don't apologise. After everything you did for us, you have nothing to be sorry about.' He sat back down. 'It's totally up to *you* now. Well, you and Arran.'

Kenzie sighed, her heart aching as she replayed her last conversation with Arran about the baby, a couple of weeks ago.

'He doesn't want me to do it. He's never wanted kids, Glenn, and I knew that.' She paused. 'Neither did I, until Olivia died, then everything seemed to change.' Her voice faltered as he reached across the table and briefly squeezed her hand.

'I know. I'm sorry.' He sat back, his eyes going to the closed blinds, obscuring the view of the river. 'This has been harder on you than me, I think.'

'I doubt that.' Surprised, she shook her head. 'I've lost my sister, but you've lost your wife, Glenn. The love of your life.'

At this, his eyes seemed to cloud over, his chin dipping as he combed his fingers through his hair again.

'Yeah.'

The tone of his voice was strangely hollow, and her sense that he'd been holding something back renewed itself as she took her barely touched plate to the counter, by the stove.

All the years she'd known Glenn, he had always been honest with her, at least as far as she knew, so this disquieting lack of transparency was not something Kenzie was used to dealing with. As she watched him, shoving the food around on his plate rather than shovelling it into his mouth as he usually would, something inside her snapped, and she blurted, 'If there's something I should know, Glenn, you'd better tell me now. Was the sperm donor in jail for murder or something, because if I decide to do this, there's no going back.'

His eyes snapped to hers and he took her in for a second before a smile tugged at his mouth. 'No, nothing like that. He's some kind of mechanical engineer, from Aberdeen.' He paused. 'If you feel you want to do this, Kenzie, for the record, I think you'd be a brilliant mum. And Arran would be a great dad if he could just get on board. Olivia and I used to talk about that. What fab parents you two would be. She never could understand why you were so adamant about not having children. You, *or* Arran.'

Kenzie walked over and stood behind her chair. She wasn't

going to share Arran's deepest fears, his motivation for saying no to having a family. If he hadn't told Glenn why he didn't want children, then it was not her place to say anything now.

'A lot of thought went into our decision, but now, many of the reasons that seemed sound have lost their oomph.' She made a fist and jabbed the air. 'I just keep thinking what Olivia would say if I let it go.' She made a sweeping motion with her hand. 'I know she'd have been gutted, so I'm afraid that, if I did walk away, I'd never forgive myself.'

Glenn closed his eyes for a moment, then met her gaze.

'I know how much you loved her, Kenzie, and that you feel this is something you should do for *her*, but you're putting way too much store on what she said she wanted. Believe me.'

'What do you mean?' Kenzie frowned, unsure where he was going with this, her last conversation with Olivia coming back to her. 'She said she had something to tell me, after the climb.' Kenzie swallowed hard, seeing her sister's face, the pale eyes bright and full of mystery. 'Do you know what it was?'

He took a moment, his jaw twitching, then he shook his head, avoiding her eyes.

'All I can say is that if you do decide to do this, do it for *you*. Not for Olivia, or me, or anyone else.' He paused. 'You deserve all the happiness in the world and if this little sprog will give that to you, no one – not even Arran – has the right to get in the way.'

Surprise held her still, this being the first time Glenn had ever been anything other than completely positive about Arran.

'But I love him, Glenn. He is my world.'

'He's a good man. One of the best I've ever known, honestly. But if you truly want this...' he shrugged. 'It's your prerogative. Your choice. End of story.'

Kenzie let his statements permeate, Arran's words about consequences simultaneously doing battle with Glenn's clear-cut logic. Despite all the conflict, the painful suck of loss every time she thought about her sister, the fate of the embryo, the new longing she'd been experiencing, and her worry over Arran's understandably negative reaction to what she'd told him, deep inside there was another sensation that was gaining momentum.

As she walked to the window, and raised the blind, the last traces of daylight smudging the outline of the hills beyond the river against the grey-blue sky, she let the feeling have air. Staring at the distinct peaks on the horizon, Kenzie let the nugget of excitement at potentially becoming a mother loose, its release like the flutter of a spring breeze on her face as she closed her eyes and floated on it.

16

Glenn had heated her plate in the microwave and insisted she eat while he sat across from her. His eyes had taken on their customary twinkle as he'd told her about his new job, the bright woman he was reporting to and the things he'd discovered about Perth, a city that Kenzie had always enjoyed visiting.

Now, with some coffee and a box of dark chocolate mints, they sat at either end of the sofa in the living room. The dark outline of the peaks and glens on the mountain that her sister had loved so much felt intrusive, so Kenzie got up and drew the curtains.

'You can't shut it out forever, you know.' Glenn wrapped his hands around his mug. 'It kind of comes with the territory.'

Kenzie huffed, pointing in the direction of Ben Nevis. 'That bastard can go straight to hell, for all I care.'

Glenn gave a huffing laugh. 'Right, well that's practical.'

She flopped back onto the sofa and tucked her feet under her, then deliberately changed the subject.

'So, when are you going back to Perth?'

'Monday morning. I need to pack up some more clothes and

then rent a van to move some of the bigger stuff, next weekend.' He sipped some coffee, his eyes on the dark curtains.

'What're you going to do with the flat?' Kenzie hugged her mug in her lap as he looked over at her.

'Kenzie, the flat is yours to do what you want with.'

The reminder sent a little shock wave through her.

'Oh, right. I forgot.' She nodded sadly. 'It still feels wrong, Glenn. It's your home.'

'It *was*. And it was a great home, with Olivia in it.' His voice grew raspy. 'But now, it's just a nice flat with a great view, and some pretty dodgy neighbours.' He gave a little snort as Kenzie laughed, despite the nut of pain that was lodged in her chest at the prospect of him not being upstairs. 'I do have an idea, though, if you're open to it.'

She set her mug on the coffee table. 'Oh, yes?'

'There's this guy at work. A real stand-up bloke, in the CID unit. He's a single dad, from Glasgow, and he's looking for a place to rent, for him and his daughter.'

Kenzie frowned at him, the concept foreign, and surprising. 'Rent it out?'

'Why not?' He shrugged. 'It makes no sense to have it sitting empty, and you could make a bit of money with a tenant in there.'

Kenzie tried to picture someone other than her sister and brother-in-law in the flat that they'd spent years in, but she couldn't visualise it without feeling overwhelmingly sad.

'I don't know. Seems weird.'

Glenn put his cup on the coffee table and stood up, yawning.

'His name is Colm Duggan. He's about thirty-five, I'm guessing. I can give you his number if you want to talk to him.'

Kenzie stood and picked up the two mugs.

'I'm not sure. A single dad?'

'Yes. His wife died a year or so ago, so it's just him and his wee girl.'

'Oh, that's really sad.' Kenzie's mouth dipped. 'How old is his daughter?'

Glen shrugged. 'Five or six, I think. Why not give him a call and just talk to him. See how you feel?'

Kenzie walked ahead of him down the hall, and into the kitchen.

'I'll think about it.' She put the mugs in the sink. 'Are you sure, though?' She leaned against the sink and met Glenn's eyes. 'What if Perth doesn't work out and you want to come home at some point?' She hoped she'd kept her voice even, not letting the strength of her wish that this might be the case come through.

'Cheers for the vote of confidence, Kenz.' He squinted at her.

'I didn't mean it like that,' she huffed. 'But renting it out is a long-term commitment, and whatever you say, or whose name is on the deed, this will always be your home.'

Glenn smiled at her. 'You're a stubborn wee bism, Kenzie Ford.'

'You just realised that?' she quipped.

'No. It's been a while.' He moved in next to her and nudged her arm with his. 'Just think about it, OK? I'll text you his info. No pressure, either way, but he does need to find somewhere soon.'

'Oh, *no* pressure.' She nudged him back. 'Well played.'

'Are you going to be OK?' His eyes were full of concern again.

'Of course. We'll sort things out. It's just a blip.' Kenzie's mind went straight to Arran and the strained atmosphere that was keeping them apart at the moment.

'I don't mean you and Arran. I'm asking about you.' Glenn

smiled sadly. 'You need to make the right decision for you. Promise me?'

Kenzie swallowed hard.

'I'm going to miss you so much.' She lifted her arms, and Glenn pulled her into a hug.

'Me too, little bean. But I'll be back to visit, and you can come to Perth, once I get settled.' He stepped back from her, his hands sliding into his pockets.

'I know, but it won't be the same. Nothing will ever be the same,' she hiccupped, a sob throbbing in her chest.

'The one thing that is guaranteed in life is change, Kenzie. It's not always what we want, but you are strong enough to take it.'

She nodded, his faith in her, while flattering, feeling misplaced given everything that was going on. 'Thanks. You too.' She found a smile, then followed him down the hall to the front door.

'Night then. Give my best to your man, and think about the Colm thing.'

'God, all right.' She nodded, rolled her eyes and gently shoved him out the door into the cool of the night. 'Sod off, PC Plod.'

Laughing, Glenn walked away from her, waving over his shoulder.

Within a few moments of Kenzie turning off the lights and heading into the bedroom, her phone chimed in the back pocket of her jeans. She took it out and saw a text from Glenn with the word Colm, then a phone number, and an emoji with its tongue stuck out.

Smiling, she typed, *Now who's the stubborn one?* : P.

She waited for a few moments, then his reply bloomed on the screen.

It makes sense. Just do it.

Putting her phone on the charger next to the bed, Kenzie

sighed, the sight of Arran's smooth pillow sending a dart of pain through her. Not much made sense at the moment, so perhaps Glenn was right. Change was well and truly here, and even if she wanted to, she couldn't stop its progress or the butterfly effect of havoc it was wreaking in her life. Maybe becoming a landlady wasn't a completely mad idea.

Moving around the room, tugging off her clothes, then pulling on an old Highlands and Islands University T-shirt of Arran's, Kenzie considered the possibility of this Colm person becoming her neighbour. Then, she tried to picture a little girl of five or six living upstairs. Perhaps with long blonde hair and pretty blue eyes, a tinkling laugh, and a battery of soft toys that would occupy the window seat in the smaller bedroom that had once been Kenzie's as a child.

As she padded into the bathroom, cleansed her face and cleaned her teeth, instead of conjuring the face of a girl, she pictured a little boy. A round-faced child with deep blue eyes and soft tufts of red hair, his pudgy hand gripping her finger as she sniffed his milky head.

The image was startling, as was the bubble of excitement it sparked, and as she spat foam into the sink, suddenly Arran's face materialised behind her eyes. She needed to talk to him before she made any decisions about the flat, but more importantly, this massive choice she had to make that could alter their entire future.

Back in the bedroom, lying on top of the duvet, Kenzie texted him, her stomach doing flips as she deleted what she'd written, then started again. Things were fragile between them, and that was down to her, so every word she wrote felt weighted with significance. After a couple more attempts, when she was finally happy with it, she sent the message.

I know things are weird between us, and I'm sorry for that. Nothing makes sense without you to talk to. Is there any way you can come home tomorrow? x

She slid down and bunched the pillow behind her head, expecting to wait a while for him to reply, so when she saw that he was already typing, she sat bolt upright, and waited.

I was just about to message you. I'll be back around noon. Lots to talk about. Love you x

Kenzie let out a little yelp of relief, then replied.

Perfect. See you then x

As she switched off her phone and then the lamp, sliding under the duvet, she visualised his message. *Lots to talk about.* That could be taken in a couple of ways, one of them not particularly positive, which made her stomach ache to think about. But then he'd said, *Love you x*. She pictured the two words, immediately afraid that he might not feel the same anymore if she went ahead with this pregnancy.

Staring at the ceiling, Glenn's statement buzzed inside her head. *If you want to do this, do it for you.* Letting the thought fill her head, Kenzie turned on her side and closed her eyes, trying to picture what her life might look like if she took that advice. Then, her mind was drawn back to the way he'd emphasised the words, but *you're putting way too much store on what she said she wanted,* when referring to Olivia, and the worm of worry burrowed deeper inside Kenzie. What had he meant by that?

An hour or so later, Kenzie threw the covers off and switched on the bedside light. She had slept only briefly, and dreamt of Olivia again, the soulful eyes filled with sadness, and her sister's voice gentle but insistent. The message had been the same as the previous dream, the words *last chance* now reverberating in Kenzie's head.

As she stared at the dark window, a sliver of silvery moonlight creeping in between the curtains, her eyes blurred. The image of the little red-haired boy flashed behind her eyes again, and she pressed her fingertips to her eyelids, increasing the pressure until it began to hurt. The deep longing was gathering momentum, the sense of there being a void in her life that only this mythical child would fill making her shake her head against the pillow.

There were so many emotions swirling inside her that she felt she might burst, so she got up and walked along the hall into the kitchen. Opening the blinds, she scanned the silhouette of the hills beyond the river, the scattering of glens like dark fingerprints on the familiar peaks. As she blinked her vision clear, she whispered, 'I love you, Olivia. I always will. And I think I want to do this – not just for you, but for me.' She swallowed over a nut of sadness. 'But I'm scared. I'm scared that I'll lose Arran, and lose myself, too. Be a crap mother, while trying to be you. Which I could never do.' A sob broke loose and Kenzie clamped her hand over her mouth, her breathing rapid. 'You had all the grace and class in this family. I was the loud one, the messy sister. The loose cannon. The one most likely to flop at things, and now you've gone and left me to deal with all this, alone. What am I supposed to do?' She let the tears come, her stomach knotting as she bent forward, her hands on her knees. 'I need you, Olivia. I can't make this decision without you.'

As she rocked slowly forward and back on her heels, Kenzie's sobs gradually subsided and she straightened up, then grabbed a piece of kitchen paper and blew her nose loudly, something that always made Arran laugh. She missed him until even her skin ached, every muscle, tendon and sinew of her body craving him. What if he came home with a 'we've got to talk' face on? What if he gave her an ultimatum? Me or a baby? What if...

She shook her head. 'Stop it. This is Arran we're talking about. Just stop it.'

Drawing the blinds again, she turned her back on the window and let out a low moan, the wall of pain that had built along with the wave of sobs beginning to ease. She walked to the door, then stopped, staring down the hall to the silent bedroom. As she tried to picture the big chest of drawers empty of Arran's things, the wardrobe without his mess of clothes, the images were so painful, her chest ached. Then, she looked across the hall to the smaller bedroom which he used as an office, and without analysing why, she made her way along the hall and into the dark room.

Kenzie flipped on the overhead light and stood in the doorway, taking in the old roll-top desk under the window, the view of Ben Nevis beyond now mercifully dark and indistinct. There was a low filing cabinet to the left of the desk and a small shredder to the right, next to the old Victorian fireplace with the original green and white Paisley-patterned tiles on the surround. She had wanted to remove them when Arran had moved in, but he'd resisted.

'I like them. They've got character, and anything we put in there instead just won't look as good.'

She'd protested, but then seeing how much he appreciated the original features of their home had been sweet. Now, she walked across the narrow room and touched the back of the wooden chair he used. Feeling the warmth of the oak beneath her fingers, she turned and took in the space. Suddenly, as she scanned the few pieces of furniture, she pictured a cot. A pretty, wooden-sided cot with a soft cotton bumper on the inside. Perhaps a mobile hanging above it, with starfish and conch shells turning gently in a circle as she leaned over the side and adjusted a tiny blanket.

A wave of disbelief sent her back out into the hall, her hand shaking as she switched off the light. Could she really be thinking this? Could she really be thinking about replacing Arran, filling the unthinkable gap he might leave in her life, with a child?

17

The following day, Arran sat across from Kenzie in the living room, his feet up on the coffee table. She'd made him a giant sandwich for lunch, and they'd eaten an entire pound of strawberries he'd picked up from a farm shop on the way home from Sutherland.

Kenzie had hugged him so tightly when he'd walked in the door that he'd laughed.

'I need to stay away more often.' His arms had circled her waist.

Though his hug had felt genuine, there had been something guarded in his tone that had scared her, but Kenzie had pushed down the flash of concern, as she'd asked him about work and diverted their conversation to her having seen Glenn, and his suggestion that she rent out the flat.

Now, Arran was yawning, his arms straight up above his head. 'It's up to you, of course, but I think renting it out makes sense, if Glenn isn't coming back any time soon.'

'Yes, I suppose so. It feels weird, though. And I'm still not convinced that he's really thought this all through. Leaving his home, his job. Us. Giving up on the chance of having a child, after everything they went through.' Realising that she had breached the wall around the sore subject they'd been avoiding, she saw Arran wince. 'What is it?'

'Nothing.'

'Arran, what?'

'You talking about it like that, makes it feel like abandonment, on his part.'

A sudden surge of frustration lifted her from the sofa. 'Well, it's Glenn abandoning Olivia's dream for them. It's like he's discounting that completely. Making it irrelevant.' Her throat began to knot. 'What *I* did, irrelevant.'

Arran looked shocked. 'OK. I understand the sentiment, but you know what I *meant*, Kenzie. It's not quite that simple.'

'No, it's not.' Her hands were trembling.

Arran eyed her, his fingers nervously linking at the back of his neck.

'Sit down, Kenz. Please. We need to talk this through.'

She hesitated, then flopped down next to him, suddenly drained of energy.

'Look, I'm sorry. I know this all makes you super uncomfortable, but I have to be honest with you, Arran. While I still worry that Glenn could change his mind at some point, the more I contemplate it, the less I think I can just walk away.' The words out, she shifted to face Arran, her palm resting on his forearm.

His face was a mask of discomfort, his mouth pinching as he scanned her features, as if he didn't recognise her. Feeling as though everything that had held them together was crumbling, Kenzie sat back and tried to steady her nerves. What she said next had the potential to undo the last vestiges of their relationship and, knowing that, her palms grew clammy as she laced her fingers together in her lap.

'Ever since Olivia died, I just feel that there needs to be more to life than our careers. Family is the only thing that goes on. A legacy that we can leave behind. Now that she's gone, it feels so much more important. She was my one remaining relative and now that concept has so much weight and sadness around it that I can hardly function.' She pressed her palm to her chest.

'I understand that. Believe me. But I've also given this a lot of thought, and even though I love the bones of you, Kenzie, I just don't think I can do that with you.' His mouth dipped. 'With that said, I would never want to get in the way of something you really wanted.' He paused as Kenzie felt the creep of dread. This sounded like a goodbye, and the bolt of pain that sent through her was excruciating.

'But can't you even try to consider it? Take some more time before you decide?' She reached for his hand, feeling his fingers chilly.

'Kenzie, I love you. You know that. But this is something I was crystal-clear about from the first time we talked about it.' He enclosed her hand with his other one. 'I wish I could give you this, love. I do. But...' He shook his head. 'I truly wish I could.'

Her chest tightening until it was crushing the air from her lungs, she slipped her hand from between his. His face was contorted, his eyes narrowing and a frown cutting across his forehead. His pain was palpable, and in the past, Kenzie would have taken back her words, told him it was all a misunderstanding, that she didn't need this. That everything would go on as normal. But despite the sadness that was robbing her of breath, she couldn't do that this time. She scanned his face, the aquiline nose, the mossy eyes, the wide mouth that she loved to kiss, seeing the torment there.

'What are you thinking?' He shifted on the sofa, shoving the cushion behind him onto the floor.

Kenzie's thoughts were jumbled to the point where she wasn't sure what she felt, but as she looked at him, all she could focus on was that this was not his fault. This shocking U-turn that she had taken was not his fault, and regardless of everything she was considering, and the pain that it could inflict on them both, there should be no guilt for him to carry.

'Arran, I understand. I know I'm the one moving the goalposts on us, and I'm genuinely sorry about that. But I need to be honest, and while it will literally break me if you...' She paused, unable to believe that she was about to say what she was about to say. 'I will accept whatever you decide, and I will never make you feel bad about it. I love you so much, and I thought that would always be enough, but now there is this ache.' She pressed her palm into her stomach. 'This need that I can't even describe. It's like something is gnawing at me, eating me up from the inside.' Tears pressed in behind her eyes as she swallowed hard. 'Do you know what I'm saying?'

He took a moment to absorb what she'd said, then nodded miserably.

'I do. And I wish... I wish I could be different. That I could get past my own issues. But this is too big, Kenzie. It's too much.'

Her heart being stomped on by each word, Kenzie felt tears break loose. Could she really let him go over this? The love of her life?

Desperate to keep any thread of hope connecting them, she wiped her tears with her palm. 'Let's take a little more time to think about it. Then we'll talk again.'

Doctor Kennedy's warning about not waiting too long flashed back to her.

Arran surveyed her face, then, to her relief, he nodded.

'We can do that.' He gave her a sad smile. 'But I think it might be best if I stay in Sutherland, just for a while. It'll give us both the space we need, to make the right decisions.'

The statement struck her like a thunderbolt. He wanted to be away from her, and that was like another giant crevasse opening between them. A bottomless gap that they might never be able to bridge.

'I'm so sorry, Arran. I hate that you want us to be apart, but I understand.' A sob clogged her throat as he slid over and wrapped his arms around her. 'My heart is breaking.'

'Mine too, Kenzie,' he whispered.

No matter how hard he hugged her, or said that he understood, Kenzie knew that she was peeling splinters off his heart, and that was something she never, in a million years, thought she'd ever do.

WINTER

18

Three weeks later, on the first Saturday in November, and with Arran having been home only once since their heartbreaking conversation, Kenzie stood in Olivia and Glenn's kitchen.

She had been coming upstairs once a week to dust, and water the plants that Olivia had lovingly nurtured on the deep sill of the bay window – a delicate money tree, a waxy bay plant, and a spindly fern that was now wilting, despite Kenzie's efforts to keep it alive.

Behind her, Colm Duggan stood in the doorway, his thick, salt-and-pepper hair only a couple of inches below the top of the frame. Kenzie had agreed to meet him the week before and they'd had a coffee in Fort William, her wanting to get the measure of him before she agreed to show him the flat. He had greeted her politely, almost diffidently, his giant hand dwarfing hers as he shook it, and his dark-brown eyes seeming to pity her, which had instantly riled Kenzie.

True to form, she had gone for the jugular, asking him outright how much he knew of her story.

Colm had seemed taken aback, then he'd grinned, revealing

friendly crinkles at the edges of his eyes that Kenzie had found disarming.

'Glenn has told me pretty much everything.' He'd nodded to himself. 'And I still wanted to meet you. Amazing, eh?'

At this, Kenzie had laughed, taken by his easy humour.

'Well, more fool you,' she'd quipped. 'I come with a hazard warning. Did he tell you that?'

Colm had laughed again. 'Not exactly, just that you don't suffer fools, and that your say is final on the flat.'

They'd talked for an hour and Colm had showed her numerous pictures of his daughter, Nora, a dark-haired, petite child with piercing blue eyes, and skin like buttermilk.

'She's utterly gorgeous.' Kenzie's throat had tightened as he'd scrolled through various shots of Nora, as an infant sitting in the kitchen sink, surrounded by bubbles, then around two years old in a bouncy chair suspended in a door frame. In the most recent pictures of her at the age of five, she was wearing a tiny two-piece bathing costume, and her little arms were in blow-up armbands. 'Where was that one taken?'

'Paros, last summer. I took her for a week just to get away from everything. She loved the beach.' He'd smiled sadly as he'd slid his phone away. 'She's a great kiddo, really. Since Sandy died...' This had brought him to a halt.

'Oh, I'm so sorry. Glenn did tell me that you'd lost your wife.' Kenzie had seen his eyes darken.

'Yeah, it was a crap time, really. Sandy was such a great mum. I felt like a total numpty trying to fill her shoes, doing everything I could to make Nora feel safe.' He'd shrugged. 'I still screwed things up, but she is a wise wee thing. One day, when I'd burned the Sunday pancakes that Sandy always made for us, Nora patted my hand and said, *Let's make some toast today, Daddy.*'

The pain of his loss had been palpable as she'd listened to him talk more about his wife, and daughter, and by the time their coffees were done, she'd known that she'd offer him the flat, if he wanted it.

Now, as she walked across the room to the big bay window, the brazen outline of Ben Nevis etched darkly on the wintry sky beyond, she turned her back on her nemesis.

'So, what do you think? Can you see you and Nora living here?'

Colm nodded. 'Absolutely. It's a cracking flat, and that view.' He pointed at the mountain. 'Doesn't get much better than that.'

Kenzie sighed. 'Well, it's not everyone's cup of tea, but I'm glad you like it.'

Frowning, Colm walked to the end of the long room, past the two sofas that flanked the fireplace, then looked down into the empty grate. 'Does it work?'

'Yes, they all do. Olivia especially loved this room, when...' She felt her throat knot, so cleared it. 'Sorry. Yes, the fires all work. There's three of them. This one, and one in each bedroom. You'll need to get some good, solid guards, for Nora, though.' She frowned, not having considered this home in terms of it being child-friendly. 'We never needed to think about that stuff.'

'No problem. I'll manage all that.' He smiled at her, his dark eyes twinkling. 'So, do we have a deal?'

Kenzie took a second, then nodded. 'Welcome to your new home.' She paused, suddenly reminded that she had not finished cleaning out Olivia's clothes, and personal belongings, the task feeling too final a goodbye to stomach. 'I'll need a few days to get everything ready, but you could probably move in next weekend, if that works for you?'

'That's perfect. I'm taking Nora to Shetland to see her granny for a few days, so we can plan on Saturday the tenth then.' He eyed her, his expression kind. 'Are you sure you're OK with this, Kenzie?'

'Yes. It makes no sense to have the place sitting empty, when you and Nora need a home.' She swallowed hard. 'I won't lie, it'll be strange having someone else living up here, but Glenn seems sure he's not moving back, so...'

Colm walked past her and back into the kitchen area. 'I think we'll be very happy here. Thank you.' He extended his hand and Kenzie shook it firmly.

The picture of Nora in her armbands flashed behind Kenzie's eyes, the cherubic face and long dark hair giving the child an ethereal look. As Kenzie turned and walked to the front door, the irony of there being a child living upstairs in her sister's flat, after all that had happened, was bittersweet.

The following day, Kenzie walked back up the stairs to Olivia's flat with a handful of black plastic bags. When Glenn had come back on the train, packed and driven a self-hire van over to Perth the previous weekend, Kenzie had stayed away, not keen to see him removing the last of his belongings, and now, as she let herself in and walked along the hall to the kitchen, the empty coat hooks behind the door, and the lack of Olivia and Glenn's keys in the little metal dish on the long sideboard, sent a zap of sadness through Kenzie. She'd never get used to this.

In the kitchen, she had already gone through everything, removing a few specific personal items, like their mother's battered baking trays, not that Kenzie baked. She'd also taken the silver cutlery that their grandmother had left to their mother, and a set of six, paper-thin porcelain teacups and saucers that Olivia loved.

In the living area, the furniture that had been there when Glenn moved in, he had said he didn't want, so Kenzie had decided to let the flat fully furnished, the hassle of removing everything too overwhelming. What was a collection of wood, leather and glass anyway, when the precious people who had once lived here were gone?

Olivia and Glenn's bedroom had been the place Kenzie had been dreading tackling the most and as she walked into the bright room, the lingering scent in the air made her stop in her tracks.

Olivia had always worn a jasmine-based perfume that over time had become infused in the fabric of all her clothing, especially the long woollen scarves she'd hang on the hook by the front door. Even the towels in their en-suite bathroom held the delicate scent, and as Kenzie let it fill her head, a rush of loss made her hug herself, the black bags falling to the wood floor.

Images of her sister flashed through her mind, a picture show of memories, each one more precious and fragile than the next. Olivia holding her tightly as she told Kenzie about their parents' deaths. Olivia sitting with her all night when Kenzie broke up with her first boyfriend in high school. Her sister standing up clapping and shouting Kenzie's name at her graduation. Each scenario had Olivia at its centre, as Kenzie's protector, best friend and parent figure in the absence of their mother and father, and as she opened her eyes and scanned the room, Kenzie whispered, 'Thank you. You were always there. You were my saviour, and my hero. I miss you so damn much.'

Kenzie walked to the bed and sat on the edge of it, her eyes full of tears. The November sky was dull outside the window, a bank of cloud obscuring the outline of the mountain, and as she stared at the smudged lines of the peaks, a rush of anger brought her to her feet.

She walked around the bed and stopped at the window, her denim-clad thighs pressing against the sill. Placing her hands on the cool glass, she filled her lungs and screamed at her nemesis, over and over. 'I hate you. I hate you so much.' Months of pain and loss erupted from her until her throat was raw and her head threatened to explode. 'I hate you so damn much,' she finally whispered, her voice spent.

Drained, she let her hands drop to her sides and stepped back from the window, her cheeks glossy with tears. Turning to the long, light-ash wardrobe that ran the length of the room on the left of the door, she pushed out a shaky breath and opened the first door on the right, where Olivia hung her clothes.

Glenn had left them untouched, and as she looked along the row of orderly hangers, seeing the familiar patterns, skirts of various lengths, and several gauzy summer dresses that would never be needed again, Kenzie's throat knotted even tighter. Never had she imagined that she'd be tasked with this gut-wrenching job, to bag up her sister's things and donate them to the charity shop in the High Street.

Kenzie tugged the first dress off the hanger and stuffed it into one of the plastic bags, then she grabbed several cotton shirts and yanked them off the hangers in a bunch, cramming them into the bag. She repeated the motion multiple times until the first rail was empty, the remaining hangers aimlessly swinging back and forth, and a few lying at the bottom of the wardrobe. As she bent down to gather them up, she spotted a dark bag at the back of the wardrobe. It looked like a sports bag, perhaps one that Olivia had kept her climbing gear in, and yet it wasn't familiar.

Her curiosity piqued, Kenzie knelt and pulled the bag out onto the floor. It was canvas, an old-fashioned style barrel bag with leather-bound handles and a zip pocket along the front. It was clean of any marks, the handles slightly worn where the leather had been handled frequently.

Sitting back on her heels, Kenzie pulled it to her and unzipped it, bracing herself for the sight of some of Olivia's numerous, dainty climbing shoes, or a bunch of shiny carabiners attached to a length of rope, but instead all she saw was a squarish tin, the shape reminiscent of an old cash box. It had a faded tartan design, and it was dented in a couple of places, the red and green pattern all but gone from the front, where a substantial padlock with a combination lock hung.

Frowning, Kenzie tugged at the padlock, turning the tin upside down, then back again. It was fairly heavy, something sliding around inside it. What on earth would Olivia be keeping in a padlocked box at the back of her wardrobe? The very location of the tin spoke of secrets, and the padlock only heightened the knot of anxiety that was building inside Kenzie's chest.

19

Glenn took a while to answer his phone, and just when Kenzie expected to be sent to voicemail, she heard his voice.

'Hey. How are you?' He sounded preoccupied, and there was a lot of background noise, as if he might be in a car.

'Hi. I'm OK. Just going through Olivia's stuff, getting the clothes ready for the charity shop.' She swallowed hard, the weight of the box on her thigh drawing her focus, like a lightning rod.

'Oh, right. Thanks for doing that. I just couldn't...' He halted. 'Sorry to leave it to you.'

''S OK. It's a shitty job, but better that I do it than you.' She sniffed, then slid the box closer to her. 'I found something in the wardrobe, a locked box. Do you know what it is?'

She thought she heard him take a sharp breath, so frowning she pushed herself up from the floor and walked to the bed where she perched on the end.

'Glenn?'

'Yeah, sorry. I'd forgotten about that, to be honest, with everything else going on.'

'So, what's in it?' Once again, she shook the box, feeling the contents slide from side to side.

'Look, don't think I'm trying to avoid things, but I can't really talk now.' She heard a female voice in the background, then Glenn said, 'Yep. I'll be there in a minute.'

'Who's that?' Kenzie stood up and walked to the window, seeing a long twist of dark cloud rolling across the already murky view of the mountain. She shivered and pulled her navy, cable-knit sweater down over her hips.

'It's my boss. I've got to go, Kenzie.'

'Just tell me about this box.' She held it up to eye level and peered at the padlock. 'Do you know the combination of the padlock, at least?'

There was a long pause, then he said, 'Look, I really have to go, but I'm coming back next weekend. I'll text you as soon as I'm in town. Please, just trust me. It'll be better to talk about it in person.'

Kenzie was about to protest, when she heard him say, 'Right. Coming now, boss.'

'Glenn? What's going on?' Her stomach was doing flips as she tried to imagine what her sister had to hide from her, nothing coming to mind that would make any sense, unless it had something to do with whatever it was that Olivia had wanted to tell her.

'Sorry. I'll text you, and I'll see you soon. Please wait until I get there, OK? Take care, little bean.' Then he was gone, leaving Kenzie staring at her phone.

He'd never cut her off that way before and the shock of it left her shaking her head in disbelief. What the hell was going on? And what was the big mystery about this damn box?

As she shook it hard, Kenzie growled, 'If you think I'm waiting for you to open this, you're off your rocker.' Holding the box close to her chest, she strode out of the room and along the hall, back into the kitchen.

Neither Glenn nor Arran were DIY-type men, so, annoyingly, there was no handy toolbox secreted away in either of their flats, or in the tiny shed where they kept the ancient lawnmower that Olivia had used to cut the grass at the front of the house.

As Kenzie set the tin on the counter by the sink, she began trying various combinations of numbers, twisting the six dials around using elements of both her and Olivia's birth dates, their parents' anniversary, and their birthdays, but with no luck. Eventually, frustrated, she lifted the box and headed for the front door. Somewhere in the village, probably at the little hardware shop next to the tea shop she and Olivia used to frequent, she'd find a hacksaw. The bags of clothes in the bedroom forgotten, she slammed the door behind her and ran down the external staircase. She'd find out whatever was inside the tin that Olivia had decided to hide from her if it took all day to break it open.

An hour later, Kenzie unwrapped the hacksaw she'd bought and put the box on her kitchen table. Bizarrely, she'd found the saw at the village store thanks to Sally's propensity to stock a few unusual items behind the counter.

Sally had patted her hair as always, then her laugh had inevitably turned into a phlegmy cough. 'It just so happens I *do* have one. Not sure how long it's been under here, but I knew someone would want it eventually, you know, sort of thing.' The quirky catchphrase had made Kenzie suppress a smile as Sally had bent over and rummaged around under the counter, then stood up triumphantly. 'Voilà.' She'd waved the saw, in a dusty plastic cover, then put it on the counter. 'Breaking someone out of jail?' She'd winked at Kenzie, who, despite her desire to grab the saw and run home as fast as she could, had laughed sadly.

'No, nothing as juicy as that. Just need to get into an old box that I've lost the key to.'

Sally had surveyed her face, then the rheumy blue eyes had grown watery. 'How are you, love? Coping without Olivia, you know, sort of thing?' She'd paused. 'You're a wee bit peaky. Are you eating?'

Kenzie had smiled at the kind woman. 'I'm OK, Sally. Some days are better than others. You know how it is.'

Sally had nodded. 'Aye, right enough. When I lost my Joe, it took me months to be able to face folk. You're stronger than me, Kenzie. I do admire you.' She'd reached across the counter and patted Kenzie's arm. 'Any time you fancy a cuppa, or a chat, you know where I am.'

'Thanks, Sally. You're a star.' Kenzie had handed Sally a ten-pound note. 'Throw in one of those Jumbo KitKats and we'll call it quits.'

Sally had laughed again, the ubiquitous cough following as she handed Kenzie the saw and the chocolate bar. 'There you go, love. You take care, OK?'

'Thanks. You too.' Kenzie had given Sally a wave as she'd walked out into the darkening afternoon, the sky ominous with grey rain clouds that seemed to be meshing, obscuring the remains of the purply blue ones that had hung overhead as she'd walked to the shop.

Kenzie had wrapped her tartan scarf across her mouth, and as her fingers had instantly felt stingingly cold, she'd slid her free hand into the pocket of her wool coat, annoyed that in her haste, she had dashed out of the house without her fleece-lined gloves.

Back at home, Kenzie took hold of the padlock, but just as she was about to start sawing, her phone buzzed in the back pocket of her jeans. Pulling it out, she saw a message from Glenn. Short, but to the point.

Please wait until I get there. I need you to trust me on this.

Kenzie frowned, picturing his face, the way he'd dip his chin when he asked her something and was waiting for her to answer him. Annoyed how much she cared what he thought, or that she'd let him guide her decision about what to do, she huffed, 'This is bloody torture.' She tugged at the padlock. 'Are you serious?'

As if hearing her, Glenn then texted, *I promise to explain. Just try to be patient. You'll understand when we talk.*

Frustration crawling across her skin, she slammed the saw on the table. For him to ask this of her was significant, and he was obviously worried about her reaction to whatever was in this tin. Glenn had always had her best interests at heart, so while it would drive her crazy to wait, something deep inside her made her give him the benefit of the doubt.

'Damn you, Glenn Mackintosh. Whatever this is about, you better have a good reason for asking this of me,' she grumbled as she texted back.

:(*ALL RIGHT!*

Then she glared at the box as if it was the devil incarnate.

Unable to stand looking at it anymore, Kenzie lifted it from the table and shoved it into the cupboard under the stove, where she kept her frying pans. 'Out of sight, out of mind.' Slamming the door, she turned her back on the cupboard.

Having finished packing up Olivia's clothes, Kenzie lugged five bulging plastic bags down the stairs and loaded them into the back of her car. The charity shop was in Fort William and if she hurried, she'd just make it before they closed. Having the bags in her possession now felt as if she was holding onto explosives that might go off at any time, and her need to have them gone was overwhelming.

As she drove out of the driveway, and headed left towards Fort William, the river stretched out on her right, and Adele's voice floated from the radio, making Kenzie's eyes burn. The lyrics to 'Easy on Me' filled the car, their referral to there being hope in these waters, so she stared at the river, her vision blurring.

Olivia had adored Adele, and each time they'd gone anywhere together in her battered old Land Rover, she'd slip a CD in and they'd sing at the tops of their voices, laughing at Kenzie's tone-deaf wails.

As she steered the car carefully down the road, Kenzie swallowed over a lump, then began singing, tears trickling down her face as she laughed between the words, hiccupping, and missing her sister with every bone in her body.

They'd had no secrets from each other, but now that Olivia was gone, with the slightly hooded comment from Glenn and now this mysterious box, for the first time in her life, Kenzie wondered if perhaps she didn't know her sister as well as she thought she did.

20

A week later, on the Saturday at exactly 10.00 a.m., Colm arrived with Nora and a car full of bags and suitcases.

Startled, Kenzie swore when the bell rang and dashed along the hall, glancing at herself in the mirror, her hair a wild mess of red curls and her blue eyes hooded with lack of sleep. She'd been wakeful all night again, as Arran's absence was loud everywhere in the house, but especially in their king-size bed.

She tugged his oversized sweatshirt down at the sides, hoping to cover more of her baggy pyjama bottoms, then opened the door.

'You made it, then.' She smiled at Colm, seeing Nora, her soft-pink cheeks puffing out slightly as she moved behind her father's leg. She was angelic, the sight of her big shy eyes sending an odd flutter of something through Kenzie that she didn't recognise. 'You must be Nora. Hi. I'm Kenzie.'

Nora slid a little further behind Colm, and Kenzie caught the child's cheeks dimpling as she stuck a finger in her mouth.

'Say hello to Kenzie, sweetheart.' Colm eased his daughter out from behind him, his big hand on her back.

'Hello.' Nora looked up at Kenzie from beneath impossibly

long, dark lashes, her tiny teeth pearly as she gave a flicker of a smile.

'I'm glad we're going to be neighbours.' Kenzie crouched down, her sheepskin slippers sliding off the back of her heels. 'Do you have a favourite biscuit? You look like a biscuit girl.'

Colm laughed, then swept Nora onto his hip, so Kenzie stood up, anxious to stay connected to this beautiful child.

'Yes, we do, actually.' He tipped his head towards his daughter's.

Kenzie widened her eyes. 'Let me see if I can guess it.'

At this, Nora giggled.

'I think it's Jaffa Cakes.' Kenzie wiggled her eyebrows. 'Am I right?'

Nora shook her head, her glossy dark hair bouncing over her shoulder, her lilac-coloured coat making her eyes look so blue that Kenzie couldn't stop staring at them.

'Hmm OK. How about custard creams?'

'No.' Nora shook her head again. 'It's chocolate digies.'

Kenzie feigned surprise. 'That's *my* favourite, too. My sister and I like the milk ones the best.' Mentioning Olivia in the present tense made Kenzie press her mouth closed, the compulsion to correct herself being squashed by her desire to make Colm and his daughter feel welcome, and not awkward.

'No way!' Colm laughed. 'We always have some of those in our tin, so you can come up and share them any time. Right, Nora?' He smiled fondly at his daughter, who leaned her cheek against his. Seeing how he looked at her sent a jolt of envy through Kenzie, Arran's angular face flashing behind her eyes as she took a second to centre herself.

'Yes, but she can't have *mine*.' Nora sounded concerned, her hand going back to her mouth.

The child's expression was adorable, so Kenzie laughed, taken by the transparent flash of panic in the little face. 'Don't worry. I'd never take yours.'

Colm gave her a grateful smile. 'Are we OK to move some stuff in now?'

'Of course. Let me get you the key.' Kenzie stepped back into the hall and lifted the keys from the dish on the sideboard. She'd had a new set cut and had put them on a Marine Institute key ring, Olivia's set being tucked safely away in a drawer. 'There you go. If you need anything, just give me a call. I'm around most of the weekend.'

'Thanks. I will.' Colm set Nora back on the ground. 'Right, Miss Nora. Shall we make a start?'

Nora took his hand, her fingers circling his thumb. 'Uh-huh. I want to see my room.'

'See you later.' Kenzie began to close the door, a pop of sadness to see the little girl leave taking her by surprise, when Nora took a step towards her.

'Do you like Squishmallows?'

Kenzie re-opened the door, taken aback, but touched that the child had addressed her directly. 'Um, I don't know. What are they?'

Nora's eyes widened. 'Squishmallows. Cailey Crab and Connor Cow.'

Kenzie looked at Colm for help.

'They're her favourite toys at the moment. It's a set of squishy, pocket-sized animals. You can build an entire zoo.' He shrugged. 'Flavour of the month right now.'

Kenzie laughed. 'Well, I'd love to see your Squishmallows, Nora. You can teach me all their names, OK?' The joy that Kenzie felt at Nora engaging with her was something she had never experienced before.

Nora nodded. 'Conor Cow is the best, then Cailey Crab.'

Colm stepped back from the door. 'Right. Let's let Miss Kenzie get on with her day.' He turned towards his car, then stopped. 'Oh, sorry. I used your side of the driveway.'

'No problem. You have your own over there, but that's fine.'

She gestured towards the opposite side of the house. 'Best of luck with the unpacking.'

'Thanks. I'll make the long drive over there.' Colm laughed, then put Nora back in the car seat as Kenzie closed her door, her chest tightening as she walked to the kitchen and poured herself another cup of coffee from the press. As she sipped some, carefully walking into the living room, she pictured the love radiating from Colm's eyes as he'd looked at his daughter. It was wonderful to witness, and even though she knew that Arran almost certainly couldn't get there, even for her, the longing that had taken up residence at her core seemed to swell, making her close her eyes briefly.

A few moments with Nora, and everything Kenzie was feeling about becoming a mother felt heightened, and even though that might erode her precious, and newly fragile foundation just a little bit more, she couldn't deny the feeling anymore.

21

The following day, Arran arrived home around 10.30 a.m., surprising Kenzie, who was reading in the bath. She heard the keys in the lock and jumped out of the water, dashed into the bedroom and pulled on her robe, just as Arran walked into the room.

'What are you doing home?' She checked the time on the clock on the bedside table, calculating that he must have left Wick around 5.30 a.m.

'Sorry. Did I scare you?' He sounded tired as he dumped his laptop bag on the chair by the window, and she waited for him to open his arms to her as he always did, but, instead, he hovered by the window.

'I wasn't expecting you. It's a good surprise, though.' Kenzie swallowed her disappointment at the coldness of his greeting as she closed the gap between them and buried her face in his chest, the faint smell of coffee on his tweed jacket making her sigh.

'I couldn't sleep, so decided to leave at five this morning. I also have a meeting at Glenfinnan tomorrow early, so...' He halted as she stepped back from him.

'Oh, right. So that's why you decided to come home?' She hoped she hadn't sounded petulant, but she hadn't expected this.

His face coloured slightly, his hand going to the back of his neck as it did whenever he was uncomfortable.

'Not the only reason, no.' He gave her a lopsided smile. 'But it made sense, logistically.'

'Right.' Stung, Kenzie pulled the belt of her robe tighter and reknotted it.

He dipped his chin. 'Kenz. Come on.'

'What?' She heard the hurt in her voice, as did he.

'Look, I'm sorry. I didn't mean it to come out like that. I wanted to see you, of course.' He shrugged his jacket off and dumped it on top of his laptop bag. 'It's been hard being away from you.'

Seeing his broad shoulders under the dark-green Shetland wool sweater, the thick hair swept back from his forehead, and the lean waist she loved to wrap her arms around, Kenzie forced a swallow. She'd missed him so much that even the tiny slight he'd just delivered wasn't enough to keep her separate from him now that he was in front of her.

'I've missed you.' She gave him a half-smile. 'Though I'm not sure why. It's cleaner, tidier and a lot less smelly here without you.'

The palpable tension eased in the air, and his sudden laugh propelled her forward, and back into his arms.

'You're an arse sometimes, Arran Ford. But you're *my* arse.' Even as she said it, the ridiculousness of the statement struck her, and she laughed, pressing her fingertips to his lips. 'Don't even say it.'

He lightly kissed the top of her head, the gesture what she craved despite being a little formal and distant compared to the way he'd normally have kissed her, having been away for a while.

My Sister's Only Hope

'I'm starving. Any chance of some breakfast?'

'There's only some lasagna from last night, in the fridge.' She looked up at him, his green eyes locked on hers. 'Or toast and peanut butter.'

He looked at the ceiling as if considering his options, then bent down and kissed her on the mouth. Kenzie leaned into the kiss, her body melting slowly into his as the pressure of his arms felt good behind her back.

Just as she began to lose herself in the moment, he pulled back, the physical separation jarring.

'What is it?' She frowned as he released her and moved towards the door.

'Nothing. Just tired from the drive.' He stretched, his arms locking in a circle above his head. 'Let's eat, then we can talk.'

Wounded, and her anxiety over the way he was acting ratcheting up a notch, Kenzie aimed for an unreadable expression. 'How do you know I haven't already eaten?'

He eyed her for a second, then a gentle smile wrinkled his eyes. 'Because it's only half-ten, and it's a Sunday, and you were still in the bath. I know you, Kenzie.'

She tutted, then tried to walk past him, but he caught her arm and gently tucked some hair behind her ear. That he knew her so well was as reassuring as it was annoying, and Kenzie pulled a face.

'Well, maybe you do, but you don't have to be a smart-arse about it.' She gave him a warning look. 'Come on then.' She eased past him and headed along the hall, towards the kitchen, her chest tight as the words *then we can talk* pulsed in her mind, like the warning of an impending storm.

She made toast and a fresh pot of coffee while Arran sat at the table and talked about his week. The Glenfinnan eco-habitat project was progressing well, the collaboration between the

Scottish railways and the forestry group proving to be productive. As he talked, it was obvious that him continuing to coordinate the meetings in person, while time-consuming, was helping to move things along faster than all parties had anticipated.

As she sat opposite him, her elbow on the table and her jaw propped up by her palm, Kenzie let the familiar rumble of his voice lull her into a semi-doze, her eyelids gradually becoming heavy, so, a few minutes later, when he put his mug down and said, 'So, what do you think? Should I get them to agree to more field days?' she jolted upright and blinked.

'Um, yes. Field days are always a good idea. Hands in the dirt, so to speak.'

He scanned her face, his expression expectant, then, startling her, he tutted, 'You weren't listening, were you?'

She shoved her hair over her shoulder and avoided his eyes. 'Of course I was.' She mocked offence. 'Field days.'

Arran stood up, took his plate to the sink and rinsed it before sliding it into the dishwasher.

Embarrassed that she'd been caught out, Kenzie pushed the chairs in close to the table and refilled their coffee mugs. She was still in her robe, and suddenly felt odd about it, as if she needed more protection from whatever he wanted to talk about next.

As he turned to face her, she saw the light had left his eyes, and he was frowning slightly.

Taking it as a cue, she said, 'I'm going to get dressed, then we can have that talk you wanted.'

Arran took his mug from her. 'Thanks. I'll be in the living room.'

Kenzie padded along the hall, and closed the bedroom door behind her, her heart beginning to thump under her breastbone.

Twenty minutes later, she sat across from him, each of them at one end of the L-shaped sofa. While she'd been dressing, he'd lit the fire, and the homely smell of woodsmoke made her smile as she entered the room.

Arran's feet were crossed on the coffee table and as he sat up and planted them on the Persian rug that had been her parents' prized possession, Kenzie took this as a sign that now he meant business.

Anxious to get on with it, the waiting and guessing unbearable, she leaned forward, her elbows on her knees.

'Right. What's on your mind?'

He took a moment, mimicking her stance, then linked his long fingers.

'Being away from you has been really hard, Kenzie, but it's also given me time to think. To give what we talked about the last time the consideration it deserves.'

'Right.' She nodded, her insides feeling as if he had reached right through her skin and wound his fingers around them.

'You know how much I love you, don't you?' His eyes seemed to bore into hers.

'Yes, I do,' she said, hoarsely.

'And I'd never do anything that would hurt you or make you unhappy.' He unlaced his fingers and dragged them through his hair.

'I know that,' she whispered. His guarded tone was a red flag, and as she tried to tell herself that there was no 'but' coming, she knew there was.

'I've asked myself every question under the sun, tried to picture the various scenarios, us going on as we are now that you've told me how you feel, us with a child, then us staying on different sides of this decision again.' His voice caught, and Kenzie leaned further forward, as if his pain and conflict was directly connected to her body, sucking her in. 'But no matter how much I try to see myself in the picture of the family you want now, in a father role, I just can't.' He laid his palms on his thighs, his skin pale against the dark denim. 'I want to be the man you need, Kenzie. God knows I do. But everything in me is straining against the idea of having a child.' He paused, nervously scanning her features. 'I know that I'm a disappointment to you, and I'd do anything not to let you down, but it's the way I feel. It's who I am.' He sank back against the cushion, his face drained of colour.

Kenzie let his words sink in, the raw honesty feeling like acid on her skin, but even as it burned her, she felt pity for him. He was tortured about this decision, that was obvious. She could see that this had been eating him alive and for that she felt responsible and guilty in equal measure.

Mustering every iota of willpower she had to control her voice and quell the tears that were pressing in behind her eyes, she held his gaze.

'Arran, you are the best man I have ever met. The kindest, most supportive, generous, fair man...' Her voice caught, so she cleared her throat. 'Every part of me wants to try to persuade you that this will be good for us, for *you*, but I love you too much to force you into anything you feel so strongly about *not* doing.' She took a second, then continued. 'I can't imagine life without you. Without us being us.' She traced a line in the air between them. 'But as much as you have been honest about how you feel, so have I.'

Arran nodded, his mouth dipping miserably.

'I know it wasn't fair of me to spring this on you, but it's as if it's out of my control. My body, my heart, my very soul wants this baby with a force I can't ignore.' She pressed her palm to her chest. 'I am so sorry, my love. And I can't believe I am going to say this, but I need to have this child, or at least try to. I want you with me, for this and for everything, forever, but I can't expect you to be untrue to yourself, just as I can't be to *my*self. So, if you can't be part of it with me, then you need to do what is best for you, live your life as I am choosing to live mine. And without regrets.'

His mouth was slack, his head shaking so minimally that it looked as if he was trembling. 'Kenzie, I'm truly sorry. I wish I was a different, braver guy. One who could put my fears aside and jump into parenthood with you.' He took a juddering breath. 'But I'm not.'

Unable to witness his pain anymore, Kenzie got up and rounded the coffee table, lifting his hand in hers as she sat beside him. His skin was cool to the touch and, as she faced him, she saw tears fill his eyes.

'Don't do that. Don't take it all on. You've done nothing wrong. I knew how you felt from day one.' She wound her fingers through his. 'I'm the one who's changed.'

Arran shook his head. 'But I'm the one who can't get past the past. Past losing Danny.' He shrugged. 'Well, you know.'

Kenzie moved in closer to his side, tears winning out and slipping down her cheeks. There was nothing left to say. No plan B, or C, or any manner of cobbled-together compromise that might save them from the world of hurt they were both preparing to face, and as she leaned her head against his chest, his tears dripping onto her face and merging with hers, the one person she wanted to run to, to share her pain with, was gone.

Olivia would have known what to say. How to comfort and advise her. But from now on, Kenzie would have to learn to cope, alone. The very thing that had scared her most in life was coming to be.

22

Kenzie and Arran had sat still, holding one another for over an hour until the fire had burned down to a pile of crimson ash. Her forearms beginning to tingle under the weight of his, she had eventually unwound herself from him and suggested they go for a walk.

Arran had proposed that they drive to Caol Beach, a favourite spot that they'd frequented for summer picnics with Olivia and Glenn near the famous local wreck of an old fishing boat. Kenzie had been reluctant, not feeling ready for another reminder of everything she had lost, and had yet to lose, but seeing his hopeful expression and needing to get out of the house, she'd agreed.

It was a little after midday now, and the November sky was a flat lilac colour, dotted with blobs of grey-black clouds. As they drove past Old Inverlochy castle, the thirteenth-century ruins overlooking the river, Kenzie was overcome with another memory, of her mother, Hazel, taking them there one Sunday when Olivia had been twelve and Kenzie eight.

Hazel, a keen amateur historian, had taken great pains to explain the history of the castle during the War of the Three

My Sister's Only Hope

Kingdoms and the famous battle of Inverlochy in 1645 when the 1st Marquis of Montrose's Royalist Highlanders and confederate Irish troops had almost destroyed the forces of the 1st Marquis of Argyll who'd been encamped under the walls of the castle.

Kenzie had quickly become bored, but as she'd skipped around the inside of the remains of the castle wall, singing to herself, Olivia had grabbed her hand and whispered, 'Kenzie, try to listen. It makes Mummy happy.'

Even at eight years old, Kenzie had felt guilty at having been so selfish, and as she'd then walked a little behind her sister and mother, swinging a stick that she'd picked up from the ground near the wall, she'd felt like an outsider. A barnacle on the smooth rock of her sister's intrinsic connection to their mother.

Now, as Arran parked in front of the row of pretty white homes behind the footpath that ran along the edge of the shore, Kenzie stared out at the water. The hills beyond looked dark and unyielding, as the wintry light sucked any remaining colour from them, rendering them giant piles of ash.

'Come on. Let's walk on the path for bit.' Arran got out and slammed his door.

Kenzie tightened the knot of her scarf and slid her gloves on, then got out of the car.

The wind was cutting across from the west, its fierce whistle tugging at her woollen hat, and sending her scarf flapping behind her in a cartoonish way.

'Wow. Was this a good idea?' She shivered, then trotted over to where Arran was waiting for her.

'It's not that bad.' He smiled at her. 'Be thankful you're not in Wick on a wintry day. That cold gets inside your bones and makes them ache. Literally.' He mimed a shudder.

Kenzie stared back at him, suddenly flooded with images of him in the upper north-east corner of Scotland, but this time with no plans to come home, and the reality of that taking shape was gut-wrenching.

Seeing her expression change, Arran took her hand, his grip tight through their thick gloves. 'Come on. Just a quick walk, then we'll go for a drink, or some lunch in town.'

He guided her along the footpath, with the water to their right, and the expansive view of it disappearing out of sight, in between the hills in the Straight Glen, was as impressive as ever. Taking it in, Kenzie felt the knot at her core tighten a little.

Despite their conversation earlier, and the devastating conclusion that had shockingly left them looking at separate paths into the future, she was sure that Arran would always be in her life. He might not be with her every day, waking up next to her, or drawing her in to his middle when he was cold at night, but he would always occupy the better part of her heart and that kind of love never went away. At least it wouldn't for her.

That evening, back at the house, after finishing a bottle of wine in front of the fire, Arran sat across from her, his thick socks pooled around his ankles and his tracksuit bottoms riding up his shins. His hooded sweatshirt was faded, but the Greenpeace logo was still visible. He'd been given it by a friend fifteen years earlier and it had become his comfort top that came out when he was ill or upset, or needing some coddling, so seeing it, Kenzie knew that under the apparent calm of his face, he was hurting as much as she was.

'Are you OK?' She tucked her feet under her, adjusting the blanket that she'd draped over her knees. The fire was once again glowing, and the big cathedral candle on the coffee table flickered in an invisible breeze, casting long, finger-like shadows up the wall by the window.

'Yeah, I suppose so. I mean, no.' He shrugged.

'I know. Me too.' Her throat had been tight since they'd got back from their walk, and Kenzie was afraid to speak now, in case she gave in to the mess of emotion she was barely holding at bay.

'So, if we are being real about this, I suppose I should make some plans.'

Kenzie's eyes snapped to his. 'What kind of plans?'

He took a moment, then spoke quietly.

'I was thinking I might make Wick more of a permanent base. Move some stuff up there.'

Kenzie felt something tear at her core, his words, while not meant to be cruel, like a quiver of arrows slicing into her, one after the other, all hitting the exact same spot.

'Oh, God. Really?' she croaked. 'Do you have to do that, already?'

Arran sighed. 'If not now, then when? Once you're pregnant?' His eyes were glittering in the firelight. 'That seems even worse. Waiting until the very end, then jumping ship.' His voice was hoarse, loaded with pain. 'I don't know if I can handle that, Kenz.'

'But I'm not even sure it'll work yet. It might not take. I mean, it could all go wrong. It could be weeks until we know for sure.' She knitted her fingers together, afraid to hear his response.

'Kenz, you rarely fail at anything, and there's no reason to think you will at this.' He smiled sadly. 'The fact that you are going down this path in itself takes you away from me, and honestly, I can't bear to be here to see it, like a gradual erosion of who we were, with me holding on like a sad limpet.'

Their eyes locked as his words sank in. She had always believed in ripping the Band-Aid off rather than peeling it, but now she'd have given anything to have more time, to pare away the wonderful life she knew and let this drastic new direction emerge into the light.

Having a child still felt surreal, and the only anchor she had in life now was Arran. Without him, she would be adrift, and yet, putting him first was the only way she could prove to him how much she loved him, so if this was what he needed, then she would find a way to survive it.

'If that's what you want, then I understand.' Seeing the tension in his face ease a little, she added, 'I'll always be here.'

Arran looked startled. 'You need to focus on you, and the child, Kenzie. Building a future. Please don't wait around for me to change my mind.'

'That's not what I meant.' She stood up, letting the blanket fall to the floor. 'I just meant that I'll always be here for *you*. Whatever you need. Whenever you need it.' She walked over and sat down next to him. 'You are the love of my life, and I'll always have that.' She placed her palm on her chest.

He shifted forwards and wrapped his arms around her, pulling her in to his side. As she felt his heart thumping against her ribs, all she could think about was being closer to him. Her flesh melting into his, his weight on top of her and their breath merged as they closed their eyes to this new reality.

'Come to bed,' she whispered, all at once afraid that he'd say no.

He kissed the top of her head, his lips pressed to her hair for a few, elongated moments before he let her go and stood up, his hand extended to her.

As they walked to the bedroom hand-in-hand, she leaned against his arm, the thought that this might be the last time ripping her tattered heart a little more.

23

Kenzie hadn't checked her phone since Arran had got home, so, at midnight, while he slept, she tiptoed out of the bedroom and went into the living room where the glow from the embers in the fire was the only light.

Yawning, she lifted her phone from the coffee table and touched the screen. A text icon emerged, so she clicked on it, seeing it was from Glenn.

Back earlier than expected. Staying at the Black Dog in town. Let me know what time works tomorrow.

Relieved that he was close, if not next door, she texted back.

Arran's leaving early. How about brunch? 11 at the BD?

As she turned her back to the fire and felt the gentle heat crawl up her calves, she saw that he was replying.

Fine. See you there. Why aren't you sleeping?

She tutted softly, then wrote, *Why aren't you?*

Glenn sent an emoji of a new moon and a smiley face.

Kenzie stared at the phone for a few moments, relieved that she would finally find out what was in the mysterious tin. It was still tucked away in the kitchen cupboard where she'd left it. Arran's unexpected arrival and then the emotional rollercoaster of the day had taken her focus hostage, but now, as she crouched down and knelt on the fireside rug, she pictured the padlock and the faded pattern of the box. Her sadness at what was happening between her and Arran now making the mysterious contents of the tin feel somewhat less significant, she pinched the bridge of her nose to relieve the headache that she always got after crying. Whatever was in the tin, she'd find out soon enough and, after the events of today, there wasn't anything left that could hurt her more than she already was.

Or was there?

Glenn met her at the door of the pub in Fort William. His hair was shorter than usual, and he wore pressed khaki trousers which Kenzie had never seen him in before. The ubiquitous lumpy leather boots were gone, and, in their place, a pair of smart brogues echoed the stylish lines of the brown leather jacket he wore over a cream sweater.

Feeling embarrassed by her messy hair, the pilled, navy peacoat, baggy grey sweater, and ripped jeans she had thrown on, Kenzie hugged his neck tightly, the tin swinging from her free hand in a canvas bag.

'Look at you, Captain Smooth. Nice togs.'

Glenn gave a short laugh, his hug brief but reassuring. 'Ta. I'm undercover.'

Kenzie's eyebrows lifted. 'Really?'

'No, you wally.' He rolled his eyes. 'Gullible much?'

'Oh, shut up.' Kenzie thumped his bicep. 'I've missed you.'

He slung an arm around her shoulder. 'Come on. They do a decent brunch in here.' He held the door open, then followed her into the pub.

It was busy in the bar area, the low hum of conversation buzzing around them, the smell of bacon, and something vinegary, hanging in the air. Many of the square wooden tables were occupied and, directly ahead of them, red leather padded benches flanked a huge wood-burning stove set into a field-stone wall. To their left was a long, L-shaped bar with a ringed, but shiny copper top, and above them, the broad beams in the ceiling had tiny lights strung between them, the giant skylights above the beams sending shards of light across the flagstone floor.

'I saved us a spot near the fire.' Glenn took her arm and led her between two occupied tables to where an empty one stood. He gestured to the chair facing the fireplace. 'What do you want to drink? I'll grab some menus from the bar.'

'A bloody Mary, please. Extra spicy.' Kenzie sat and shrugged out of her coat.

'Got it.' Glenn nodded, and walked away, towards the bar.

Kenzie hooked the canvas bag over the back of the chair and scraped her fingers through her hair, her nails catching on the knots behind her neck. As she watched her brother-in-law standing at the bar, then talking to the tall redhead who was serving him, she was struck again by Glenn's new look.

Olivia had never been bothered by his sightly scruffy clothes, the way he let his hair get a little too long, or the permanent five o'clock shadow he sported, so seeing him looking so uncharacteristically put together was as if the distance growing between him and Olivia's memory was widening. It hurt Kenzie to see it, but as he walked back towards her, she consciously kept her expression neutral, not wanting to inflict any more pain on him than he'd already endured.

He dropped a menu on the table, then handed her a tall glass.

'Extra spicy as ordered.' He smiled, scanning her features as if noticing something for the first time. 'You look tired, little bean.'

'I am a bit. Not sleeping well at the moment.'

Glenn sat down.

'Arran's been away a lot, right?'

Kenzie's chest ached as she nodded. 'Yep.' She wasn't willing to go into what was happening in her marriage, a tiny seed of hope that Arran might have a change of heart something that she wanted to keep alive inside her. Telling Glenn about their conversation, and devastating conclusion, would make it real and, for now, she wasn't ready for that. 'So, how's the new job?'

They talked about his work, the flat he'd rented in Perth, and the new climbing group he was getting to know. He'd been to Ben Lawers, an almost four-thousand-foot Munro north of Loch Tay, the previous weekend, the first climb he'd made since Olivia's death. Kenzie let him talk, trying to banish images of her sister in her climbing gear, smiling as she headed up Ben Nevis for the last time, but when Kenzie could no longer keep the images at bay, she diverted the conversation again.

'I brought the tin. It's been driving me mad, so can you tell me the combination?'

Glenn looked taken aback at the sudden change of tack, but he nodded slowly.

'I will, but I want to talk to you about it first.'

'Why all the mystery?' She was getting annoyed now. She had waited long enough.

He shifted forward and leaned his elbows on the table. 'This isn't going to be easy for you, Kenzie. Are you sure you want to do this here?'

Her stomach dipped as she pictured him making a hurtful or incendiary revelation. 'Just tell me what's in there, please.'

'OK. Well, there's no easy way to say this, but shortly after I met Olivia, about two years after your parents died, she told me that she felt bad, but had kept something from you.'

Kenzie felt as if she'd been slapped, the idea that Olivia had knowingly kept something secret from her inconceivable. 'What are you talking about?'

He hesitated. 'Olivia had found that tin among your mum's things, hidden in an old trunk in the attic.'

'OK.' Kenzie's heart was racing now.

'She opened it and found a bunch of letters to your mum, from a man called Russell.'

The name unfamiliar, Kenzie frowned, nervous, but unwilling to believe the worst. 'OK.'

'According to Olivia, in his letters, he referred to their agreement that your mum was going to leave your dad.' He sighed. 'I'm really sorry, Kenzie. I know it's not what you wanted to hear, but...'

Kenzie felt the air leave her in a rush as her mouth went slack. This couldn't be right. Olivia, and he, had to have made a terrible mistake. Her mother would never have done this.

'Wait a minute.' She sat forward and, to stop them shaking, she planted both her palms on the tabletop. 'Are you saying that our mum was having an affair with this Russell person?'

Glenn nodded. 'Olivia said it seemed clear that she was.'

Kenzie heard an odd buzzing in her ears as her breathing became ragged. 'No. That's not possible. She loved our dad. They were... they were happy.' She shook her head, unable to reconcile this momentous mistake that Olivia *had* to have made.

'I'm sorry. I don't know what to say other than to tell you what Olivia told me.' He shrugged.

Kenzie slammed back in her chair, her mouth feeling suddenly dry and her face tingling as if she was being blasted by an icy wind. 'I don't believe it. It can't be true.' She blinked as if trying to clear something unpleasant from her vision. 'And if Olivia knew, why didn't she tell me about it?'

Glenn smiled sadly. 'She did it to protect you. Like she always did.'

Kenzie shook her head again. 'No. We didn't have secrets from each other. We never did.' As she said it, she felt the creep of doubt at her core, unsure if she believed this anymore.

Glenn's face seemed to sag, his eyes narrowing. 'Everyone has secrets, Kenzie. Even Olivia.'

'No. I don't believe it.' Unable to bear not seeing this for herself, for another second, she twisted around and unhooked the canvas bag from the back of the chair. Taking the tin out, she placed it on the table between them. 'How did she open it? She must've had the combination?'

'It didn't have the padlock on it, originally. Olivia put that on.' He pointed at the box.

Kenzie's jaw dropped. 'Why would she do that?'

'She said it was in case you found it, by mistake.'

Kenzie squinted at the box, trying to imagine her sister, the most transparent and honest person she'd ever met, consciously keeping something like this from her. Whether Olivia had thought she was protecting Kenzie or not, the concept was baffling and went against everything Kenzie had known to be true of her sister.

As Kenzie's breath snagged in her chest, she felt the press of tears.

Seeing her distress, Glenn leaned in a little closer. 'I'll tell you the combination and you can read the letters for yourself. OK? I just wanted to prepare you.' His eyes were full of concern. 'You've been through so much already; I didn't want this to just pile on more shock.'

Kenzie focused on his familiar features, asking herself was it possible that her mother had been unfaithful to her father. It still felt unbelievable, but, if it *was* true, why hadn't Olivia told Kenzie about it when she'd got older? A grown woman who deserved to know the truth about her parents.

'What's the combination?' Kenzie's hands were shaking as she pulled out her phone.

'Seven, nine, four, nine, three, six.' Glen sat back, his hands dropping to his lap.

Kenzie typed the numbers in, then slid her phone into her

pocket. When she looked back at Glenn, he was staring at her expectantly.

'Are you going to open it?'

She slid the tin closer to herself, the idea of opening it here suddenly feeling like stripping in public. 'No. After what you've told me, I'll do it at home.' She lifted the tin and put it back into the bag.

Glenn seemed relieved. 'Good idea.'

She eyed him, the sense that he was holding something back, overpowering.

'Have you read the letters?'

He shook his head emphatically. 'No.'

She considered his expression, his eyes wide and his mouth set firmly. He had never lied to her, even when she might have preferred that he did, and so she believed him now.

'OK.' She lifted her drink and took a long sip, her hand shaking as the tang of Tabasco in the bloody Mary made her tongue tingle.

'I'm here until tomorrow morning, as I'm off work until Tuesday. If you need to talk later, just call me.'

Kenzie set the glass down and nodded. 'Thanks. I will.'

'Shall we order some food?' He lifted the menu and scanned it.

The thought of food made Kenzie shudder.

'Do you mind if I skip brunch?'

He looked up. 'Um, no. I suppose not.'

'Thanks, Glenn.' She tried to smile. 'And thanks for handling this so... carefully.'

He nodded. 'Of course. I'm just sorry that it happened, and that Olivia didn't feel she could tell you.'

Kenzie took in his deep frown, and the slight shake of his head, the gesture speaking to disappointment in his wife, not something Kenzie remembered ever having witnessed before. And yet, now she also felt the sting of that too.

Her instinct, however, was still to protect Olivia, so she said, 'I suppose she had her reasons.'

He hesitated, then spoke quietly. 'You always had Olivia on a pedestal, Kenzie. She was only human.'

Puzzled by yet another hooded remark about her sister, Kenzie frowned. 'What do you mean by that?'

'You know how much I loved her, right? But she wasn't perfect.' He slid down in the chair a little. 'None of us are.'

The knot of anxiety tightened in Kenzie's chest, the implication that he thought her sister had made mistakes, while not impossible, was hard to imagine. 'Are you all right, Glenn?'

She watched his eyes flick to the door, then back to her.

'Yeah. It's still hard to talk about her, that's all.' His mouth dipped.

Unsure whether she believed this, but unwilling to make him feel any worse, she nodded. 'I know. I'm sorry. I feel the same way.' Her voice caught. 'I'm going to go. I'll call you later. OK?'

He looked up, nodding. 'Sure. Talk to you then.'

He stood and hugged her goodbye, then Kenzie pulled on her coat, took the bag from the back of the chair and headed for the door.

There were twenty-one letters. Each with an old-fashioned post-office stamp from Tayside. Kenzie knew of no one they'd ever known who lived there, so as she leafed through the pile of envelopes, seeing the blocky handwriting, with random letters capitalised, she frowned.

The letters were kept in date order and as she was about to open the first one, she paused. This felt wrong and, even though her mother was long gone, like a betrayal.

As she put the letter back at the bottom of the pile, she lifted the most recent one instead. The envelope was stained,

My Sister's Only Hope

and the back flap all but torn off. It felt heavy in her palm as Kenzie considered, for a moment, tossing the entire pile onto the fire and letting her mother's, and her sister's consequent secret, remain secret.

Kenzie stood up, holding the letter away from her as if it were toxic, then, curiosity winning out, and before she could stop herself, she pulled the single sheet of paper out and unfolded it.

It was dated six months after she'd been born, and as she scanned the first few paragraphs, the words swimming around on the page, her focus was drawn to the bottom of the sheet. As she read the last few lines, then re-read them, her heart felt as if it was crawling up the back of her throat.

This could not be happening. Surely her mother could not have lied so profoundly, and consistently, to her family. But if it were true, and Olivia had found out about it, perhaps Kenzie hadn't truly known her mother, *or* her sister, at all.

24

Kenzie sat at the kitchen table, her hands shaking as she read the last lines of the letter again, the words seeming to float up from the paper.

> *I'm not sure how much longer I can wait, Hazel. This is killing me. You have to tell him everything so that we can make a fresh start over here. All the secrets are eating me alive.*
>
> *Please, Hazel. Be brave.*
> *I love you.*

Russell

Kenzie dropped the letter onto the table, her hand covering her mouth. The words were surreal, and as she stared at them, she was frozen to the spot by shock, and then a surge of anger that was so real it threatened to choke her.

Two of the people she trusted most in the world had hidden this momentous truth from her, and the crumbling of yet another pillar of her life's foundation dealt Kenzie a painful blow.

How could their mother have done this to their father, the kindest, most gentle man Kenzie had ever known? Hazel had been a good mother, a role model whom both the girls had adored and wished to emulate when they grew up. Had they known that she'd been living a lie, the effect on their childhood would have been incalculable.

As she stood up and walked to the sink, filled a glass of water and gulped it down, Kenzie was flooded with images of her mother, smiling as she made shortbread in this same sunny kitchen. Singing to them when they were in the bath, then hiding in the big linen cupboard in the upper hall so that she could jump out and scare them witless. Laughing softly while Kenzie complained melodramatically about the family outings to the mountain, then encouraging her when she felt uncoordinated and clumsy navigating terrain that Olivia seemed to glide over, just as their father did.

Kenzie let the images come and as they tugged painfully at her mind, a question began to surface. If Hazel had truly been in love with this Russell person, why hadn't she gone to him? Left her family and joined him.

Kenzie frowned, then walked back to the table, looking at the pile of letters and wondering if she might find answers in them, but no sooner had she had the thought than she dismissed it. The letter she had read had been the last one, and not having any idea what her mother's reply was, but evidenced by her never having left them, Hazel had obviously chosen her family over Russell, in the end.

Gathering all the letters into a pile, Kenzie dumped them back in the box, slid the padlock on and twisted the dials. She was blindingly angry with her mother, not for herself but for their father, but then, as Kenzie sank onto the chair and leaned forward, her forehead on her folded arms, her anger began to redirect itself.

Their mother had done an unthinkable thing to their dad,

but, despite her feelings for this Russell, she had stayed, and for that she deserved some quarter. They would never know how difficult that decision had been for Hazel, but she had obviously sacrificed being with her lover to do the right thing.

As Kenzie processed the concept of sacrifice for family, Olivia's face materialised in her mind. How could Olivia have kept this from her? What had given her the right to decide what Kenzie did and did not need to know about their mother? It was arrogant and condescending of Olivia to make a command decision like that and yet to tell Glenn about it. What was it about Kenzie that had made Olivia feel that, even as a thirty-year-old woman, she was incapable of handling this revelation?

Standing up, Kenzie steadied herself, lifted the box and once again stuffed it in the cupboard under the stove. She slammed the door closed, then turned her back on it, her breathing shallow and rapid. While she wanted to understand how this had happened, there was too much going on in her life, in the present, to have the bandwidth to go back in time and try to get inside her mother's or her sister's heads. To figure out why they both did what they did. If she wanted to survive, she'd have to compartmentalise it all, and deal with what she was able to control, rather than dwell on things she couldn't. If that was possible.

By 9 p.m., Kenzie was staring into the living-room fire as it died down, her empty wineglass on the coffee table between her slippered feet. Chinese takeout boxes were on the table next to a pile of sticky napkins and the warmth of the fire was making the wine bottle sweat, the bottom of it stuck to a copy of *Field and Stream* that Arran had been reading the day before.

He had texted her from Glenfinnan to say that he was heading back to Wick and would phone her in a day or so, the obvious distancing in his message sending her rushing to the bathroom, where she blotted her eyes, blew her nose and stared at herself in the mirror.

Her face was blotchy and her nose rosy from all the tissue action. Her hair was wild, the wiry curls sitting away from her head like a rust-red halo. Her blue eyes were cupped by dark shadows and as she tried to brush her hair and scrape it into a ponytail, tears trickled down her cheeks, her bloodshot eyes feeling gritty as she blinked.

She had stayed out of the bedroom when Arran had been packing a large suitcase, the sight of him emptying drawers and hangers too much for her to witness.

Splashing a little water on her face, then dabbing it with a towel, she started to refold the towel, then scrunched it up and threw it against the wall instead. She was desperate to talk to Arran. Tell him what she had discovered. But she had promised to respect his need for space, and even though it was breaking her, she'd keep her word on that score. On a scale of one to ten, this weekend had surpassed itself, at a resounding ten, as the most devastating since Olivia had passed.

Kicking the bathmat out of the way, Kenzie flipped off the light and walked towards the bedroom. It might only be 9.15 p.m. but all she could think about was crawling into bed and burying herself under the duvet.

Just as she reached the bedroom door, the front doorbell rang. For a second, her heart lifted at the prospect that it could be Arran. Perhaps he'd changed his mind, decided that he needed her more than he needed to be child-free?

As she walked back along the hall to the door, pulling a large umbrella out of the rack to protect herself in case it wasn't Arran, she caught sight of herself in the hall mirror. She looked ridiculous, her pyjamas twisted up around her waist, her ponytail sagging down the back of her neck, and her face still flushed from all the crying.

Dropping the umbrella back in the stand, she straightened her pyjamas and approached the door.

'Who is it?' She spoke firmly, squinting at the small glass panel above the letter box.

'It's just me.' Glenn sounded amused. 'Not the bogeyman.'

Relief coursing through her, she opened the door. 'What are you doing here?'

'Charming.' He mocked offence. 'Lovely to see you again, too.'

Kenzie gave a little huff. 'Come in.'

'Sorry it's a bit late, but you weren't asleep, were you?'

'No,' she grumbled, making her way back to the living room.

'It's chilly in here.' He frowned at the small pile of glowing ash.

'The heating is off, and I let the fire go out.' Kenzie shrugged.

Glenn lifted a log and placed it on top of the embers, then replaced the fireguard.

'Thanks.' She curled up on the sofa and wrapped the tartan blanket around herself. 'Want some wine? Or some cold Chinese veggies?' She pointed at the mess on the table.

'Surprisingly, no. But thanks.' He grimaced as he sat on the opposite end of the sofa.

'So, what's up?' She pulled the blanket tighter around her and shivered.

'I wanted to see how you were.' He tossed the cushion behind him onto the floor just as Arran always did, the reminder a painful jab to her heart.

'I'm great.' She rolled her eyes. 'Never better.'

'Sorry. I know that was rough today.'

'Yeah, not the best.' She tucked her feet under herself. 'I'm just letting it all percolate.'

He nodded. 'Right.'

'The thing I can't get over – almost more than what Mum

did – was Olivia keeping it from me. Like I was a child she needed to filter the truth for.' The truth of the statement was something she didn't want to admit out loud.

He eyed her. 'Yes, I get that.'

'Why didn't she tell me, when she told you? It feels like a betrayal. If she could just have been honest with me...'

Glenn's face seemed to sag as he leaned back and ran a palm over his new short haircut. 'Like I said, she wasn't perfect.'

There it was again. The disappointed tone that spoke of something unsaid.

Kenzie took a moment, then, heartily sick of secrets and hidden truths, she launched in.

'Look, if there's something else I need to know, for God's sake tell me. Whatever it is, I can take it. I can deal with anything except more secrets, or lies.' She stared at him, her pulse ticking at her temple.

Glenn sat forward and scanned her face, as if determining whether it was safe to share whatever it was he was holding back.

'Glenn, just tell me or I swear I'm going to lose it.' She thumped back in the seat and slapped her palms on her knees.

'OK. Don't flip out.' He pressed his palms down in mid-air. 'I'll tell you.'

'Good.' Kenzie folded her arms protectively across her body, her senses tingling as she waited for the next blow.

'Since I saw you earlier, I've been thinking a lot. I know the whole thing with the letters was rough for you, today, but I also understand how upset you are that Olivia kept the truth from you.'

Kenzie nodded, silently, her heart thumping wildly.

'Ever since the last time we talked about the embryo, I've been feeling bad.'

Her eyebrows jumped. This was not the direction she thought this conversation was going. 'OK.'

'I didn't do a good job of explaining everything behind my reason for taking myself out of the equation so quickly.' He halted, then glanced at the fire, collecting his thoughts.

Unable to help herself, suddenly afraid that he might feel differently now, Kenzie blurted, 'Have you changed your mind?'

'No, I haven't, but I think you deserve to know everything that went into my decision. It was more than Olivia being gone, or my fear of doing it alone.'

Kenzie frowned and leaned forward, her elbows digging into her knees. 'What was it then?' Seeing his pained expression, anxiety grabbed at her throat.

He took a moment, then spoke deliberately, as if he had rehearsed this and needed to get it exactly right.

'No marriage is perfect. We all try our best, but mistakes happen, and laying blame isn't helpful,' he said, haltingly. 'I was so distracted by work, spending too much time off on the bike, or with the climbing crew, and not seeing Olivia becoming unhappy.'

Olivia, unhappy? Kenzie felt the air leave her, her insides turning over as she saw the misery in his face. He wasn't going to say what she thought he was, was he?

'Just say it, Glenn. Please.'

He took a moment, his jaw twitching.

'I found out about a few weeks before she died that Olivia had started seeing this guy at the climbing club. Eddie. One of the instructors.'

Shock ricocheted through Kenzie, her legs beginning to tremble under her elbows. Her stomach twisted, sending shards of heat along her limbs as she tried to wrap her head around this information. Surely she had misheard him? Olivia unfaithful? It just wasn't possible.

'There's no way. Not Olivia.' Kenzie hesitated, seeing the intensity of his stare. 'How did you find out?'

'She told me. Confessed it. She said she couldn't stand the guilt anymore.' He stood up, lifted the wine bottle and shook it, before pouring the remains of the wine into the glass Kenzie had been using earlier. 'We had this huge argument, a couple of weeks after you did the egg retrieval.'

The air seemed to be being sucked from the room, so Kenzie threw off the blanket and stood up, walking unsteadily to the window. The unexplained, gradual waning of Olivia's excitement and her delay in scheduling the implantation suddenly began to make sense.

Glenn turned towards where she stood and continued.

'She told me that she was going to leave me, to be with Eddie, and that she was going to tell you that she couldn't go ahead with the pregnancy.' His voice cracked and Glenn swiped his eyes with his palm as his last words circled Kenzie's heart like a thousand needles, ready to pierce what was left of it if she moved.

'But it was all she ever wanted. To have a baby, and keep the family line going,' Kenzie whispered.

'I know. It was. But apparently Eddie had other ideas. She had told him about the IVF cycle, and us using a sperm donor, and apparently, he told her that *they* should try having a child together because he wanted to be a father.' Glenn dropped his hand to his knee. 'I confronted him at her funeral. The sheer gall of the guy to turn up there.' He shook his head. 'Bloody unbelievable.'

Kenzie's eyes widened as she recalled the tall, Scandic-looking man that Glenn had had an altercation with at the service. 'I remember him that day. At the funeral.' She gulped. 'But, Glenn, are you sure about all this? It just doesn't sound like her.' Kenzie blinked away fresh tears, then made her way back to the sofa and sank down onto it.

'Olivia told me herself, Kenzie.' He shrugged miserably.

'We were trying to figure out a way to tell you, when...' he halted. 'When the accident happened.'

Stunned, and unable to believe not only that her sister had been unfaithful to her husband but that she had kept so *many* secrets from her, Kenzie buried her face in her palms. As she exhaled into her hands, wishing that she could rewind time, sit across from Olivia and ask her *why* she would do something as monumental and life-changing without telling Kenzie, from beneath the shock and confusion, hurt bubbled to the surface, making Kenzie sit upright, just as she felt Glenn settle next to her on the sofa.

'Sorry, Kenzie. I know this is shitty timing, but seeing you today, I knew that I had to tell you everything. Especially given that you'd been prepared to give us the ultimate gift. The chance to have a child that now, you can give to yourself.'

The sense that her chest was being crushed made it hard to breathe. How could Olivia have done this?

'You deserve that, Kenzie. If it's what you want, you have to do it.' His cheeks were glistening, his voice raw.

As Kenzie took in his wounded expression, the pain in his eyes palpable, she swiped at her cheeks. All she had wanted was to give this to her sister, the one thing that Olivia had wanted more than anything in the world. But now, as she pictured the tall, fair-haired man, Eddie, who had entered her sister's life and derailed everything, even though she wanted to, she couldn't make *him* responsible for the carnage.

The fact that Olivia had let Kenzie believe that she wanted to go ahead with the pregnancy, knowing that she had already decided not to, was the most gut-wrenching element in this whole mess. Whatever the motivation, or reason, that her sister was summarily prepared to discard the priceless gift that Kenzie was offering her might be unforgiveable, and that was something Kenzie didn't know if she would ever get over.

25

Glenn stayed another hour, the two of them sitting in the dark, staring into the fire as they talked about Olivia, what he thought had contributed to her growing unhappiness, and how responsible he felt.

Kenzie had listened to him, at times telling him not to take it all on himself, but even as she had tried to stay focused on what he was saying, her mind kept going back to the devastating truth about her parents' marriage, the secrets that Olivia had kept from her, one betrayal upon another, and the heartbreaking irony of history repeating itself, aspects of Olivia's story reflecting their mother's so closely.

By 11.45 p.m., she was unable to keep her eyes open, and seeing him also yawning, she folded the blanket and stood up.

'I'm sorry, Glenn. I have to go to bed. I have an early start, and I need to get some sleep.'

He looked startled, then checked his watch. 'God, sorry. I lost track of time.' He stood up and stretched out his back, then met her eyes. 'Are you going to be all right?'

She gave an unhappy laugh. 'Sure. My world is in tatters. My mum was a cheat. My sister, my best friend, couldn't trust me with her problems, and then outright lied to me. I need to make a decision about having this baby when my husband has checked out...' She caught herself, as Glenn looked startled.

'What?'

Kenzie sighed. 'Sorry. I was keeping that for another time.' She paused, an image of Arran flashing behind her eyes. 'He definitely doesn't want the whole fatherhood thing, so he's going to stay up in Wick for a while.' Her throat began to narrow, so she forced a swallow.

'Oh, Kenzie. I'm really sorry. If I'd known, I'd have kept that last piece of news for another day, too.'

'It's OK.' She shook her head. 'I'm glad you told me and that you, at least, are always honest with me. There's only so low someone can get and I'm pretty much at rock bottom, so one more gut punch makes little difference.'

He looked at her sadly. 'Is there anything I can do?'

'No, but thanks.' She waited for him to cross the room and, needing to feel in safe hands, for a second, she hugged him. 'I just need some time.'

'I understand. I wish Arran was here. You need support.'

'I'm tougher than I look, you know. Don't worry about me.' She nodded, knowing that she'd sounded unconvincing.

He gave her a look that said, *yeah right*, then hugged her again.

'I'm only a phone call away. I can be back here in a few hours if you need me.'

Kenzie smiled gratefully at him, her fondness for her brother-in-law as intact and precious as it ever had been. 'I know, and thank you.'

She walked into the hall, Glenn at her side.

'Try to forgive her.' He surprised her, his voice suddenly intense. 'I am.'

Kenzie took in his face, the stoic smile, undermined by the sadness floating in his eyes.

'You're amazing, Glenn.' She touched his arm. 'I know you've had longer to process everything, but still.' She shook her head. 'I'm too angry, and I'm not sure if I can be that big of a person.'

'All I can say is, from my perspective, it's not worth holding onto grudges. They do more damage than good, to all involved. There was much more good than bad to remember. So, I'm hanging on to that.'

She watched him pull his jacket on, then she opened the door. As he stepped outside, Kenzie was overwhelmed by wanting to make him proud of her, the way he used to be when she achieved something worthy of praise. He was the last remaining member of her family, and his approval was suddenly paramount.

'If I do get there, at some point, it will be for you.'

Glenn smiled. 'Do it for *you*.'

She held his gaze. 'I'm mad as hell, Glenn. I'm hurt, and shocked, and...' She gulped. 'I've been an idiot, and I can't figure out why Olivia did what she did.' She paused. Seeing his eyes fill and wanting to give him something to hold on to, she whispered, 'But, I'll try.'

'Phone me. Any time. OK?' Nodding, he walked down the steps and onto the front path turning up the collar of his jacket as a gust of wind blasted Kenzie's face, the mulchy smell of the river at night-time filling her lungs.

As she watched him walk away, Kenzie's mind was flooded with all the questions she had that she might never get answers to. Why had her mother strayed? Why had she then stayed? Why had Olivia followed that same path, too, and if she'd been that unhappy, why hadn't she confided in Kenzie? The turmoil of emotions that she was working through was overwhelming, but blinding her to everything else, louder in her heart and her head than all the rest, was the resounding throb of disappointment in her sister.

. . .

Two days later, on the following Wednesday, having had little to no contact with Arran and spending the previous two days at the research centre analysing the crab project data with Harry, Kenzie was working from home.

It was a frigid morning, typical of mid-November, and, her feet cold in her thick socks, she'd moved from sitting at the kitchen table into the living room, intending to light the fire. Just as she set her laptop on the coffee table, her phone chimed in her back pocket.

As always happened when she heard a text notification, her heart skipped, hoping it was Arran, so seeing Colm Duggan's name on the screen was something of a disappointment.

Hi. Hope I'm not disturbing you. I saw your car. Are you home today?

A swoop of loneliness tugging at her, Kenzie set her laptop on the coffee table, then replied.

Working from home. What's up? All OK?

A few moments later, she read his reply.

All good. Was wondering if you wanted to have an early dinner with Nora and me. It's lasagna.

Frowning, she sat on the edge of the sofa and considered this unexpected invitation. Unsure exactly how to take it, but recognising that having some company would be good for her as opposed to another night in front of the fire with the TV on mute, she typed her response.

That's very kind. Lasagne is my favorite. Time?

After a few moments, he replied.

6 OK? Early, I know, but it's a school night.

Kenzie smiled to herself, picturing the petite child, the glossy dark hair and piercing blue eyes, and thinking about seeing her again sent a buzz of joy through Kenzie that numbed her loneliness, a little.

Perfect. Can I bring anything? All out of Squishmallows tho, I'm afraid ;)

LOL. No need. See you then.

Kenzie tossed her phone onto the sofa cushion next to her and checked her watch. She had a lot of analysis to do for Harry that was due by the next morning, but knowing that she had something to look forward to that evening had lifted her spirits.

As she sat and drew the laptop onto her knees, Kenzie's phone chimed again. Thinking it was a follow-up from Colm, she grabbed it, then her eyebrows jumped. It was a reminder about her next appointment with Doctor Kennedy that Friday, and seeing the date and time, with the *Reply Yes to confirm or No to cancel* links, she hesitated.

After everything that had happened this past week – Arran coming home, their crushingly hard decision, then the letters, followed by Glenn's revelation about Olivia – Kenzie had been lost in a maelstrom of emotion. Staring at the phone, Glenn's words came rushing back to her: *You'd been prepared to give us the ultimate gift... that now, you can give to yourself.* The statement was newly significant in a way that made Kenzie's mind begin to spin.

With Arran leaving, and with everything she now knew about both her sister's and her mother's truths and lies, Kenzie's desire to rebuild her family felt magnified, the questions and doubts surrounding her decision falling away. She had always feared being alone in the world, and now that ostensibly she was, she had a chance to change that.

If Arran and Olivia, and even Glenn, weren't going to be present, be right here with her, then she would take this leap, send a message to the universe that she was capable of turning the tide of recent events and of bringing a child, *her* child, into her world. Something that now felt more important than anything that had come to pass so far or might in the future. She was going to have this baby, and what's more, she was going to do it alone.

She held the phone up and, staring at the screen, hit *Yes to confirm*, then sat back and, smiling, opened the report on the data findings she'd been working on, a rush of excitement making her hands tremble as she typed.

Colm sat across from her in the spot where Olivia had always sat, at the end of the leather sofa, facing the window.

Kenzie had cleared her plate of lasagna and had offered to do the dishes while Colm put Nora to bed, and now Kenzie nursed a healthy brandy that he'd poured for her.

Nora had been a delight at dinner, chattering to Kenzie about her best friend at school, Brody, and, of course, her Squishmallows that had made an appearance at the table, Kenzie being told to pick her favourite.

'I think I like Cameron the cat best.' Kenzie had lifted the small, egg-shaped toy, with one brown ear and one black. 'He looks cheeky.'

Nora had giggled, squirming on Colm's knee, and Kenzie had had the overwhelming desire to move closer to the little girl, to have her tiny hand in hers. 'He's naughty sometimes. But I like him, too.' Nora had twisted around and grinned up at her father. 'Daddy likes Winston best. He says he's clever.'

A warmth seeping into her soul at the gentle young voice, Kenzie had looked at the teal-coloured owl, as, behind Nora, Colm had widened his eyes.

'I do. But he's a smarty-pants sometimes, just like Nora.' He'd tickled her, his big hands around her tiny ribs as the music of her laughter penetrated Kenzie's soul. 'As is Brody, when they have play dates.'

'Brody is funny.' She'd wriggled off his knee, walking

around to where Kenzie sat. 'Auntie Kenzie. Do you have someone to play with? A best friend.'

Taken aback at the sweet familiarity of the title, and the maturity and compassion of the question, Kenzie had looked at Colm, silently asking for help.

Rescuing her, Colm had said, 'I'm sure Auntie Kenzie has lots of friends, Nora. And not ones as cheeky as you, or Brody.'

Kenzie had laughed, relieved that Colm had stepped in, but then a little embarrassed that the truth of it was, she didn't. Olivia had been her best friend, and their closeness had meant that neither of them had looked for friendship elsewhere. Not for the first time, Kenzie regretted that, especially given what she had recently discovered, but rather than let the devastating sense of betrayal seep into the evening and squash the joy she was feeling being around Nora, Kenzie had swiftly changed the subject. She'd refused to confess to being a sad loner who now felt as isolated from the world as she ever had in her life.

Now, as Colm kicked his shoes off and crossed his feet on the old chest that Olivia had bought at a garage sale in Oban, Kenzie sipped her brandy, the welcome burn easing her tight throat.

'Nora's wonderful, Colm. You're very lucky.'

Colm smiled, the brandy glass balanced on his thigh. 'Thanks. She is my world.' He nodded to himself. 'Sometimes I'd kill for a boys' weekend, or a two-day camping trip up in the hills, but, honestly, I wouldn't change a thing.' He paused. 'Except of course that Sandy isn't here to see her grow up.'

'I'm sorry. I know how hard that must be.' Kenzie sighed, her mind jumping forward to what her life might look like soon. 'How do you cope, being on your own? I mean, it can't be easy to be a single dad.'

As he studied her face, she suddenly regretted not treading more carefully, but as she was about to apologise for her ubiquitous hobnail boots, he said, 'I've sort of grown into it. I stank at the beginning, always doing the wrong thing, or *not* doing things quite the way Sandy did. The constant second-guessing myself was crippling. But then Nora helped me. She's a wise little bird, really.' He smiled. 'It was hard not to want to compensate for what she had lost, but when I figured out that I didn't need to fill Sandy's shoes, just be the best dad I could, it got easier.'

'Right. That makes sense.' Kenzie nodded, her admiration for this man growing. 'But practically, I mean. How do you cope when you're working full time? Do you have help?'

He considered her question. 'I do, thankfully. I have a great babysitter called Bridgette, who's the daughter of a guy on the force with me. I knew the family from when he and I were both stationed over in Glasgow together, so when I moved here, Bridgette offered to help with Nora.' He swirled the brandy around his glass, then took a sip. 'I also have a cousin who lives in Oban, which helps. She has a five-year-old son, so if I ever need to work weekends, or a week of nights, she takes Nora for me. Then, sometimes, Ben comes to us so I can give her a break.'

Kenzie nodded, the stark reality of what she had decided to take on, completely alone, hitting home. Colm was coping well, but he had a support network, which was something she did not. What on earth made her think that she could do this by herself?

26

Colm set his glass on the chest and leaned back, his dark-brown eyes narrowing.

'That's a lot of questions about my single parenting. Why do you ask?' He dipped his chin and gave her a curious smile.

'No reason.' The lie tasted salty, so she sipped some more brandy.

It was oddly peaceful being up here in the flat, Colm and Nora's presence, and a few of their personal belongings, seeming to cleanse the space of sad memories, which was unexpected. Not knowing this man well enough to share her innermost feelings or fears was saving her from making a fool of herself and asking him outright to please be her friend. To help her navigate becoming a single parent. To share his help, be it Bridgette or whoever else could step in when Kenzie would inevitably feel overwhelmed.

As she skimmed through all the frightening what ifs that arose when she thought about what she was about to do, he spoke softly.

'I know we don't know each other well, Kenzie, but you can talk to me. I swear I'm non-threatening. Benign. Just a friendly ear, if you ever need one.' He paused. 'Glenn's told me what a hard time you've had lately. It can't be easy.'

The kindness could potentially undo her, so Kenzie lifted her chin deliberately.

'Thanks, Colm. I have a few things to figure out, and a few things to learn to let go of, but I'll get there.'

'I'm sure you will.' He nodded. 'Just don't try to handle everything alone. We humans weren't designed to be islands, you know. Support saved me, and you'll need some, too.'

She met his eyes, seeing the genuine concern there, and an understanding that was disarming. How much did he know? Had Glenn shared the fact that Arran had gone to Wick?

The people she would normally have shared her worries with had let her down, and now were gone, so perhaps it was time to make new connections, even if it was scary.

'Be careful. You might wish you hadn't said that.'

'Try me.'

Kenzie stared at him, the need to spill the contents of her heart, overwhelming. So, she drained her glass and, deciding to be brave, started to talk, unsure how far she would go.

Two hours later, as the clock on the wall by the fire chimed nine times, Kenzie started.

'Oh my God, is that the time?' She made to get up. 'I'm sorry. I've prattled on for two hours.'

Colm shifted forward on the sofa. 'It's fine. Do you know how long it's been since I had a decent adult conversation?' He laughed softly. 'I'm just grateful that you felt you could talk to me about everything you're dealing with.'

Suddenly embarrassed and questioning the wisdom of the amount she had shared, the floodgates opening on Olivia, the letters, Arran and the dilemma they had faced, her decision about the embryo, she turned away from him and walked into the kitchen area.

'I'm sure that was more than you bargained for, though.'

He crossed the room and put his glass in the sink.

'Not a problem. This just means that you owe me, and I have a pass to do the same to you, sometime.'

'Deal.' She watched him move around the space that had been her sister's domain, the fact that he was so much bigger than Olivia, not just in stature but in the way he moved, making the kitchen feel small.

While she had previously felt at peace being in the flat, Kenzie was suddenly overwhelmed with wanting to escape this place. Disappointment in her sister still roiled inside Kenzie, making her want to scream it out, to see it all plastered on the wall behind Colm, a messy collage of all that she was feeling.

Before she could edit herself, she blurted, 'I'm just so bloody furious with her.'

Colm looked surprised, as if they'd jumped back several topics and he was trying to find context. 'With Olivia?'

'Yes. She kept me in the dark about our mum. Basically, lying by omission. Then to go and do that to Glenn. Why couldn't she talk to me about it? What did I do that made her feel she had to keep something that important from me?' Sharing with Colm earlier, that her sister had had an affair, had happened almost without Kenzie realising it, and now, having brought it up again, guilt at betraying Olivia, by sharing her most intimate secret, threatened to choke Kenzie. 'Sorry, Colm. What must you think of me.' She shrugged miserably. 'I'm a truly shitty person.'

He leaned back against the sink and crossed his arms. 'I don't want to be patronising, but can I share something my counsellor told me?'

Kenzie tried to keep from looking surprised. He hadn't mentioned a counsellor up to now. 'Sure.'

'He said that I had to let myself be angry, and hurt, and scared. To let all that stuff in, then let it go.' He paused. 'I held on to some things about Sandy's illness. Decisions about her treatment that she overrode me on. In the end, it was just stuff I got wound up about that meant nothing, after she was gone. But it takes time. That kind of release doesn't happen overnight.'

Kenzie watched him nodding to himself, as if reliving what he was describing to her. As she tried to imagine what it would feel like to be rid of the painful pieces and just immerse herself in all the happy, precious memories of her mother and sister, Kenzie felt drained.

'I don't know if I can. Glenn told me the same thing, but I'm not as good as him, or you, by the sounds of it.' Her throat tightened, and despite having shared her innermost secrets with this man she barely knew, crying in front of him was a step too far.

'From what I know of you, and from what Glenn has told me, you're a freaking rock star.' His eyebrows lifted. 'You did something utterly amazing and put your sister first. That is heroic.'

Kenzie surveyed his face, looking for any signs of practised flattery, but all she saw was openness, and maybe even a little admiration.

'Thanks, but she spent her *life* putting me first. That was just something that I could finally do, for *her*.' She stopped herself, as Glenn's revelation came back to her. 'But then she changed her mind.' She shrugged sadly, Olivia's betrayal stinging like an open wound.

'That wasn't on you, Kenzie. Their marriage was obviously in trouble, so regardless of what ended up happening, I mean the tragedy of Olivia dying, bringing a child into that might not have been the best move.'

Kenzie felt winded, the logic behind what he was saying striking directly at her core. With all the thoughts she'd been having about her sister's decision not to go ahead with the IVF cycle and to discard what Kenzie had done for her, Kenzie hadn't considered this.

'I suppose that might be true.' She stared at him, amazed that a relative stranger could open up an entirely new perspective that might help her reconcile the decision she had just taken.

Two days later, Kenzie had spent only fifteen minutes with Doctor Kennedy and when she walked out of his office, the date for the transfer was set. In two weeks, just as December arrived, they would implant the embryo. Doctor Kennedy had told her that it would take around two weeks until they'd know if it had taken, and a blood test would confirm whether she was pregnant.

Having the dates in her phone was both exciting and terrifying, this next step one she would not be able to turn back from. If all went to plan, in roughly thirty days she would know whether her momentous decision had paid off, and the course of her life would be changed, forever.

Arran was on her mind constantly and not having seen him since he'd packed his suitcase and driven back to Wick, Kenzie now sat in the café in Inverlochy and stared at her phone. It was Saturday, and after picking up a few things at the shop, and having a chat to Sally, Kenzie hadn't wanted to go home to the empty flat. Colm and Nora were in Shetland again, seeing his mother, and knowing that the entire house was void of company and heavy with silence was depressing.

This whole being alone thing was new to her, and still as scary as it ever had been, so the magnitude of what she was doing seemed to glow behind every feeling she was experiencing. If she was lonely, *she* had done that. If she felt isolated, she had chosen this path. If she felt abandoned, she had set things in motion for Arran to go, and no manner of logicising or rationalising could change that.

As she stirred the frothy drink, watching the carefully created leaf design disappear into the milky foam, she desperately wanted to talk to Arran, to hear him say that everything would be OK, but that was too much to ask of him, and she wasn't selfish enough to phone him looking for understanding, or support. She had broken them, and he deserved space to lick his wounds.

Scanning the café, Kenzie took in the occupants of the various, tile-topped tables. Next to her sat an older woman with a young girl of five or six, probably her granddaughter, both with ice-cream floats and doughnuts of some kind in front of them. Over near the leaded-light window at the front of the café sat a young man, with long wavy hair and a black leather jacket. He was hunched over a laptop, a half-eaten scone next to him as he squinted at the computer screen.

Directly across the room, at a long wooden table near the counter, four women in their thirties were drinking hot chocolates with piles of whipped cream on top, their laughter rising and falling in waves that, when it reached a crescendo, made the older woman with the child glance over, a tiny disapproving frown sending a message that the women summarily ignored.

As Kenzie stared into her cup fighting a wave of self-pity, life was going on around her in a disconcerting way, and while it was galling, she needed to witness it, to stay connected to people, even if she couldn't entirely relate to their circumstances.

The young woman who had served her was now back behind the counter, her long blonde hair in a fish-tail plait and a shiny nose ring pulling focus from her giant grey almond-shaped eyes. She had brought Kenzie's latte and scone to the table and Kenzie had caught the scent of patchouli from the loose, crocheted sweater the girl wore. The smell had instantly transported Kenzie into a memory of having gone to a concert with Olivia a few years ago. It was a folk group from Inverness that Olivia loved, and Kenzie was dubious about, but Olivia had been visibly excited about getting them tickets.

'Come on, Kenz. You'll enjoy it.' Olivia had nudged her shoulder as they stood next to the cannon, near the Old Fort William fort ruin, rain pelting onto the big golf umbrella they were sheltering under.

'Is it all hippy tambourines and frou-frou stuff? I swear to God, Olivia, if there are pan pipes...' Kenzie had made a crazy face.

Olivia had laughed, her eyes closing sightly as they did when she was really amused. 'No. It's not plinky-plinky spa music. It's folk. Acoustic, with Celtic fiddles and guitars.'

Kenzie had looked at her sister, and seeing the hopeful anticipation in her face, Kenzie's defences had crumbled. 'OK, fine. But if I catch one whiff of patchouli, I will bolt. I'm just warning you.'

'OK deal.' Olivia had slung an arm around Kenzie's shoulder and tipped her head to meet Kenzie's. 'It'll be much more fun with you there. Glenn just grumbles about going, then falls asleep at these things.'

Kenzie had laughed. 'I knew I liked that man.'

At the concert in Oban, their seats had been a few rows from the front of the stage, and as soon as they had eased past the people already seated in their row, the smell of patchouli had been overwhelming.

Kenzie had thumped down in her seat and pulled Olivia close, then whispered in her ear, 'You are dead.'

Olivia had laughed so hard, tears had trickled down her cheeks until Kenzie had joined her, and now, as she sipped her latte, letting herself linger in the memory of that shared moment, just one of so many that there was no way to count them, Kenzie missed her sister so much that she could barely breathe.

She took a gulp of coffee to force down the knot clogging her throat, then, grabbing a paper napkin, she wrapped the scone in it and shoved it in her bag. Slinging her peacoat over her shoulders, she headed for the door, the flat suddenly feeling like the only place she could be comfortable with herself and the choice she had made to blow up her marriage for the chance to be a mother.

27

Time had taken on its own pace, the days bleeding into each other, and being at work, driving back and forth to Oban, doing laundry on autopilot and eating takeout in front of the TV had become Kenzie's new normal.

Almost exactly three weeks from her consultation with Doctor Kennedy, and just a week after the implantation, she now sat on top of the toilet seat in the flat, a used pregnancy test balanced on the edge of the sink. Doctor Kennedy had told her to try to resist taking at-home tests until her blood test came back, but she had been unable to.

She had resolved not to tell the doctor that she'd done this, regardless of the results, and as she checked her watch again, the minutes dragging by like satiated maggots on a rotten corpse, Kenzie tapped her fingertips on her thigh.

The only person who knew that she was taking a test today, oddly, was Colm. They'd had several coffees together, a couple of lunchtime walks when he was off shift and she was working from home, and twice, she'd had him and Nora over for dinner.

In the six weeks that they had been her neighbours, Kenzie and Colm had become friends, a gentle energy existing between them, with no weird sexual tension or undercurrents, which Kenzie was grateful for. What she needed more than anything, and now knew that Colm did too, was a confidante, a trusted friend, to vent to with no judgement, and a safe place to share their hopes and fears. They had provided that for each other and knowing that had helped Kenzie get through the past few weeks, when her best friend, and love, Arran had been so painfully absent from her life.

Colm was up in the flat with Nora and had told her to phone him as soon as she knew, one way or the other.

'I'll have a pot of decaf tea ready for outcome A, and a nice bottle of Bordeaux ready for outcome B.' He'd laughed into the phone that morning, as Kenzie had paced around the coffee table, chewing at her thumbnail.

'Great, thanks.' She'd closed her eyes briefly, trying to picture the digital letters on the white stick reading *Pregnant*. 'I'm scared.' It had escaped her before she could stop it.

'I know, but you'll be OK. Whatever happens. You're going to be OK.'

She'd walked to the window, seeing the outline of Ben Nevis etched clearly against the sky of the clear afternoon. The tall peaks seemed to be leaning in towards her as she watched a shawl of lacy cloud wrap itself around the summit, a comfort that she felt the mountain didn't deserve.

Turning her back on it, she'd told Colm she was off to take the test and to wish her luck.

When the alarm on her watch pinged, she jumped. Standing up, she averted her eyes from the wand and took in her reflection in the mirror above the sink. Her cheeks were flushed, her hair unusually calm, even slightly glossy, the long red twists splitting obediently over her shoulders. Her eyes were clear, the turquoise irises seeming extra bright, as she blinked at herself, wondering if her baby son would have her crazy hair, or her slender nose, or her tendency to blurt things out before she'd thought them through.

As she stared at her reflection, Kenzie's hand strayed to the plastic wand, her fingers curling around it.

'You have to look. It's all right. Whatever it says, it's all right.' She nodded to herself, then, standing a little taller, lifted the wand up and stared at it.

As she read the words, her heart dipped, then lifted under her breastbone, her insides instantly on a fairground ride that tugged her, at warp speed, from high on a mountaintop to floating just above the earth's surface, her whole body trembling as she waited for her feet to touch down.

Her vision blurred, so she blinked furiously, then smudged the tears in her eyes with her free thumb. She dropped the test in the bin by the toilet, blew her nose, then, flipping the light off, headed for the hall.

Colm stood in the open doorway, a tentative smile on his face.

'So?'

She took a second and nodded. 'Tea it is.'

'Christ alive, that's fantastic.' He grinned, then, without warning, stepped forward and hugged her. He smelled of bacon and toast and comfort, and overcome with needing that more than oxygen, Kenzie stifled a sob.

Stepping back from her, Colm ushered her inside and closed the door.

'Are you OK?' He studied her face, as Kenzie blotted her nose with the tissue she'd grabbed on the way out of her flat.

'Yes. Just a bit overwhelmed.' She sniffed, then found a smile. 'I'm fine.'

He looked relieved. 'Good. Come on through. Nora's watching telly, and the kettle is not long boiled.'

Kenzie followed him along the hall and into the living area, seeing Nora, her head barely visible above the back of the sofa as she stared at the TV where Paddington bear was dribbling marmalade onto his knees while sitting on a park bench somewhere.

'Hi, Nora.' Kenzie made her way to the sofa and waited for the little girl to look up at her. 'Is that Paddington?'

Nora glanced at her, nodded, then looked back at the TV, her cheeks rosy and her favourite little square of fluffy blanket held up to her cheek as she sucked her thumb.

'What's he up to?' A rush of affection drew Kenzie onto the seat next to Nora, catching the scent of baby powder and something milky coming from the child.

'He's lost.' Nora stared straight ahead; her free fingers tightly curled around the remote control.

'Oh no. Where is Mr Brown?' Kenzie smiled to herself as Nora gave an exaggerated shrug.

'Don't know. At home maybe.'

Kenzie laughed softly, moving a long strand of silky hair behind Nora's shoulder. 'Well, I'm sure he'll find Paddington soon.'

Nora nodded, then, as Kenzie made to get up, the child turned to her.

'Auntie Kenzie?' The new moniker still sent a spark of pleasure through Kenzie whenever she heard it.

'Yes, love.'

'Can Santa bring me a Paddington?' Nora looked at her earnestly, the blanket square now covering her tiny thigh.

'Well, I think you'll have to send him a letter and ask him.' Kenzie smiled into the blue eyes, the innocence of them so beautiful it threatened to unseat her. Would her son's eyes be this blue?

'Daddy says if I'm good, then maybe.' Nora shrugged, then turned back to the TV, lifting her little piece of blanket again and rubbing it against her face.

'You *are* a good girl,' Kenzie's voice cracked, a cocktail of gratitude and sadness swirling together, filled her to bursting.

Approaching the sofa, Colm held their teas, his big hands dwarfing the ceramic mugs.

'Let's sit over here.' He gestured towards the kitchen island, so Kenzie nodded, standing up and tugging her lavender cashmere sweater down at the back. She'd slipped her sheepskin slippers on rather than shoes, and her jeans were her best ones, no holes or tears, which, given the circumstances, felt appropriate.

Settling herself on the stool next to Colm, she accepted a steaming mug from him, catching a whiff of bergamot, the familiar smell of her favourite Earl Grey tea. Instead of the light floral scent that she loved, this smelled bitter, like gone-off milk, or mouldy yogurt, and without realising it, she shuddered.

'Well, my friend, you really are up the duff.' He chucked softly. 'And so, it begins.'

By 10 p.m., Kenzie was tucked up in bed with a hot-water bottle at her feet. The radiator by the bed was ticking as it cooled and, looking over at Arran's smooth pillow, Kenzie sighed. He had texted her earlier, before she'd taken the pregnancy test, to check in, and she'd asked him to call her back later, but as of now, he still hadn't.

Lifting her phone from the charger on her bedside table, she checked, for the umpteenth time, for any missed calls. Seeing none, she put the phone back and curled up, facing away from it.

Outside, the wind was howling, the tall fir trees at the side of the house bending to its will, their long boughs scraping the window, like fingernails on the glass. Kenzie closed her eyes and pictured the river across the street, the water undulating with row after row of white-topped waves, and beyond the water, the dark hills keeping watch.

As she practised the yoga breathing that Olivia had taught her for when she was stressed, Kenzie felt her jaw begin to relax and the pull of sleep at her limbs. Just as she was ready to surrender to it, her eyelids feeling pleasantly weighted, the phone rang, making her jump.

Flipping over, she grabbed it, a lift of pleasure bringing her to a sitting position.

'Hi. I didn't think you were going to call.'

'Sorry it's so late. I got caught in an after-work thing, then driving home I got a flat tyre.' Arran sounded tired. 'Did I wake you?'

'No. I was just reading,' Kenzie lied, then grimaced. 'So, how are you? I mean, apart from the flat.' She pictured him having been at a work function, perhaps in a pub, or a wine bar with some colleagues, a small group of environmental biologists equally as passionate about what they did as Arran was. Perhaps there were women amongst them, maybe clever, pretty ones that thought he was good-looking, or funny, or worse, available now.

Clamping her eyes shut to banish the thoughts, Kenzie waited.

'I'm OK. Tired and wet. It's pouring here today.' He grumbled. 'But I've got a wee dram, and the electric fire is on, so I'll warm up soon.'

When he'd gone back to Wick, he had described the flat he'd rented, short term, a one-bedroom above a bakery. He'd then shown her on a video call the big picture window in the living room overlooking a park, and the skinny, galley kitchen with a two-ring stove, a microwave, and the smallest fridge Kenzie had ever seen. The bedroom was long and narrow with an old fireplace that had been boarded up, and an ancient brass bed frame with porcelain knobs on each corner. When she'd seen it on the screen, she'd laughed, despite a stab of sadness at him making a home base, anywhere other than with her. 'God, is there a washbowl and jug in there?'

Arran had laughed, too. 'Yes, and a chamber pot under the bed. We have all the mod cons here in Sutherland.'

Now, feeling chilly, she pulled the duvet up under her armpits.

'So how was your day?' He suppressed a sneeze. 'Sorry.'

'You need to have a hot shower, Arran. Want to call me later?'

'No. I'm fine. Tell me about your day.'

She shifted up against the padded headboard, her pulse beginning to quicken. She'd known this moment would come, but now that it had, she wasn't sure how to deal with it.

'It was OK. I did some shopping. Saw Sally for a quick chat, then had a coffee in the village. My usual Saturday.' She paused, hoping he'd interject with a question that would give her an out, but all she heard was silence. 'I popped in for a cuppa with Colm and Nora and then had a long soak in the bath.' She pictured the tub where she'd lain an hour or so ago, the bubbles up around her throat, and the odd sensation of pressing her hands to her stomach, this time knowing that beneath her palms, under the skin, muscle and sinew, there was a presence, hopefully beginning its journey into her life.

'How's it going with them? Still being good neighbours?'

'Yes, they're great. Nora is a little honey, and Colm is a really good person.'

'That's good. I don't like to think of you in that big house by yourself.'

More than anything, she wanted to say, 'Then come home,' but instead she just whispered, 'Yep.'

'So, what else? Have you spoken to Glenn? I tried phoning him the other day, but he hasn't got back to me.'

She frowned, hoping that Glenn wasn't freezing Arran out

because of what was going on between her and him. Arran and Glenn had always got on well, and neither of them having a lot of male friends, she didn't want her situation to cause a rift there.

'He sometimes takes a while to get back to me, too.' She pulled her knees up to her chest and wedged the phone under her jaw. Delaying tactics were only going to work for so long, and if she didn't bite the bullet and tell him *everything* that had happened today, he might end the call, leaving her gagging on guilt at keeping him in the dark. 'So, I need to tell you something, Arran.'

'OK.' He sounded guarded. 'I'm listening.'

Steeling herself, Kenzie began to talk.

28

Arran was quiet, Kenzie's news, a metaphorical nail in the coffin of their marriage, obviously hard to hear.

Feeling suddenly confined, she threw the covers off and sat on the edge of the bed. 'Are you there?'

'Yes.' His voice was low. 'It *is* hard, but I'm happy for you.' He sounded exhausted. 'I know how much you want this, Kenzie. I'm just sorry I couldn't give it to you.'

She closed her eyes, picturing him doing the same, in his odd little living room in Wick.

'Thank you for saying that.'

'How are you feeling?'

She stood up and walked to the window, pushing the curtain aside. The night sky was indigo-black, the moon almost full, the right side smudged, like a disc of fluorescent watercolour that had leaked into the darker background.

'I'm OK. A bit queasy today, but otherwise all right.'

'Already?'

'Yes, it was weird. Colm made me some Earl Grey tea and I nearly barfed.' She forced a little laugh, but even the memory of the smell made her grimace.

'Wow. Well, I suppose it comes with the territory.'

'I suppose so.' Kenzie pressed her palm to the glass, the chill a pleasant jolt against her warm skin. As she looked at her fingers splayed out, her wedding ring drawing her eye, her mind began to spin forward in time.

She saw her shape beginning to change, the smaller bedroom being rearranged to make room for a cot, the car seat and stroller that would eventually be parked in the hallway, all inevitable, and still feeling surreal.

More alarming than exciting, she thought about the short term, and the year drawing to a close, and suddenly, she felt so lonely, her bones ached.

Both Olivia and Arran had always made Christmas special, full of warmth, and fun, plenty of good food, and sometimes mischief. The idea of her first Christmas without them both was brutal, so she readied herself for a moment, then tried not to sound desperate.

'I know it's a way off yet, but are you planning to come back for Christmas?' She grimaced again, picturing him frowning as he weighed up the pros and cons of spending time with his wife, who was forging ahead with a plan that would ultimately exclude him from her life.

There weren't a lot of pros for him, as far as Kenzie could see, but she held her breath as tightly as she held onto hope.

'Kenz, I want to be there. I really do.' He paused, while she braced herself for disappointment. 'Can I think about it for a while?'

Relieved at being spared a categoric *no*, Kenzie nodded. 'Of course. No need to decide right now.' She bit her bottom lip, the temptation to say more, and push too hard, overwhelming.

'OK. I'll let you know soon, I promise.'

'That's fine.' She pulled the curtain closed and returned to the bed, then slid under the duvet. She didn't want to say goodnight, but she couldn't think of how to keep him on the phone without coming over as needy, or self-serving. She'd asked enough of him for one conversation.

'You must be tired. Go and have a hot shower and we'll talk soon.' She pulled the covers tighter under her chin and shivered, the bed feeling chilly and inhospitable without him.

'Thanks. I am pretty knackered.' He hesitated, then said, 'Are you sure you're all right?'

Afraid to be too honest, and empty her heart to him, she took a moment to formulate her reply.

'I'm fine. Just adjusting to a lot of new normals. It'll take time, Arran. I'm not going to lie; I'm a bit freaked out. I go between scared and excited, then back to scared again. But I think that's probably normal.' She swallowed hard. 'I miss you so much.' Damn. That wasn't how she'd wanted to end that little monologue.

'I'd say it's normal. This is a huge thing you're taking on. I miss you too, Kenz. So much.' He halted, and as she waited, and hoped for the *but I'll be here for you*, the seconds ticked by until the silence became awkward.

Turning on her side, she bunched the pillow up under her jaw. 'Right. Have a good sleep, love.'

There were a few more seconds of silence that felt endless.

'You too. I'll phone you soon.'

Tears pressing in, Kenzie nodded. 'Night.'

As she put the phone on silent and laid it back on the charger, her chest tight and her head beginning to throb, she closed her eyes. What had she expected? He had made his position clear, and she had made her choice. Arran had done nothing wrong, and she now had to face the new landscape that she had designed for herself and stop expecting to be rescued from her own decision.

. . .

As December slid by, and Kenzie charted that she was almost three weeks along, despite Doctor Kennedy telling her it was unusual to start so early, her nausea was increasing. She'd gone off coffee completely, munching salty crackers all day, and had switched to lemon ginger tea, rather than Earl Grey, both of which had helped her get through the mornings.

Harry had been kind, bringing her in some ginger sweets that his wife had recommended, and when she'd occasionally excuse herself from a meeting, or a video call with Anders, in Bergen, Harry would cover for her without making her feel bad.

With less than two weeks until Christmas, Kenzie was battling the dread that chilled her whenever she thought about spending the holiday alone. Arran had still not confirmed whether he would be back and while her head told her not to expect it, her heart was holding on to a sliver of hope.

It was a Tuesday, and working from home, she had taken an hour off at noon to go out and get a tree, and now the little fir stood in a bucket of water at the front door. Colm had said he'd help her get it inside and set up that evening, and the thought of the woodsy scent floating into the hall, then her decorating the tree alone, with her half of the family decorations that she and Olivia had shared, made her throat knot.

Colm and Nora were going to spend Christmas in Shetland with his mother, so they'd decided to have an early celebration together on the twenty-first when they'd exchange gifts and watch *Olaf's Frozen Adventure* with Nora. Kenzie was looking forward to spending that time with them, and to having Nora's bright energy to lift her spirits, the empathetic little girl fast becoming a presence that Kenzie treasured in her life.

As she boiled the kettle and spread some jam on a slice of toast, her go-to lunch for the past few days, her phone rang. She crossed the kitchen and grabbed it from the coffee table, smiling as she answered.

My Sister's Only Hope

'Hi.'

'Hey. How's things?' Arran sounded as if he was sheltering from a strong wind.

'Much the same. Just getting a presentation done that's due before the Christmas break. Harry is going to Bergen in early January, so we're getting him up to speed with all the field research and data we've gathered.'

'You're not going this time?'

Kenzie sat on the sofa, licking a speck of tart raspberry jam from her thumb.

'No. I'm going to join the meetings remotely. The budget is slim for travel next year, so we agreed that Harry would take this trip.'

'How are you feeling. Still icky?'

'Yes. And it's a fallacy that it's mornings only. The bastards lied. My worst time is in the evening, so I'm living on Ritz crackers and toast at the moment.'

'That doesn't sound very healthy. Can't you even eat eggs, or—'

Kenzie tutted. 'Believe me, I've tried. Pregnancy is no picnic, you know.' She instantly bit her tongue, wanting to snatch that back.

'Well, good things are worth paying the price for, I suppose.'

It sounded like a rebuke, so she winced.

'Of course. I'm not miserable or anything, just learning what I need to do to make it through the day.'

'Good. I'm sure you'll figure it out.'

Unable to fake agreement with something she wasn't even sure of herself, she switched tack. 'So, what's happening with you?'

'I wanted to let you know that I've decided to come for Christmas, if that's still OK?'

Kenzie closed her eyes and joyfully punched the air.

'Of course. That's great.' She bounced up and down a few times on the sofa. 'When do you think you'll get here?'

'I thought the twenty-third. Then I'll leave on the twenty-seventh.'

She instantly calculated the number of days, grappling with disappointment at the short stay.

'OK. Whatever works for you is fine with me. I'll be here.' She chewed the inside of her cheek, a stab of pain making her cringe.

'Great. Let me know if there's anything you want me to bring you from here. Some priceless Viking relics, or a vat of pickled herring.' He laughed softly.

'God, just the thought of it.' She shuddered. 'Thanks, but no thanks.'

'I'll speak to you before then and see you soon.'

'It'll be so good to have you here.' Her throat narrowed, but she swallowed past it. There would be no more maudlin conversations. Arran deserved better from her, so, from now on, she would present more of the positives of her situation, and, without being insensitive, even the excitement she felt when she thought about a little boy in her arms. For Arran to feel that the sacrifice they had made was worth it, she could, and must, do that for him.

That evening, Colm lay on the floor in Kenzie's living room and adjusted the tree, inside the stand.

'Is it straight now?'

Kenzie tipped her head to the side. 'Yep. That's it.'

He rolled out from under the lower branches and got up.

'Good stuff. Want me to help with the lights?'

'Please.' Kenzie dug into the cardboard box next to the fireplace.

Nora sat on one of the sofas, flipping the pages of a book about a hippopotamus that Colm had brought with them.

'It's pretty.' She looked up from her book and pointed at the tree. 'Ours is bigger.'

Colm dipped his chin and gave her a look, then Kenzie laughed.

'It is a bit wee, I suppose, but it's a nice shape, don't you think?'

Nora nodded. 'Like a triangle.' She dropped the book and made a teepee with her hands.

Kenzie's eyebrows lifted. 'That's exactly right. Aren't you a clever girl.'

Nora grinned. 'Daddy says I'm a smarty-pants.'

Kenzie sat next to Nora. 'That's funny. My husband calls me that, too.' She smiled at the little girl, mentioning Arran comforting in the current setting.

'Where is he?' Nora frowned, then looked at her father. 'Is he here?'

Kenzie noticed a flicker of angst in Colm's face, so, shaking her head a little, she smiled. 'He is working away for a while, but he'll be home for Christmas.'

Nora considered what Kenzie had said, her little mouth pursing.

'Will he bring you presents?'

Kenzie laughed. 'I'm not sure I've been good enough.'

Nora frowned. 'You are good. You are nice to me, and Daddy says you are kind.'

Kenzie pressed her palm to her chest, touched by the endorsement. 'Well thank you, both.' She caught Colm's eye. 'Maybe Santa will be good to us both, Nora.'

Nora nodded, then lifted her book and square of blanket again.

Colm was hovering in the doorway, his salt-and-pepper hair tidy and his dark jeans and pale-blue Shetland sweater looking well put together. He was going out for a drink with someone from work and Kenzie had offered to babysit.

As she stood up and walked towards him, she gave him a thumbs-up. 'Looking good. I hope this lady appreciates it.'

He dipped his chin, looking uncomfortable at being complimented. 'Yeah, we'll see. She's more a friend, really.' He shrugged, then shoved his sleeves up, one at a time.

'That's good. Arran and I were friends before anything else,' Kenzie said, then instantly realised that their relationship might not be the best benchmark anymore, which brought with it the familiar surge of sadness. 'Just enjoy it and don't overthink.'

He nodded. 'I'll try.' He lowered his voice to a whisper. 'I feel like I'm cheating on Sandy. It makes it hard to just be present.'

'I understand that. I mean, I think I do.' She patted his forearm, catching a whiff of a citrusy cologne she hadn't noticed before. 'It's been a year and a half. I'm sure Sandy would want you to explore new friendships, at least.'

Colm met her gaze, a grateful smile lighting his eyes. 'Thanks, Kenzie. Are you sure you'll be OK?' He nodded towards Nora.

'Perfectly fine.' She patted her stomach. 'I need the practice, anyway.'

'True. And Nora won't hold back if you mess anything up.' He laughed. 'Just don't let her boss you around.'

'I won't.' Kenzie mock saluted. 'We're going to binge-watch Frozen films and eat chocolate digestives.'

When Colm widened his eyes, she laughed softly.

'Just one or two, don't worry. Now go and have a good time.'

He passed her, leaned over the back of the sofa and kissed the top of Nora's head. 'Be good for Auntie Kenzie, OK?'

Nora nodded, then, as he straightened up to go, she dropped her book, stood up on the sofa and wrapped her arms around his neck. 'Bye, Daddy.'

Colm hugged her, then kissed her cheek. 'Bye, Tinkerbell. See you later.'

Kenzie smiled at the sweet nickname, her heart swelling at the obvious, mutual affection between father and daughter, the inextricable bond that she was hoping for with her son.

If only Arran had had the same wish.

29

By the twenty-first of December, there was a crisp frost on the front lawn, the river frothy and high, and Kenzie had done all her Christmas shopping. She'd found two Squishmallow characters that Nora didn't have, and for Colm, she'd bought a delicate crystal decanter for the port he enjoyed sometimes after dinner.

Arran's gifts had been more challenging, her wish to get him personal things rather than resorting to a new kettle, or a set of wooden spoons for his sparsely furnished flat. Buying him those things not only felt sad, and impersonal, but it also helped to solidify the new distance between them, not something Kenzie was ready to do. She'd settled on a new laptop case and a couple of audiobooks in a series she knew he was enjoying. Along with a few stocking fillers and a bottle of his favourite Macallan whisky, she was satisfied.

Not shopping for Olivia had been even harder than Kenzie had anticipated. While she was still hurt and angry with her sister for her deception, knowing that there would be no Christmas Eve with the four of them in front of Olivia and Glenn's fire, with a glass too many of wine and a late-night game of Monopoly that always ended with the two guys throwing little plastic hotels and houses at each other, was gut-wrenching.

One thing that Kenzie had learned since her parents had died was that grief doesn't diminish over time. It stays the same, while we learn to craft our lives around it. It becomes part of our make-up, and as a result, it changes us – the very shape of our heart.

Since Olivia had passed, Kenzie's grief had become compounded, and each new experience she had that her sister was not a part of added another layer of loss to what she already carried. Knowing that would be the pattern of her life made Kenzie want to change things that she would normally have done at this time of year, the creation of new patterns seeming essential to her survival.

This being the last Saturday before Christmas, she had decided to go to Perth for the day, albeit a two-hour drive each way. She'd told herself it was to get away from the village, and Fort William, just for a change of scenery, but, in reality, she wanted to see Glenn.

She'd had a quick breakfast of crackers and a cup of lemon ginger tea, then she'd called Colm to let him know that she'd be gone all day.

'Nice. I hope the traffic's OK. Phone me when you get there.'

She'd been touched by his concern, feeling good to have someone keeping an eye on her whereabouts in Arran's absence.

'Thanks, Colm. I'll be fine.' She'd smiled to herself. 'See you later.'

As she locked the door, slid her leather gloves on and walked to her car, the crisp morning air chilled her face. The river smelled briny in the mornings, the westerly wind kicking up legions of white horses that danced across the water. Taking in the familiar view, she blinked her vision clear. For the first time since Olivia had died, Kenzie suddenly was compelled to see the mountain, to face her nemesis, so she turned around, taking in the vista that she'd been avoiding for months.

Ben Nevis towered behind the village, the jagged slopes and majestic summit clearly visible against the crystal-clear sky. As she stared at it, letting the chilly air fill her lungs, she pictured Olivia, her face alight as she packed her backpack, her favourite climbing shoes tied together by the ends of the laces and looped around her neck like a stethoscope.

Kenzie had always teased her about consistently using the oldest, most battered pair of shoes, and Olivia would laugh and say, 'Just because they're not pretty, doesn't mean they're not the best choice.'

Kenzie let the memory come, and along with it another memory of how Olivia's description of the shoes had sometimes made Kenzie feel. She had always known that she wasn't the prettier one, that Olivia outshone her in that department, but when Arran had come into her life, for the first time, Kenzie had felt that he saw her for more than her looks. He had fallen for her heart, her big, stubborn, loyal, imperfect heart, and that had made Kenzie feel like the most beautiful person in the world.

As she breathed past the gathering pain in her chest, she reminded herself that in just two more days he'd be back, and while she knew it would be different, potentially even awkward between them, just having him in the same room would be the best gift she could receive.

Glenn had booked a little French bistro for lunch, and by the time Kenzie got there, he was sitting at the table, tucked into a corner near the window overlooking the street. The restaurant was warm, Kenzie's cheeks freezing from the short walk from where she'd parked her car near Saint Ninian's Cathedral.

In the five minutes she'd been outside, it had started to sleet, and not having a hood or umbrella, her hair was already damp, curling into tight twists as she shoved it off her forehead and crossed the room.

Glenn stood up. 'Hi. Is it raining?'

Surprised by a rush of emotion at seeing him, she shook her hair, feeling the icy slip of droplets inching down her neck. 'Sleeting. Just started.'

He helped her off with her coat and sat across from her.

'White Christmas, maybe?'

'Maybe.' Kenzie sat and draped her damp coat over the back of her chair. 'Nice place. I like the décor.' She pointed at the long strands of dried lavender that hung behind the well-stocked bar on the far wall. The handful of tables all had crisp white covers and at the centre of each one was a small dish of salt flakes and a single pink rose in a slender vase. The floor was a black-and-white tile, and, on the walls, a creamy damask wallpaper gave the space a homey feel. A silky voice was singing in French in the background and there were baskets of sliced baguette lining the bar.

'It's my posh go-to place.' He smiled at her. 'I thought you deserved a treat.'

'And here was me hoping you'd take me for some chips from the food truck back there.' She gestured over her shoulder, a smile twisting her mouth.

Glenn laughed. 'How's the sickness? Still bad? He'd been delighted for her when she'd called to tell him she was pregnant, his voice cracking as he'd said, 'Wow', over and over.

'It's rough most days. I'm getting by, though. Thank God for all things ginger.' She grimaced. 'It's mostly smells that do it to me.' She glanced over at the blackboard behind the bar where the daily specials were listed in chalk. 'But this place is fine. No mega garlic pongs.'

'I didn't even think of that. Are you sure you're OK?' He looked suddenly anxious.

'I'm fine. A mixture of excited, and paralysed by fear, but

overall...' She made a little huffing sound. 'I'm doing OK, Glenn.'

'Good to hear.' He smiled at her, then lifted the menu.

As they ordered lunch, and sipped their sparkling water, Kenzie relaxed into their familiar banter, and the little jabs they'd take at the other, all the while smiling behind the fond barbs. She'd missed this feeling of belonging, of being with her own people, and when her herb omelette arrived, she met Glenn's eyes.

'Thanks for doing this today.' Grateful at him taking the day off to see her, her throat began to knot, so she gulped down some water. The pregnancy hormones were wreaking havoc with her tear ducts.

'It's great to see you. I was just a bit worried about you doing all this driving in one day. Got to make sure you don't overdo it and take care of yourself now.' He nodded at her stomach. 'Can I ask you something?'

'Of course.' She took a bite of omelette, the peppery tang of thyme making her pause before she swallowed.

'Can you feel anything yet?'

Kenzie hesitated, ready to make a sarcastic comment about only being four weeks pregnant and the baby being approximately the size of a poppy seed, but seeing his slight frown, she edited herself.

'No. All I feel is tired. Hungry but not hungry exactly. Sick, and I need to pee a lot.' She shrugged.

Glenn looked a little embarrassed. 'Right. Of course.'

She smiled at his endearing naivety. 'It'll be months before I feel any movement or anything.'

He nodded, focusing on his steak.

'I'll let you know as soon as I get the first wriggle, or poke.' She placed her hand on her stomach, a new, minuscule and all but invisible rise that had caused her to loosen the belt on her jeans that morning.

My Sister's Only Hope

Glenn chewed, then he put his fork down.

'I'm glad you came because I've been wanting to tell you something.'

Kenzie's stomach feeling curdled, she put her fork down and gave him an exaggerated frown. 'Oh, God. What now? I don't think I can take any more secrets or revelations.'

'No. It's nothing like that. I just wanted to make sure that you knew that *all* I ever wanted was to give Olivia her wish, to keep the family line going. But when I found out about the affair, and then she died, it was really all that bottled-up hurt that made me disconnect so quickly from the idea of being a parent. Then I had to get away. To give myself a chance to come to terms with everything.'

She took a moment, unsure how this was any different to what he'd told her the last time they'd talked about it, but sensing there was more to come, she waited for him to continue.

'It's just that now she's gone, and I know you're pregnant, I think I want to be involved in this child's life – albeit as an uncle.' He held his hands up, palm out. 'I mean, if that's OK with you.'

Kenzie's face split into a wide grin. This was exactly what she had hoped for, that Glenn would still be in her and the baby's life, but it had felt like a pipe dream. 'Oh my God, of course it's OK.' She nodded enthusiastically. 'I wouldn't have it any other way.'

He looked relieved, his eyes brightening. 'OK great. I know I've gone and put distance between us, but I'll still be the funcle, who comes to visit and ruins him. Breaks all the rules, then hands him back.' He smiled, then instantly looked pensive.

'What is it?' She took in the slight dip to his mouth.

'I know it's weird, but in a way, even though it's not hers and mine anymore, the baby coming makes me feel like we haven't lost Olivia completely.' He shook his head. 'Does that make any sense?'

Kenzie nodded, her eyes prickling at the touching sentiment that echoed her own secret thoughts. 'It does make sense. I've felt the same way. I'm processing all the new stuff I've learned, and to be honest, I'm still angry with her for keeping me in the dark, and for what she did to you. But then the next minute, all I can think of is how much I miss her, and how easy and closely linked our lives used to be.' She swallowed hard. 'If this little one can keep *us* connected to each other, and to Olivia, then that can only be a good thing.'

Glenn sniffed, then blinked repeatedly.

'You are my family, and I was so afraid that I'd lose you, too,' she whispered.

'No chance.' He nodded, took a long draught of water, then set his empty glass down. 'So, what's happening with Arran? Is he really, one hundred per cent out?'

Kenzie felt the question like a dagger, its point hitting her most exposed pain right between the eyes.

'I think so.'

Glenn nodded slowly. 'I'm sorry, little bean.'

She avoided his eyes; sympathy more than she could handle without her practised bravery crumbling.

'It's not his fault, Glenn. I knew how he felt. My eyes were wide open, so to speak.'

Glenn nodded. 'But still.'

'I'll be OK. We both will.' She patted her stomach. 'Especially if Funcle Glenn is around.'

He laughed softly, then sat back. 'I'm only a couple of hours away, Kenzie, so if you need me over the next few months... if you need any help at all.'

'Thanks.' She croaked, then shoved her plate away, the pale omelette already congealing. 'I'll tell you what I *do* need.'

He sat up straight, waiting for his orders. 'Name it?'

'Some bloody chips.' She was able to keep her face straight

for a moment before they both melted into laughter. 'Hold the vinegar though, or I'm likely to barf.'

Glenn shoved his barely touched meal away, then stood up. 'Let's go.' He held his hand out to her, which she accepted as she stood. 'Funcle Glenn to the rescue.'

Kenzie let him help her on with her coat, waited while he paid the bill at the bar, then followed him out of the restaurant. The sleet had stopped, but the pavement was slick and shiny, the sky a greyish purple that held the promise of rain.

'You need to make tracks. Looks like some nasty weather coming in.' He pointed at the sky.

As they walked down the street towards her car, passing the nineteenth-century cathedral, the stunning, high, Gothic arches, intricate stained-glass windows and dark slate roof towering above them, they linked arms.

Kenzie leaned into Glenn's side and, for the first time in weeks, she felt at peace. Glenn had her back, and even though she knew she could do this alone, without Arran, it was good to know that she might not have to, completely.

30

Kenzie's drive home had been mercifully easy, and dinner with Colm and Nora that night had been fun, the little girl so excited that she was allowed to open her present from Kenzie early that she had run rings around the coffee table while Kenzie and Colm laughed.

Colm had done a decent job of making a roast chicken with mixed vegetables and creamy mashed potatoes, Nora's favourite. The apple pie that Kenzie had bought at the village bakery had gone down a treat and after the *Olaf* film was finished, when it was time to leave, Kenzie had hugged Nora tightly.

'Have fun with your grandma, and I'll see you next week.' She'd kissed Nora's flushed cheek, feeling the child's arms tighten around her neck, the sensation like warm water filling her insides.

'Six sleeps at Grandma's.' Nora had released Kenzie, then looked at her father for confirmation.

'That's right.' Colm had nodded. 'Six sleeps and then we'll be home.'

Kenzie had felt a jolt of joy at him referring to the flat as home, and as she'd smiled at him, he'd nodded, as if doubling down on the truth of what he'd said.

'Have fun, you two.' Kenzie had picked up her gift from them, a soft blanket with a wide weave and long fringes the colour of purple heather. 'Thanks again for my lovely present.' She'd held the blanket up to her face. 'I'm going to go and snuggle up in it right now.'

As she'd waved goodbye to her new friends, walked down the stairs and let herself into the flat, for the first time since Colm had moved in, she'd realised that, while upstairs, she hadn't missed Olivia quite so much, and though she was grateful for it, Kenzie had also felt a little surprised.

Two days later, December twenty-third was finally here, and Arran was due to arrive within the hour. Kenzie had cleaned the flat, changed the bed, gone to the village shop and stocked up on a few provisions.

Sally had been happy to see her.

'Oh, Kenzie. You're looking well.' She'd nodded. 'It'll be a different Christmas for you, pet, without your sister, you know, sort of thing.'

Kenzie had smiled at the kind woman, noticing that her hair was a soft mauve shade, rather than the usual silver-grey. 'Yes, it's not easy. Especially as Glenn's gone to Perth now.' She'd picked up her two bags of groceries and taken a step towards the door.

'Right enough, although I understand the need for a fresh start.' Sally had smiled sadly at her. 'But you and Arran will have a good time, you know, sort of thing.'

Unwilling to share more of her personal situation, Kenzie had nodded. 'We're having a quiet one. Just some festive grub and a few good films in front of the fire.'

Sally had sighed. 'Ah, yes. The best kind of Christmas.'

Kenzie had taken one more step towards the door, not wanting to be rude, but keen to get home and finish preparing for Arran's arrival. 'Well, I'd better be off, Sally. Have a lovely Christmas and enjoy your family coming over.'

Sally had walked around the counter and opened the door for her. For a moment, Kenzie had thought she'd seen Sally looking at her middle, then a knowing smile had tickled Sally's mouth.

'Give my best to that lovely husband of yours.' She'd waited for Kenzie to pass her, then closed the door, waving as Kenzie headed for home.

Kenzie now stood at the window overlooking the drive, waiting for Arran's car to turn in from the street. Across the road, the river was wild, high winds puckering the surface and rolls of foam gathering on the near shore as the water pounded the smooth stones beneath the surface. Beyond it, the hills were shrouded in mist, the slopes a brackish colour, and the scattering of white houses close to the shore all but obscured from view.

Kenzie shivered and pulled her new blanket tighter around her shoulders, the vague scent of pine lingering on the soft wool. She had put on Arran's favourite of her sweaters, a red V-neck with fine ribbing, and a row of tiny seed pearls lining the deep V. Her best jeans were a little tight now, but with the sweater over the top of the waistband, when she'd checked herself in the mirror in the bathroom, she hadn't looked any different to the last time he'd seen her.

She had recently read that her baby bump wouldn't start to show in earnest until around fourteen weeks, and it was a relief. She didn't want to look different to Arran, her altered appearance a potential gut punch – a reminder of the situation she'd put them in – so as she'd smoothed her hair, she'd whispered, 'It's just me. I'm just the same.'

As she'd then walked along the hall and into the living

room, lifting the blanket from the sofa and draping it around her shoulders, the truth of the profound change that *had* taken place had sent a fizz of excitement through her. She was going to be a mother, and there was nothing small, or insignificant about that. Aside from her wish to be gentle with Arran, not to overwhelm him with the new path she was on, she also recognised that she didn't want to shy away from it, either.

Kenzie checked her watch again and seeing it was almost noon, she turned and perched her backside on the windowsill, taking in the room. The tree was glittering in the corner by the fire, and she'd bought a new cathedral candle for the coffee table. The florist next to Sally's shop had been selling fir boughs, so Kenzie had bought two long lengths of the fragrant greenery that she'd pinned along the mantel. Her and Arran's stockings were folded neatly over the old brass log box that sat at the fireside and the fire was laid, ready to light. She'd decided to wait until he got here, but now, as she stared at the neat crisscrossed pile of logs, it felt less than welcoming.

Taking the fire lighter from the drawer in the sideboard by the window, she crossed the room, knelt and lit the scrunched-up newspaper she'd shoved under the logs, the satisfying crackle of the dry kindling starting to burn making her sigh contentedly.

As she stood up and watched the flames begin to lick the sides of the logs, she heard the crunch of a car on the gravel of the drive. Taking one last glance at herself in the mirror above the fire, she squared her shoulders, then ran out of the room and along the hall.

As soon as he was inside the door, Arran dropped his bags and hugged her, his chin digging into the soft muscle of her shoulder. 'Hello, shorty.'

She had been nervous, unsure whether he'd be reserved, or weirdly formal around her, but relief flooding through her, she hugged him back as the familiar coffee scent on his jacket that she used to relish made her grimace.

'Hello, you.' Her eyes were prickling, but she blinked them clear. No tears today. That was her mandate.

He straightened up and looked at her, his eyes scanning her face. 'You look good. No green gills to see.'

Kenzie pulled a face. 'Not yet anyway. Just keep that jacket away from me.' She pointed as he took it off and hung it on a peg behind the door.

'Really?'

'Yeah, it's the coffee smell. It's like kryptonite for me at the moment.'

He took her in, then quietly said, 'Noted.'

Behind him, his old rucksack sat next to a brown paper carrier bag. As Kenzie tried to keep disappointment from her face at not seeing the huge suitcase he'd lately taken to Wick, she turned and walked along the hall.

'Tea, or a beer?' She spoke over her shoulder, aware that he was close behind her.

'Tea first.' He paused at the long table under the mirror and lifted a pile of mail that she'd been keeping for him.

'There shouldn't be anything scary in there.' She gestured at the collection of envelopes. 'I've been telling you about the important stuff.'

'Ta.' He tossed the mail back on the table and followed her into the kitchen. 'The place looks good.' He glanced at the new dried-flower wreath that she had placed on the kitchen table, a tall, amber-coloured candle standing in the centre of it.

'Thanks. I got a couple of things to Christmas it up a bit.' She filled the kettle and set it to boil.

'How are the neighbours? Still working out well?' He pulled a chair out and sat at the table, shoving the sleeves of his sweater up his forearms. His hair looked a little longer than usual and his chin was shadowed, a day's growth making his jawline even more pronounced.

'They're great. It's a shame you won't meet them as they're

not back from Shetland until the thirtieth.' She eyed him, hoping that hadn't come off as a dig at the length of his stay.

'Next time.' He shrugged, as Kenzie let the promise of another visit comfort her.

The remainder of the day had sped by, the two of them talking about her trip to Perth, Arran's progress with the Glenfinnan job, and Kenzie's report on the crab project that Harry had said was excellent work.

She had made them a simple pasta dinner, which she had been able to eat a little of, and then Arran had told her to put her feet up while he did the dishes.

Kenzie now sat in the living room, her head leaned back on the sofa, listening to the comforting sound of his presence, the clanking of dishes and the water running into the big farmhouse sink. Having Arran home was like being wrapped in her favourite blanket, and yet beneath her joy was a layer of dread at the question that kept rising to the surface.

How much longer would he be here with her – not on this trip, but ever?

31

By 9.30 p.m., Kenzie was exhausted, her eyes growing heavy as Arran talked about a trip he was planning to London with his boss in the New Year, and how he was dreading being in the city.

Across the room on the opposite end of the sofa, Kenzie was focused on his mouth, her feet up on the coffee table. His voice was fading in and out as she blinked, then started, awakening again, hoping he hadn't noticed. She didn't want the evening to end, and anxiety over them sleeping in the same bed was beginning to set in, when he caught her off guard.

'I was putting away the casserole and I noticed an old tin with a padlock on it under the stove. Where did that come from?' He was twisting a fringe on the blanket draped behind him around his index finger.

'It was Mum's.' Abruptly refocused, she sat up and crossed her legs under her.

'I've never seen it before.' He frowned, releasing the twist of wool.

'I found it a little while ago. It was at the back of Olivia's wardrobe.'

Arran's frown deepened. 'Why was it in there?'

Kenzie circled her neck to release the sudden grab of tension at the base of her skull.

'She hid it there.'

Arran leaned forward, his elbows propped on his knees. 'Sounds mysterious. What's in it?'

Kenzie took a second, unsure why she hadn't told him about the letters right away, and yet, despite her lingering anger with them, her instinct to protect Olivia and her mother from judgement simultaneously justified her delaying. He was still her husband, though, and he cared about her, regardless of where they were at now, and having him know, being able to share her feelings about what she had learned, would be a relief.

'It was a shock, to be honest.' She nodded to herself. 'But I want to tell you.'

He was studying her face, his eyes searching for clues as to what was coming. 'OK.'

Kenzie stood up, the blood rushing back to her feet making her calves tingle. As she walked towards him, Arran leaned back and, surprisingly, opened up his arm. Sitting next to him, grateful to feel the weight of it wrapping across her chest, she began to talk.

The tin sat on the coffee table, the padlock off and the lid open. Kenzie had gone to retrieve it from the kitchen while Arran poured himself a brandy, and now they were seated next to each other again.

He was staring at the tin as if it might self-destruct at any minute, and Kenzie's heart was thumping.

'Did you read them all?' He nodded at the stack of letters.

'No. I couldn't bring myself to. Only the very last one.'

He glanced at her, then back at the box. 'Why only that one?'

Kenzie shrugged. 'I suppose it felt like an invasion of Mum's privacy to read them all.'

Arran nodded. 'I get that, but at this point, I think I'd have wanted to understand all there was to their relationship. I mean, she was *your* mum, and it's up to you, of course, but...' He halted, as Kenzie shifted forward and lifted a letter from the bottom of the pile, the one dated the earliest.

'You can read them.' She held it out to him.

He looked at the letter, then took it from her. 'Do you want to know...?'

'No. I'd rather not.' Her certainty of that was like a rush of electricity coursing through her.

Arran held the envelope in his hand, then, surprising her, he handed it back. 'If you don't need to know, then neither do I.'

She was flooded with love for this thoughtful man, reminded of one of the many reasons she had fallen for him.

'Thanks, love.' She slipped the letter back to the bottom of the pile. 'But read the one I *did* read, on the top of the stack. I'm curious to know your take on it.'

He frowned slightly, then nodded. 'I can do that.'

Kenzie pushed the tin towards him. 'I'll make myself some tea.'

In the kitchen, as she boiled the kettle, she pictured him reading Russell's words, his plea to her mother to leave her family and join him. Kenzie knew Arran well and was sure he'd be saddened for both her father and her mother, his heart big enough, and his emotional intelligence developed enough, not to snap to judgement. Even with that knowledge, she was biding her time to share what she had learned about Olivia, as there, he might not be as understanding.

A few moments later, as she walked into the living room with her mug, Arran was staring at the sheet of paper, his mouth slightly agape.

'What do you think?' She settled herself across from him, balancing the mug on her thigh.

He looked over at her, then shook his head ever so slightly. 'You didn't tell me the part about you. I mean, based on the date, I'm assuming it was you he was talking about.' He flapped the paper. 'And the newspaper clipping is sad.'

Kenzie felt as if he'd literally rattled her bones, the shock of what he'd said making her squirm. 'What do you mean?' She put her mug down as her hands began to shake. 'What newspaper clipping? There wasn't one in the letter I opened.'

'Maybe I read a different one. Here.' He pointed to the page. 'See the last few lines.' He stood up and held it out to her, in his other hand, a tattered and yellowed strip of newspaper.

Kenzie took the letter and scanned it, looking for her name, but instead her eye was drawn to a line halfway down the page.

Bring the baby with you. I'll love it like my own. I want you both.

She gasped, her hand going to her mouth. 'Oh my God.' She stared at Arran, the letter shivering in her hand.

'The date is about four months before you were born, so it has to be you he's talking about.' He stared at her, his arms opening slightly as if ready to catch her if she were to fall.

Kenzie felt the floor begin to undulate beneath her feet, a strange buzzing sound mounting in her ears.

'What if she'd gone? Taken me away from here, from Dad and Olivia?' The words sounded hollow, and yet she couldn't help but imagine the scene playing out. 'I wonder if she seriously considered it.' She sank onto the sofa, her eyes beginning to burn.

'But she stayed, Kenz.' He paused, taking in her shocked expression. 'She stayed.'

The truth of his statement began to surface from beneath her shock, as she noticed that he was still holding the strip of newspaper. His big hand made it look small, and yet her instincts told her that its contents were far from insignificant.

'What's that about?' She pointed a shaky finger.

Arran looked down at the sliver of newspaper, then handed it to her.

Kenzie felt how flimsy it was, obviously having been handled multiple times and softened with age. She hesitated for a moment, then read the column of faded text.

Dated three months before her birthday, the obituary was brief. Russell Macrae, a chemist, had died in a car accident in Dundee. Forty-two years old, he was survived by his mother, an older sister and two nieces, and his younger brother who had emigrated to Canada.

As Kenzie looked at the names, all foreign to her, and summoning no images of faces she knew, or would ever know, her heart felt as if it would stop. He had died. Her mother's lover had died, and now there was no way Kenzie would ever know whether that was the only reason Hazel had stayed.

Arran was sleeping soundly, the duvet tucked up around his neck, his breathing steady and his back turned to Kenzie.

She had told him about Olivia's affair and he'd been shocked, and sad for Glenn.

'It's hard to believe she did that, but Glenn wouldn't lie.' He'd frowned. 'Poor guy must've been gutted.'

Kenzie had nodded. 'Yes, to think he might lose her to another man, then he lost her anyway.'

Arran had met her eyes, his glittering in the firelight. 'That's hard to contemplate, but you're exactly right.' He'd paused. 'No idea how the bloke is still functioning, honestly.'

The pointed response had speared through Kenzie, leaving her sure that Arran was comparing his loss to Glenn's, then multiplying it by a factor of a hundred to get inside Glenn's pain.

With the burden about Olivia shared, Kenzie had cried for a good while after they'd gone to bed, and Arran had held her, gently telling her that she was OK. She'd let him stroke her hair the way he always had, his fingertips softly combing across her temple as he moved the hair away from her face, the rhythmic movements and his touch so comforting that she had eventually fallen asleep.

Two hours later, she was wide awake again, a new pattern that was happening regularly ever since he'd moved up to Wick.

As she lay on her side and looked at the hill of his shoulder, the valley of his waist and the long, log-like shape of his legs as they stretched to the very end of the bed, she sighed. All he had to do was be in the same room as her and the world felt righted again, everything as it should be, but as she closed her eyes against the memory of having to choose between the love of her life and the baby, there was a dull, grabbing pain low down in her stomach.

She gasped, her hand cupping her middle, as tiny beads of sweat bloomed on her upper lip. *It's nothing. Just a blip. Just a normal—*

Another tug of pain made her gasp, sit up and shove the covers off.

Swinging her legs over the side of the bed, her feet dangled a few inches above the bedside rug, and her pyjama bottoms were wrinkled up around her calves. As she leaned over to pull them down, another pop of pain made her bite on her lower lip.

'Oh, God,' she whispered, her palm pressing into her stomach.

'What's up?' Arran rolled over, his hand going to her back.

'I'm having pains. Like period cramps.' She shook her head. 'This can't be happening.'

Arran sat up and switched the bedside light on. 'What do

you need?' He got out of bed and walked around to her side, then crouched down in front of her.

Afraid to move, her hand frozen to her middle, Kenzie forced strength into her voice. 'Help me to the bathroom.'

He stood, and helped her up, then, looping her hand over his forearm, he walked her carefully across the hall and into the bathroom.

'Do you want me to stay?' He stood at the side of the bath, his hands on his hips and his pyjama bottoms trailing on the floor.

'No. I'll call you if I need you.' She lifted the lid of the toilet, then waited for him to leave the room.

Kenzie closed her eyes, then pulled down her pyjama bottoms, but before she could check for any signs of bleeding, another cramp made her slump down onto the seat.

'No. No. No,' she whispered, grabbing a length of paper from the roll. 'Please, no.'

32

Three hours later, Kenzie lay in a bed in the Belford hospital, the same place Olivia had been taken after her accident. Arran had driven her to the accident and emergency department and within minutes she'd been taken back to a room.

With it now being Christmas Eve morning, she had not expected Doctor Kennedy to answer the call that the attending obstetrician had made, but within ninety minutes of her being admitted, all the while nauseated and panicked that this could be the end, that she might lose the baby and her last tenuous connection to Olivia, Doctor Kennedy had walked into her room.

He'd been calm as he'd shaken Arran's hand and then he'd talked Kenzie through the result of the ultrasound they'd done.

'This is called a subchorionic hematoma, Kenzie. It's essentially a small amount of blood that collects between the outer membrane of the foetus, and the uterine wall.' He'd looked over at Arran, who was wearing his long coat over his pyjamas, his eyes wide as he stood by the window. 'It's frightening, but not uncommon in women who've undergone fertility treatments. Often there's light bleeding, and lower abdominal pain, but everything else looks fine on the scan.' He'd patted her shin through the thin blanket. 'These things generally resolve themselves in a few weeks, so we'll monitor you through a series of ultrasounds just to be sure things are settling down.'

Kenzie had taken in everything he was saying, her eyes drilling into his, and typically, rather than let herself exhale fully, she had peppered him with questions.

'So, the baby is OK? What if it doesn't settle down, though? What if it continues, or gets worse? I mean, what is the worst that can happen?'

He'd smiled kindly at her. 'It's best not to focus on the what ifs, Kenzie. Let's keep positive and I'll monitor you closely. If there are any changes, we'll be on it right away.'

She'd blinked her vision clear, still not convinced that she'd heard everything she needed to. 'I understand that, but what *is* the worst-case scenario? I need to be prepared, just in case.'

He'd taken a moment before answering.

'It's highly unlikely, but in some rare cases, a subchorionic hematoma can lead to miscarriage, placental abruption or preterm labour.' He'd dipped his chin and locked eyes with her. 'You need to rest, make sure you're getting plenty of fluids, and sleep, and try not to worry.'

'Easier said than done.' She'd given a little huff, looking at Arran, who was now standing next to her.

'Does she have to be on bed rest or anything?' Arran's question had made Kenzie feel stupid. She should have had the wherewithal to ask that.

'No. If she takes it easy for a day or so, she can get on with life as usual. Light exercise is a good thing, so gentle walks, some swimming, et cetera...' He'd halted, seeing Kenzie begin to chew her thumbnail. 'I know it's a worrying time, Kenzie, but stress is not your friend. Try to find ways to minimise it, if you can. Yoga. Meditation.'

At this, Arran had moved to the end of the bed, as if

distancing himself from that part of what Kenzie was dealing with. Seeing him step away, right at that moment, delivered a message that hit Kenzie like a tidal wave. While doing the right thing by her tonight, he was truly out, and the sooner she came to terms with that, the better.

Christmas came and went, and Arran had barely left her side. Initially, he'd been uptight, nagging her if she was bustling about the flat. He'd then banished her to the sofa and taken on all the cooking, cleaning up, and done a couple of loads of laundry.

After she'd got home from the hospital, Kenzie had taken a while to relax, but then she'd decided to lean into his care for however long he was here, and once she did that, the atmosphere between them relaxed a little.

On Boxing Day, after they'd had lunch at the kitchen table, and he had walked to Sally's shop to get a few provisions for them, he was in the office making a call when Kenzie walked in. He was standing at the window, his back to her, his free hand in the pocket of his jeans.

Her sheepskin slippers, soft on the wood floor, masked her entrance and as she stood behind him, about to touch his shoulder, he said, 'Look, Calvin, she needs me to be here for a few more days, so I won't be back as planned.'

Kenzie was about to protest, but then something held her back. This was what she wanted, what she needed, so if he was willing to change his plans, even for a couple more days, she'd gladly accept his help, however selfish that made her.

'Right. Thanks, mate. I'll phone you when I know when I'll be back.' He nodded, then turned, seeing her standing there. Looking mildly alarmed, he rolled his eyes theatrically. 'Yeah, OK, mate. Talk soon.'

Kenzie waited until he'd ended the call, then tentatively

touched his arm. 'Thank you.' She was about to say, *you didn't have to do that*, but she stopped herself, knowing that he would know that she'd be playing a part, so she stayed silent. He understood her better than anyone on the planet, and this gift he was giving her might be the last thing he *could* give her before their paths separated permanently.

'Right, back to the couch for you.' He took her arm in his.

Kenzie leaned on him, the firm muscle beneath the soft cashmere sending strength into her bones by osmosis.

By the twenty-eighth of December, Kenzie was feeling back to normal. Her pains had stopped, as had the spotting, and her appetite was back with a vengeance. For the first time since becoming pregnant, she found she was craving odd foods.

They'd decided to order a pizza for dinner from a place in Fort William that delivered, and as they scanned the menu on Arran's laptop, picking their toppings, Kenzie pointed at the screen.

'Oo, I want anchovies.'

'What?' He stared at her. 'You hate them.'

'I know.' She shook her head. 'But I need them.'

Arran laughed softly, then clicked the appropriate box.

'Anything else?'

She looked at the list again, then said, 'Pineapple.'

At this, Arran laughed hard, his head going back for a second.

'Are you serious? What happened to the *people who put pineapple on pizza are deranged* thing you've had ever since I've known you?'

He completed the order and paid with his credit card.

Kenzie slid back on the sofa next to him and hugged a soft cushion to her middle. 'Don't judge, my friend. It's a woman's prerogative to change her mind.'

He looked fleetingly wounded, then the statement seemed to take on water, obliterating their light mood as effectively as an ice-cold shower.

'Sorry. I didn't mean anything by it.'

He shook his head. 'It's OK.' He got up, closed the laptop and checked his watch. 'It said thirty minutes until the delivery, so I think I'll jump in the shower.'

'All right.' She felt the sink of disappointment, the delicate membrane of their connection so easily ruptured these days. 'I'll be here. Glued to the sofa.' She patted the cushion next to her and found a smile.

He simply nodded, then walked out into the hall.

Kenzie's gut instinct was to grab her phone and call Olivia. To ask her sister what she should do, how she should navigate this new, awkward way she and Arran were relating, and as soon as the impulse passed, loss clamped around Kenzie's insides like a vice.

That night, Arran had stayed up later than Kenzie, saying he wanted to get some work done, but Kenzie had sensed that, in truth, he just needed some distance between them.

She went to bed and read for a while, until her eyes grew heavy and the book she was reading flopped onto her chest, startling her. Seeing that his side of the bed was still empty, she'd swallowed hard, turned off her bedside light and given in to sleep.

The following morning, Kenzie woke to see Arran's pillow still smooth, and the covers undisturbed on his side. Instantly afraid that he'd gone, perhaps for good this time, she rolled out of bed, put her slippers and robe on and went down the hall to the living room.

The room was dark, the curtains still closed, so she walked to the window and drew them.

Behind her, Arran yawned, making her jump.

'Oh, God. Sorry. I didn't know you were there.' She covered her mouth with her hand.

He scrubbed the top of his head, his hair sticking up at the crown like a cockscomb.

''S OK. I was up pretty late, and I didn't want to wake you.' He was lying on the sofa, covered in the old quilt that she kept in the linen cupboard. 'So, I just bunked out here.'

'You wouldn't have woken me.' She gathered her mane of hair into her fists and twisted it into a long coil. 'But thanks.' Hurt bubbled in her chest, but she pushed it down. He was entitled to need his space from her, and she'd be gracious about it, even if it felt like she was digging her own heart out with a spoon. 'Want some breakfast?'

'No, thanks. Just a cuppa.' Arran stood up and began folding the quilt, his faded T-shirt, stripey boxers and Argyle socks looking comical as he moved around the room, replacing the cushions he'd tossed off the sofa to make room for his long legs.

Kenzie watched him for a few seconds, the urge to close the distance between them and wrap herself around him like an addict craving a hit. Once again putting the lid firmly back on what *she* wanted, she handed him his jeans from the back of the opposite sofa.

'Tea or coffee?'

He took the jeans and looked momentarily coy, as he quickly slipped them on.

'Coffee, but I'll make it. I don't want you to barf in it.' He gave her a half-smile, then tucked the front of his T-shirt into his jeans.

'Probably a good idea.' She nodded. Then, seeing him checking his watch, she added, 'What's on your agenda today?'

He raked both hands though his hair, then tightened his belt.

My Sister's Only Hope

'Actually, I spoke to Calvin last night and I think, now that you're doing better, I'll head back to Wick today.'

Kenzie's stomach went into free fall. 'Oh, right.'

'You are OK to be on your own now, aren't you?' He frowned.

'Of course.' She forced a smile. 'You're fine to go. I'm right as rain.'

He scanned her face. 'Are you sure?'

Kenzie nodded, afraid that her poor acting skills would give her away if she tried to be overly positive. She mentally calculated the dates, today being the twenty-ninth of December. She had hoped he'd stay past New Year, but they hadn't talked about it, so she shouldn't have assumed.

'You've been an angel. Thank you for staying on.' She smiled, this time genuinely. 'I don't know what I'd have done without you.'

Arran took her in, his hands sliding into his pockets as his shoulders rolled forwards.

'You look good, Kenz. Better than when I got here. There's more colour in your face.'

She patted her cheeks. 'So, my face doesn't look pale anymore?'

His mouth twisted. 'No. No buckets or pails here.'

She laughed softly. 'You are officially off duty, Mr Ford. I'm going to be all right.'

He closed his eyes briefly, making Kenzie think she'd said something hurtful again, then he walked over to her and took her hands in his.

'Being here has been great, but the longer I stay, the harder it's going to be to...' He stopped himself, just as Kenzie worked one of her hands loose and pressed her fingertips to his lips.

'Don't say it. I understand.' A tear formed in the corner of his eye, so she gently thumbed it away. 'You are the best of men, and I love you more than you'll ever know. I know what I'm doing to you, but I can't go back now, Arran. And, if I'm honest, I don't want to.'

He released her other hand and pinched the bridge of his nose.

'I'd never ask you to. It's just that I love you so damn much, this is like a nightmare I can't wake up from. If we weren't best friends, or we'd had one of those relationships where we fought constantly...' He gave a strangled laugh. 'The problem is I love *and* like you, Kenzie. I liked us, just as we were.' He shook his head. 'Staying here now feels like I'm hiding from where we're going, and I can't do that anymore. I have to face what's coming.'

Kenzie's vision blurred, her *no crying* resolution crumbling as she wrapped her arms around his waist and leaned her head against his chest. 'I'm so sorry, Arran. I'm just so sorry.'

'Me too.' He hugged her tightly, his chest heaving under her cheek as she inhaled his smell, the warm, leathery, we're-in-this-together smell, that had always made her feel safe.

It was time to face the choice she had made head on, and she had to be the stronger one, from now on.

33

Arran was packed and ready to leave shortly after twelve. Kenzie had given him space to gather his things together and when he came to find her to say goodbye, she was lying on top of the bed reading.

'I'm off, then.' He hovered in the doorway, his jacket on, and his car keys looped around his forefinger. 'Don't get up.'

She closed her book and sat on the edge of the bed, a band of sadness tightening around her heart like a tourniquet.

'Will you let me know when you get there?'

'Sure. I'll text you.' He slid the keys into his pocket, and just as she thought he might simply wave as he left, he crossed the room and sat next to her. 'You take care of yourself, and don't overdo things.' He lifted her hand in his. 'Promise?'

She nodded, unable to trust her voice.

'I'll always be in your corner, Kenzie. You know that, right?' He locked eyes with her, his full of pain.

'I know,' she whispered. 'And I will always be in yours.'

He wrapped his arm around her and hugged her to his side, his finger digging into her upper arm as if searching for a climbing hold.

They stayed like that for a few moments, then he stood up. 'Right.'

She pulled her shoulders back, her chin setting in a firm line.

'Thank you for everything you've done. For all the love, and fun, and brilliant years of us.' She placed her palm on her chest, then rose onto tiptoe and planted a soft kiss on each of his eyelids. 'You deserve the best, Arran.'

'You do too. Good luck, Kenz.' He pointed at her middle. 'That baby is the luckiest little sprout on the planet.'

She cupped her stomach as he turned and walked from the bedroom, then she sat, rolled onto her side and let the tears come.

The next twenty-four hours trickled by, Kenzie too miserable to get out of her pyjamas, dozing in bed, and on the sofa with the TV on mute, and picking at whatever was in the fridge whenever her stomach twinged with hunger.

Arran had texted from Wick to say he'd arrived safely, and she'd responded with a thumbs-up emoji, which felt cripplingly impersonal and yet a portend for the next phase of their separation.

As she stared at the clock on the mantel, calculating that it could be a couple of hours until Colm and Nora got home, her phone lit up on the coffee table.

Colm's text, albeit simple, felt like a well-timed lifeline.

Almost home. Do you need anything from the shops?

She sniffed, wiped her nose on the sleeve of her sweatshirt, then replied.

Nope, but thanks. See you soon.

He sent her a crazy-face emoji and the words *Nora says hello,* which made Kenzie smile as she hoisted herself from the sofa and made her way to the bathroom to shower, wash her face and put on some clothes. The prospect of seeing the little girl was the brightest light of her day, so far.

Just over an hour later, a little before 2 p.m., Kenzie heard the car on the gravel, so she walked to the window and looked out at the drive.

Colm opened the driver's door of his Volvo and got out and folded forward at the waist, stretching out his long back. As he straightened up, he looked over at the window, so Kenzie waved to catch his eye.

He waved back, beckoned to her, and mimed drinking something, then pointed to the side of the house where the stairs to his flat were.

Gratitude making her eyes sting, she gave him a thumbs up before flattening her two palms, fingers splayed, to indicate ten minutes. He returned the thumbs up, then opened the back door and got Nora out of her car seat.

She was wearing a new, pink puffy coat with a fur-lined hood. Her dark-blue leggings ended in pale-pink Ugg boots, and her glossy dark hair swung around her shoulders as she spotted Kenzie and waved, too.

Kenzie waved again, longing spiralling through her as she watched Colm lift Nora to his hip, grab a big bag from the back seat, then head for the stairs.

Kenzie walked through the flat to the bedroom and checked herself in the mirror above the dressing table. Her cheeks were flushed, her eyes puffy and her hair, though newly washed, was twisting away from her head as if she'd been electrocuted, so, tutting, she headed back into the bathroom.

She dragged her brush through the web of hair, and as often happened when she did this, Olivia's face floated into Kenzie's mind. It had been almost a whole day since she'd thought about her sister, or considered how she felt about everything she now knew to be true, so letting those feelings back into the light, Kenzie brushed, each stroke easing some of the tension that was stretched across her back.

Putting the brush back in the small cabinet next to the bath, she sighed, 'Why couldn't you talk to me, Olivia?' She frowned at her reflection in the mirror, looking for signs of unapproachability, or worse, judgement, but all she saw was her face.

As Kenzie stared at the stubborn chin, the wide-set blue eyes, the long nose and the wide mouth that curved down slightly when she concentrated, something struck her. There was an edge to her features that was missing from Olivia's. A certain line to her jaw that said *I know what I want, so don't waste your time trying to change me,* and as Kenzie took it in, a moment of clarity made her eyebrows lift.

From a young age, she had been more outgoing than Olivia, more confident in her place in the world. Olivia had always deferred to her, letting Kenzie have the limelight, be the focus of their parents' attention. Then, after their parents' accident, Olivia had taken on the role of provider, putting herself and her own needs aside to make sure Kenzie's life stayed as close to her plan as possible.

Kenzie had, of course, been grateful but had perhaps too easily accepted Olivia's sacrifice as reasonable, and now, feeling the long-overdue truth of that was humbling.

Olivia had been her best friend, and champion, and in making the choices she'd made, taking a job she disliked, giving up on her dreams of university and studying overseas, she'd passed her licence to dream on to Kenzie, Olivia's being stamped out by the practical requirements of their new life.

Recalling all the times that Olivia had insisted that she was fine working at the call centre, that Kenzie should enjoy university, go on those field trips to Scandinavia, and Egypt, to study the marine life, essentially embracing life for them both, Kenzie closed her eyes, shame chilling her insides.

The more the incidences piled up in her mind, the more ashamed she felt, and the more her question of just moments ago to Olivia was answered. Her sister had been so concerned with Kenzie's happiness, and protecting her from anything unpleasant, or sad, that Olivia could not confide in Kenzie about her troubled marriage, or her growing love for another man, and that knowledge was as painful as it was revealing.

When they'd talked about Olivia a couple of months earlier, Glenn had told her that she'd had her sister on a pedestal, and now, finally accepting how unfair it had been to put that kind of pressure on her, Kenzie's hurt at Olivia not confiding in her began to dissipate. In its place was the beginnings of understanding, sadness at her own lack of emotional maturity and, in the wake of all that, forgiveness.

There was nothing to hold against Olivia that Kenzie wasn't partly responsible for, and as she let the reality of that permeate, she whispered, 'I'm so sorry, Olivia. I wasn't there for you when you needed me the most. I see that now.' She swallowed over a knot of regret. 'Please forgive me.'

Turning her back on her reflection, Kenzie took a ragged breath, every fibre of her being yearning for one more chance to hug her sister, tell her that she finally, fully appreciated everything that she had done for her. But not having the opportunity to hear Olivia say the words left only one way forward for Kenzie. She would have to try to forgive herself.

34

Two weeks later, and a new year having begun, being back at work was a relief. Not only was it good to get out of the flat, but being in the lab, seeing Harry and her colleagues and getting back into her research, was giving Kenzie a mood boost.

She'd reasoned that perhaps it was being over six weeks pregnant now, and her nausea having eased a little, but whatever the cause, she felt energised.

Harry's wife, Celia, had sent him in with a selection of herbal teas and some tiny woollen booties, along with a note saying how happy she was for Kenzie. She'd been so touched that she'd had a little cry in the ladies' room, the booties balanced on her knee as she hid in the cubicle.

Arran had been keeping in touch via texts and emails, but as the days passed and she carved herself a new routine, training herself to function without hearing his voice every day, Kenzie was growing to accept whatever he *could* give her, and be grateful.

The Norwegian crab study was progressing well, and Anders had told Harry, when he'd been in Bergen, that everyone at the research institute there was impressed with

Kenzie's work. Harry had been like a proud parent when he'd returned a few days earlier. They'd had a brief video call, and he'd told her he'd fill her in on the next stage of the project when she was back at work.

Kenzie had stopped on the way in to work and picked up two bacon rolls for her lunch. Bacon had become her favourite food, and along with the recent additions of buttery mashed potatoes, oranges and the sour, dill pickles from Sally's shop, the list of foods she could tolerate was expanding a little.

As she made herself a cup of ginger tea at the drinks station on the counter against the far wall in the laboratory, she could smell the bacon from the rolls in her desk drawer. Contemplating having a bite or two before Harry came in for their meeting at 9 a.m., her mouth began to water.

Suddenly starving, she turned towards the door just as Harry came in, a covered cup in his hand and a pile of file folders against his middle.

'Happy New Year.' He smiled broadly. 'Good to see you. How was your wee break over Christmas?' He set the cup down on her desk and then slid the files down next to it.

'It was nice, thanks. Quiet, but a good break.' She nodded, dunking the teabag in the mug. 'How was yours?'

'Good. Good.' He nodded, then pulled the chair out opposite Kenzie's desk and sat down. 'Well, actually, Celia had Covid a few days before Christmas, so we were isolating inside the house.' He rolled his eyes. 'But she tested negative before I went to Bergen, so we were able to spend New Year together.'

'Oh, that was a pain for you both. Sorry.' Kenzie's mouth dipped. 'Is she fully recovered?' She sat at her desk and put her mug on the coaster with a bird's-eye view of Ben Nevis that Olivia had given her when she'd got her job at the institute. As she adjusted the mug to cover as much as possible of the image, Harry sipped some of his coffee.

'Yes, she's fine. Gone to a white-water rafting group meet up near Boat of Garten for a couple of days. There are some good rapids up there apparently.'

Kenzie nodded, picturing his petite blonde wife steering a kayak through class-three rapids in the sometimes-treacherous Highland rivers, the very thought of which made Kenzie grimace. 'She's amazing. How often does she do this stuff now, and in winter, too?'

Harry chuckled. 'Not usually at this time of year, but she says she's landlocked and stir-crazy after spending two weeks in the house with only me to talk to.' He pulled a face. 'Can't blame her, really.'

Kenzie laughed. 'I'm sure that's not the reason, but I do admire her. My idea of adventure these days is to put honey in my tea instead of milk.'

Harry gave a snorty laugh. 'You and me both.' He set his cup down and lifted a file from the top of the pile. 'So, to work. Let me get you up to speed on the study, my meeting with Anders and co, and then, I have a proposal for you.'

Kenzie's eyebrows danced as she wiggled her left hand at him. 'I'm flattered, but, Harry, we're both married.' She'd said it without thinking, just as she would have at any other point over the past four-plus years, but now there was a shadow over her marital situation, a sad reality that she was yet to share with Harry.

'Funny lady.' He shook his head at her. 'Let's save that part until later. We've got lots of data to look at first.'

'Right.' Kenzie took another sip of tea, averting her eyes from the coaster, the view of the mountains still making her eyes sting.

Half an hour later, Kenzie stood at the window behind her desk, overlooking the Garbh Àrd point, and the prominent peak of Glenn Lora, her fingernails drumming the wooden sill. What

Harry had just told her had knocked the wind from her and as it was sinking in, he was waiting patiently for her to say something, his large stomach pressed up against the far side of her desk.

'There's no pressure to decide right now, as they don't need you there until the end of November. Obviously, Anders doesn't know your personal situation with the baby, and I wasn't about to tell him, or attempt to answer for you. He was just feeling me out, to see if I thought you'd be remotely interested. So, take your time and think it over. Talk to Arran about it, and then you and I can regroup.'

As she turned to face him, he took off his glasses, cleaned them with the bottom of his lab coat and put them back on.

'But he said they want me to be based over there, for a year?' It didn't seem real, but saying it out loud was giving it form. As the initial shock began to abate, Kenzie mentally calculated the timing, instantly struck that, by November, she'd be a mother. Her and her son would only have had a few weeks together by then, and as she tried to picture her life that way – and, what's more, doing it alone – she was overcome with a mixture of excitement and trepidation.

'Yes, a year. They're bringing biologists in from Alaska, Antarctica, the Azores and the Baltic regions to form an environmental think tank. He felt you'd be perfect for it with your field experience from Egypt, and your knowledge of the local marine life environment.' Harry drew an arc in the air. 'If I were younger, I'd jump at it, but honestly, I think you're the better man for the job anyway.' He nodded. 'You're sharp as a whip, have the necessary thirst for growth, and a year on secondment would be good for your CV.'

She locked eyes with him, her mind spinning forwards in time, everything she had planned for the next eighteen months feeling as if it could be obliterated by this new, exciting opportunity.

'I don't know what to say, Harry.' She shook her head, her hands diving into the pockets of her lab coat.

'Well, that's a first.' He chuckled. 'As I said, take some time, talk it over with Arran. You two are a great team and if you decide you want to do this, I'm sure he'll support you.'

Kenzie kept her face still, hoping for unreadable, as she nodded.

'I'll think it all through and I'll let you know.'

Harry stood up, lifted the pile of files and his empty cup.

'Good. Now, back to work, Mrs Ford. No rest for the wicked.' He smiled warmly at her, then walked out into the corridor.

All the way home in the car, Kenzie was having a mental conversation with herself, with Arran, with Glenn and even the baby, talking through the pros and cons, the logistics of taking this opportunity to expand her horizons, open herself up to new challenges and, in doing that, giving her child an entirely different start to life than she had had.

While Kenzie had never felt confined growing up in the big house on the river, her world revolving around her family, the mountain and the simple and yet beautiful way they lived their lives, thinking about blowing the sides off the box she'd found herself in recently was intoxicating. Inevitably, though, as she imagined taking her baby son to Norway, setting herself up in a new place to live, a new job, making new friends, while finding the support she needed with childcare, and someone to talk to who'd let her be one hundred per cent herself, Arran's face kept sliding into her mind.

As she passed through Fort William, and turned the car towards Inverlochy, she tutted.

'Stop it. You can do this by yourself, if you want to.' She

My Sister's Only Hope

indicated, then turned the Volkswagen into her street. 'You just have to take the leap.'

As she pulled into the drive, she was pleased to see Colm's car parked at the far side of the house. Since he and Nora had got back from Shetland, they'd been getting together regularly for meals and taking Nora on walks along the beach when the weather permitted. This evening, they'd planned on cooking together at Kenzie's place, so she'd bought in everything they needed for a shepherd's pie, plus a couple of chocolate eclairs from Sally's shop, which she knew Nora loved.

Kenzie turned off the engine and got out of the car, a relieved smile tugging at her mouth. With everything that was swirling inside her head now, she needed to talk to a friend, tonight, more than ever.

35

Nora was in a fleecy tracksuit, installed on the sofa watching *At Home with Olaf*. Her eyes were glued to the screen and her slippers, two bright yellow chicks with black beads for eyes and tiny orange beaks, were bouncing in time with the music.

They'd had their dinner at the kitchen table and now that Nora was settled, Colm followed Kenzie into the small bedroom, where a large cardboard box was propped up against the wall. She'd told him she needed help with something, so to please bring a screwdriver, and when he'd turned up with a giant blue toolbox and a pair of leather work gloves, she'd laughed.

'Settle down, MacGyver. It's just a simple assembly job.'

Colm had shrugged, then grinned. 'I was a scout. Always be prepared.'

Now, as she rolled Arran's desk chair out into the hall to make room, Colm was looking at the box.

'So, what is it?'

She instinctively placed her hand on her tiny bump. 'A cot.'

Colm looked surprised. 'Right.'

'I know it's early, but I'm excited.' She grinned at him. 'So, shoot me.'

He laughed, then levered the top of the box away from the wall. 'Are the instructions in Swedish, or Chinese?'

'Neither.' Kenzie mocked offence. 'It was hand-made by an artisan on the Isle of Skye, from local rowan wood. It's sustainable and, of course, it's the wood of protection.'

Colm frowned. 'Really?'

'Yes. Rowan trees are known as protection trees, faerie trees, you know, from Scottish folklore?' She paused, this obviously being new information for Colm. 'The fact that rowan also wards off witches, and protects against enchantments, is just a bonus.' She laughed at his look of surprise. 'A perfect way to look out for this wee one.' She cupped her stomach again.

Colm smiled, walked the box into the middle of the room, then laid it flat on the floor.

'So, it'll protect me from you if I do this wrong?' He took a Stanley knife out of his toolbox and sliced through the thick tape along the long edge of the box.

'Not necessarily.' She gave him a warning look. 'Focus, Sergeant Duggan. Focus.'

Kenzie stood in the doorway, taking in the room. The cot was beautiful, the pale yellow of the wood, with a deep-brown heartwood, was perfect. She had had to blow her nose when Colm had finished it, him being kind enough to pretend that he hadn't seen her welling up, and now it stood against the wall on the left of the room in the space that Kenzie had cleared the previous weekend.

She had boxed up some of Arran's old university textbooks, environmental magazines and several ring binders full of closed project information so that she could take down the three open shelves on the wall, and now she could picture the room as it would be when she was finished. With some new curtains and a coat of paint, a changing bay in the corner by the door, and Arran's desk pushed tight into the far corner, rather than centred under the window, the room felt much bigger.

Colm was standing behind her, and the trace of coffee she picked up didn't seem to bother her anymore. She'd talked to him about Norway as he'd worked, handing him pieces of the beautifully turned wood, and he'd listened, asking a few questions, but mostly letting her work through her excitement and her fears, uninterrupted, which had not been lost on Kenzie, her gratitude for her new friend making her eyes fill again.

'Looks good, boss. This is a nice room for a little one. Lots of light, but still quiet. Cosy, and right across the hall from Mum. Perfect.'

'Yes. I think so, too.'

'Ready for a break?' He lifted his toolbox and moved into the hall.

'Yes. Thanks a million, Colm. You're an angel.' She followed him along the hall and into the living room, where Nora was now fast asleep on the sofa, tucked up under Kenzie's new blanket. 'Bless her heart,' Kenzie whispered, pulling the blanket over one exposed yellow slipper.

'So, when do you need to decide about Bergen?' He spoke softly, setting the toolbox by the door, and then hovered near the sofa, across from where Nora lay.

Kenzie motioned for him to sit, as she sat in the armchair by the fire.

'Not sure exactly, but Harry said there was no immediate rush. The project kick-off isn't until end November, so I have some time,' she whispered.

Colm sat down, propping one ankle on the opposite knee.

'It sounds like a no-brainer to me. Scandinavian countries are the best for single parents. Healthcare is stellar, and childcare is supposed to be great, too, and easy to come by. Plus, I think they even supplement your rent and stuff. Unless that's only for citizens.' He frowned. 'Not sure on that one.'

Kenzie was listening to him, but her focus was hooked by the words *single parent,* the reality of that being her lot still startling.

'If you do decide to go, I'll keep an eye on this place for you.' He gestured towards the fireplace. 'I mean, unless you rent it out, too.'

'No. I can't do that,' Kenzie blurted, seeing his eyebrows jump. 'Sorry, it's just that I couldn't have anyone else living here. Besides, it's still Arran's home, too.'

'Right. I get it.' Colm nodded, then shifted forward on the sofa. 'I felt the same way about our house in Bearsden, for over a year. But without Sandy, over time it started to feel like *just* a house, and then the job came up here, and the rest is history.' He eyed her. 'I believe these opportunities come our way by some kind of divine providence, when things all align. Like the universe telling us, *Hey, wake up, I've done the ground work, stupid, now the rest is up to you.*' His hands hovered above his knees, palms up.

'Thank you, Sensei.' She made a comical face, but his words had struck a chord, and their message was clear. She had to see the signs, and take them for what they were, and if she did, the world could be her oyster, not her prison. The buzz that sent through her was undeniable, so she stood up, walked around the coffee table, opened her arms and waited. Colm seemed confused, so she said quietly, 'Get up, you big loon.'

He looked startled, then realisation dawned, so he stood up, and Kenzie walked in towards him, her arms going around his neck.

'Thank you, Colm. You're a true friend, and I need a friend right now.' She felt his arms tentatively circle her waist, his chest tense, and sensing his discomfort, she quickly released him. 'Now, you should probably take sleeping beauty home before she wakes and keeps you up half the night.'

He looked relieved. 'Right enough.' He circled the coffee table, gently removed the blanket, then lifted Nora into his arms. 'I'll get the tools tomorrow, OK?'

'Of course.' Kenzie followed him along the hall, then opened the door for him. Since they'd arrived, the rain that had been battering down had stopped, and a smoky haar had rolled in off the water, giving the front garden a mystical look. 'Go carefully.'

Colm nodded. 'Night, Kenzie. Thanks for dinner.'

'Pleasure. Thanks for all your help.' She waved, waiting until he made it safely along the path and disappeared around the side of the house, then she switched off the outside light and closed the door.

As she walked back along the hall, turning off lights as she went, a decision was forming with such clarity that she shook her head.

How her life had changed in a few short months, and how her future potentially was about to be turned on its head again. Could she really live in Bergen? Take her son away from this house?

36

The following Saturday, a chilly overcast day, she had arranged to go back to Perth to see Glenn. He'd promised her a simpler lunch this time, and then they were going to a baby shop in the High Street that Kenzie had spotted on her last visit.

As she pulled into the car park near the cathedral, Glenn was standing by the entrance. He had on a dark leather jacket, black jeans and, despite the murky sky, stylish sunglasses, and his head was bent over his phone.

Kenzie tooted her horn and laughed as he jumped, looked up and, seeing her, gave her the finger.

'Nice,' she muttered as she parked next to a sleek Mercedes.

Glenn walked to the car and waited for her to open the door.

'Smooth entrance. Daft cow.'

'Charming as always, Mackintosh.' She slammed the door and slung her giant bag over her shoulder.

'You look well. Decent drive?' He bent his elbow so she could slip her hand through his arm.

'Fine.' She squeezed his arm, then fell into step beside him as they headed for a little café on North Methven Street that Glenn had said was great.

Lunch for Kenzie was a simple, grilled halloumi sandwich and a camomile tea, while Glenn devoured a burger on a brioche bun and a pile of chips, which Kenzie pinched a few of. As they caught up on the past few weeks since they'd seen each other, covering all the updates on Kenzie's pregnancy, how things were going with Colm and Nora, Glenn's new boss and her propensity to call him Glenys, which drove him crazy, they talked animatedly around their mouthfuls, laughing at Glenn's impersonation of a colleague who whistled constantly around the police station.

Kenzie let herself lean into the comfort of being with someone she loved, the sense of being at home with Glenn making her fully relax until he stopped talking and stared at her.

'What?' She rubbed the end of her nose. 'Do I have a rogue bogey?'

Glenn laughed. 'No, you nut. I was just thinking that you are sort of shiny. All rosy-cheeked and bright-eyed.'

Kenzie was taken aback. 'Oh, thanks. Must be the hormones. The upside of being preggers, I suppose.'

He smiled at her. 'Well, it suits you, little bean.'

She heard the affection in his tone, and it felt good to be loved, with no agenda, or danger of disappointment.

'Ready to go?' He nodded towards the door, just as a noisy group of women walked in, all wearing pink sweatshirts with a walking group logo on the back.

'Definitely.' Kenzie dragged her jacket from the back of the chair and stood up. 'Lead on, MacDuff.'

They turned right out of the café, and under a now mostly clear and bright sky, started the ten-minute walk to the High Street. Kenzie liked this part of Perth, with its collection of eclectic shops, characterful pubs and wine bars, and as she walked with her brother-in-law in comfortable silence, her conversation with Colm the previous week filtered back to her, her true mission in coming today reasserting itself.

As the most invested member of her remaining family, it was time to tell Glenn what she was thinking about doing, so as they stopped to look in the window of an art gallery, the display a series of miniature oil paintings of points along the river Tay, she released his arm and turned to face him.

'Glenn, I want to tell you something.' She watched his carefree expression grow cautious.

'Oh, yes?' He slid his hands into his pockets. 'Should I be worried?'

'No. Not really. It's something good. At least *I* think so.' She gave him a nervous smile.

'OK. I'm all ears.'

Kenzie took his arm again and eased him back into the gentle flow of people walking along the road, being in an outdoor setting and away from home making it feel easier to share her news.

Glenn listened to her as he steered them around a young man pushing a baby in a stroller, a couple whose arms were hooked around each other's shoulders so they took up most of the pavement, and then an elderly man in a kilt, wielding two serious-looking walking sticks.

Kenzie talked quietly about the opportunity in Norway, careful not to sound too definite about it until she got his feedback. She had always valued his opinion on big decisions, and since he had said that he wanted to be involved in the baby's life, it was all the more important that he didn't feel excluded from this potentially life-altering change.

By the time she was finished talking, they had reached the baby shop, a narrow store wedged between a Caffè Nero and a pretty gift shop with pastel-coloured stuffed rabbits and a woodland display in the bay window.

Though ridiculously early, the baby shop window had Easter themed outfits in it, tiny onesies with fluffy chicks on them, and miniature white jeans paired with pale-blue and pink jean-jackets, each with colourful eggs embroidered on the breast pockets.

As they stood in silence, taking in the fairy-tale display, Kenzie began to feel anxious. Glenn hadn't said a word for a full five minutes, and now her chest was aching, her need for his approval paramount.

Seeming to sense her tensing up, Glenn turned towards her, his eyes bright.

'Kenzie, it's fantastic, and if you're taking this next step on your own, it sounds like an ideal set-up. So, I think you should grab it.' He made a pincer motion with both hands. 'It's an excellent opportunity that might not come along again, and home will always be here. I'll always be here, too.' He smiled at her. 'Norway isn't that far away either, so just make sure you have a spare room, or a comfy couch, for Funcle Glenn.'

Kenzie's relief made her feel as if she might float out of her body, her face splitting into a huge smile. 'Really? You won't feel abandoned?'

He shook his head. 'If anyone has the right to feel abandoned, it would be you.' His eyes glowed. 'Olivia left you, albeit not her choice. Then I upped and left you because I couldn't handle the memories. Arran... Well, I know that's a whole other story, but he's essentially left you, too.'

She made to defend Arran, but Glenn held his palm up to stop her.

'I'm not judging him, because I know there's much more to what's going on between you two than you've told me. And, honestly, most marriages are that way, so I don't *need* to know.' He surveyed her face, seeing her eyes begin to fill. 'All I know is that you are my hero, Kenzie. You might be tiny, but you are mighty, and you'll crush this new job, like you crush everything you take on. I am so proud to be your brother.' His voice caught, so she slid her arm through his.

'Thanks, Glenn. You don't know how much that means to me.' She touched her temple to his shoulder, then looked up at him. 'You will always have a place with us.' She tapped her stomach. 'This little fellow and I will love having you visit, and we'll come back home, too, of course.'

He mocked shock. 'I should think so.'

She smiled at him, feeling her throat thicken. He had given her exactly what she needed, as he always had, and in return she wanted to give him something equally as meaningful.

'So, I've decided what to call the little sprout.' She tipped her head to the side. 'Have a guess.'

Glenn's eyes brightened as he twisted his mouth to the side. 'Hmm, Jacques Cousteau Ford?'

Kenzie laughed, the tension easing in her chest. 'Close, but not quite. But now you mention it, I might have to change my mind.'

Glenn shook his head. 'Tell me what you've decided.'

She took a moment, then hugged his arm.

'Jack Glenn Ford. For Dad, and you.'

Glenn's face froze, then his jaw slackened as he ran his free hand over the top of his head.

'God, Kenz, are you sure?'

'One bazillion per cent.'

He released her arm and clasped her narrow shoulders, his eyes full. 'That's the best present I have ever been given.' He paused. 'And Olivia would have approved, I think.'

'I think so, too.' She nodded. 'Thank you, Glenn. For being the best big brother a girl could ask for, and a true friend.' She gulped down a sob, her heart so full it felt as if it might explode.

'You, and he' – he nodded at her stomach – 'are family. That's the most important thing of all.'

Kenzie pulled him into a hug, feeling his back quiver as he

took in a deep breath. Her love for this man, and her admiration for how he had loved her sister, supporting her through all their struggles with IVF, coping with the pain of her affair, then losing her to the mountain, was immense. His belief in Kenzie's ability to take this giant leap, start her life afresh with little Jack, and not only to do it, but to do it well, was worth everything to her, and more than anything, in this moment, she wanted to see him smile.

'Right.' She tugged his arm and moved towards the door to the baby shop. 'Let's go in and splurge on some way-too-pricey mini clothes that he'll grow out of in a few weeks.'

Glenn slung his arm around her shoulder and laughed softly. 'Good plan. I vote for that.' He pointed at a tiny onesie covered in honey bees. 'Do you think they do it in my size?'

Kenzie let out a laugh, then playfully nudged his shoulder. 'Probably. They do specialise in size idiot.'

As they walked into the shop, she let go of any remaining anxiety she'd had about telling him her news. Now, all she had to do was tell Arran, and with that came a new flutter of nerves, but with a very different root cause.

SPRING

37

Twelve weeks had passed since Arran had left for Wick, and as April delivered its customary showers, Kenzie was beginning to show. Her due date was September twenty-first, Olivia's birthday, and the coincidence was as shocking today as it had been when Doctor Kennedy had confirmed it, months earlier.

Arran had said it was divine providence, and that had made Kenzie cry, but in her heart, she felt the same way. With each passing week, as little Jack became more a part of her, so Olivia felt closer again and Kenzie was grateful for that.

As she drove back and forth to work or moved around the flat, she talked to her son, asking him if he liked the music she was playing, or whether he was comfy and had enough room. She'd stand with her hands on her stomach and look out at the river, picturing taking him for walks on the shore and picking up smooth stones to skip across the surface as she had done with her father.

As Kenzie leaned in to the reality of becoming a mother, she rarely pictured Arran as part of that anymore. Instead, she saw herself pushing a stroller along the pedestrian street in Fort William, settling Jack into a car seat and driving to Perth to see

Glenn, then she'd remind herself that when Jack was finally here she'd be taking him to Bergen, perhaps walking along the shore of Byfjorden – the fjord that sheltered Bergen from the North Sea – rather than her river here at home.

On her last visit to Bergen, on Anders' advice, Kenzie had taken a taxi to Bryggen. The historic harbour district dated back to the fourteenth century and was a UNESCO World Heritage Site, best known for its long row of tall wooden houses along the quayside, their pretty gables touching, and the colourful fascia painted in the rusts, golds, and dark pinks of autumn.

She had walked along the picturesque wharf, sat at an outdoor café and watched tall-masted yachts sliding in and out of their moorings. Then she'd wandered through the network of narrow alleys that twisted up the hill behind the quay, browsing in the collection of small shops, galleries and artist's studios filled with local traditional crafts.

Being there had left her with a sense of peace that at the time had felt beyond her grasp, and now, when she thought about looking for a home for her and Jack, Bryggen felt like somewhere they could be happy.

A few days after seeing Glenn, she'd had a video call with Arran to tell him about her plans. She had been nervous, but after a few moments of silence when he'd turned his face away and stared out of his window, he had then looked her in the eye and said, 'You'll be great, Kenz. You can do anything you set your mind to. I've always known that.'

Her heart had swooped low in her chest, the final flicker of hope that he might say, *please don't go*, extinguished.

'Thanks. That means a lot.' She'd found a smile, then said she'd keep him informed, the finality of this move solidified.

Today, a rainy Sunday afternoon, typical of early April, Colm and Nora were due back from the swimming pool at the leisure centre in Fort William. Nora had been having lessons and Colm had been as nervous as a kitten that, today, they were taking off the armbands, albeit in three feet of water, and with him right by her side.

Kenzie had reassured him that all would be well and told him to bring Nora over for hot chocolate when they got home, and as Kenzie stood at the window, her palm on her bump while she sang 'Flower of Scotland' to Jack, she saw Colm's car coming up the drive.

A lilt of happiness made her wave, seeing Nora also waving out of the back window. The little girl had become precious to Kenzie, Nora's gentle ways and sometimes startlingly sage observations making Kenzie even more excited to get to know her son, learn his personality, his quirks and traits.

Turning away from the window, she made her way into the kitchen and poured milk into a pan. Nora liked her hot chocolate extra frothy, and Kenzie always put some chocolate sprinkles on the top for her. As Kenzie turned the heat under the pan down low, she set three mugs on the counter and opened a new packet of chocolate digestives, laying several on a plate.

Within a few minutes, she heard the doorbell, so turned off the milk and went to open the door.

Nora's hair was damp, the long dark tresses wavy and split around her shoulders. Her eyes were bright as she stepped confidently inside, her father forgotten behind her.

'I swam on my own, Auntie Kenzie.' She beamed at Kenzie. 'All by myself.'

'Wow. That's amazing.' Kenzie clapped her hands and bent down so Nora could hug her neck. 'Well done, sweetheart.' As always, the child's spontaneous affection sent a jolt of joy through Kenzie.

Colm came inside and closed the door. Behind Nora, he mimed relief, swiping the back of his hand across his forehead.

'Yes, she did brilliantly.' He nodded as Nora looked up at him. 'The teacher said you were a very good swimmer. Didn't she?'

Nora nodded. 'Yes. I am a big girl now and I don't need armbands.' She clasped her little hands together, then strutted towards the kitchen.

'Sorry.' Colm grimaced. 'She thinks *this* is her home, too.'

Kenzie laughed softly. 'You have no idea how happy that makes me. Come on through.' She beckoned to Colm, who dumped his backpack and followed her into the kitchen.

With their mugs of hot chocolate in front of them, Colm and Kenzie talked to Nora about school, her best friend Brody, who had a new yellow Lab puppy that came with his mother to pick him up every day, and about their next trip to Shetland for Nora's sixth birthday in a few weeks.

As Kenzie listened to the little girl, her animated chatter sent another flutter of happiness through Kenzie that Colm seemed to sense, his smile reflecting Kenzie's across the table.

Once her drink was finished, Nora wiped her mouth with the back of her hand.

'Can I see Olaf?'

Colm made eyes at her. 'Not here, love. Auntie Kenzie is busy. We can watch Olaf at home.'

Nora pouted. 'I like it *here*.'

Colm made to get up, but not ready to lose her company just yet, Kenzie shook her head.

'If Daddy says it's OK, you can watch some here, then maybe finish it at home later. How would that be, Daddy?' She tipped her head to the side, seeing Colm smile.

'I don't stand a chance against you ladies, do I?'

At this, Nora looked at her father, a tiny smile curving her rosy lips. 'Girls are better. Boys are silly.'

Kenzie couldn't help laughing, her hand covering her mouth, as Colm shrugged resignedly.

'I know when I'm beaten.'

. . .

Kenzie sat on the sofa facing the window, and Colm sat on the floor across from her, his back against the sofa where Nora lay, her eyelids drooping as she battled sleep.

'She's almost gone,' Kenzie whispered, just as Nora's eyes closed. 'Aaaand, she's out.'

Colm got up and carefully draped the blanket from the back of the sofa over Nora's legs.

'I won't let her sleep for long, or we can forget bedtime in' – he checked his watch – 'three and a half hours.'

Kenzie nodded, tucking her feet under her. 'She's a doll, Colm. I'm going to miss her, and you, of course.' She grimaced. 'Her more, though.'

Colm grunted and lowered himself back onto the floor. 'I'm under no illusions there. She's always the popular one.'

Kenzie smiled at him, his salt-and-pepper hair sticking up at the back, probably still thick with chlorine. As she considered leaving her new friends, there was sadness, but also a calm that made Kenzie feel confident about her decision. Knowing that Colm and Nora were here, keeping the home fires burning, so to speak, was comforting, and with Glenn in Perth and Arran – well, Arran wherever he ended up, Kenzie needed that anchor to be able to leave.

Colm was watching her and frowning.

'What is it?' she asked.

'I was just wondering what you were thinking. You looked miles away.'

Glad of the chance to share her feelings, Kenzie sighed. 'I was just thinking about leaving here. The flat, my home, you, and Nora and Glenn.'

He eyed her. 'And Arran?'

'Yes, and Arran.' She uncurled her legs and leaned back, her heart pinching.

'You know, from the little you've told me, it's hard to give you advice. And we've not known each other that long either, so there's that, too.' He gave her a half-smile.

'No, please. Give me advice. I need it.' She made a beckoning motion. 'Have at it.'

He shifted his legs, extending them under the coffee table. 'OK. As I see it, there's no blame to assign, on either side. But if, after all this time, you are still on different paths, I'd say love him all you need to, but let him go.' He scanned her face for a reaction.

Kenzie let his words settle on her, the permission to keep loving Arran something that she hadn't thought to give herself.

'God.'

Colm looked alarmed. 'I told you I shouldn't give you advice. Sorry, just ignore me.'

'No. I mean, God, I never thought about it that way.' She squinted at him. 'I suppose I was thinking that if we're not together, then I needed to remove him from here, somehow.' She patted her chest. 'But I knew I couldn't do that, so I thought I'd be living in this perpetual state of flux. My husband here, me somewhere else with the child that technically broke us apart.' She felt her throat begin to narrow. 'You've just shown me a way forward that I think I can live with, so, thank you.' She watched relief flood his face.

'Well, I'm glad. You deserve to be happy, whatever it takes.'

'I think I'm beginning to believe it's possible again.'

As she watched Colm gently wake Nora, then walk her towards the door, Kenzie marvelled at the fluidity and contrariness of happiness. The way it enters the soul, takes up residence, then in the blink of an eye can leave you, empty, bereft and hopeless, only to come back again when you least expect it.

She had learned over the past few months, since losing Olivia, that happiness needed space to get in, and the only way to create that space was to clear out anger, disappointment and regret. She believed that acceptance was the final, golden ticket to healing, and as she waved goodnight to her friends, she had another epiphany.

Accepting that the outline of her family had changed was another form of release that would allow her to focus on the good memories, back when family had meant Olivia and Glenn, Arran and her, together. If she could do that, then she could also make space for the last part of the package: forgiveness, of herself, Olivia and, also, their mother.

Kenzie made her way along the hall, glancing at herself in the tall mirror, and feeling lighter, a weight she'd been carrying lifting from her soul. Simultaneously, her mother's face floated into her mind, the gentle smile, the blue eyes, adoring, behind her tortoise-shell glasses, and Kenzie closed her eyes for a moment.

The memory of the newspaper clipping brought her to a standstill, picturing the obituary, and the tribute to a man she would never know.

Kenzie opened her eyes and made a decision. She was choosing to believe that her mother had stayed not because Russell had died, but because she loved her family, and even their father, more, and that certainty was the final element Kenzie needed to make peace with the past.

38

By early May, as Kenzie was close to hitting the five-month mark, and not having seen Arran in person for almost four months, her plans were taking shape for the birth. She had asked Glenn if he'd come home and be at the hospital, and he had agreed.

The previous week at her prenatal check-up, she had spoken candidly with Doctor Kennedy about her birth plan, her very specific preferences for the delivery.

He had looked mildly surprised, so Kenzie had sat up a little straighter, deciding that now was the time to tell him that she would be doing this alone.

'I'm not joking, Doc. Honestly, I'm terrified about the birth, and I don't handle pain well. Believe me, you won't want to see that.' She'd shaken her head. 'Plus, Arran won't be here. I mean, he's not going to...' She'd faltered, her voice threatening to crack, but determined not to cry, she'd taken a moment and rallied. 'So, all the drugs on the menu. OK?'

The doctor had looked sympathetic, and seeing her expression, had spoken kindly.

'I'm sorry. I didn't want to ask, but he's been noticeably absent from your prenatal checks.' He'd smiled at her then. 'You're in good hands, Kenzie. We'll make this as easy for you as we possibly can. We'll take everything into account, and make sure that all the protocols are—'

She'd cut him off. 'Yes, I know about the protocols. But, with all due respect, I'm a wimp. So, don't expect me to get all altruistic at the coalface. I'll need the big guns. Epidurals. Acupuncture. Witchcraft. The works.'

Doctor Kennedy had sat back in his chair and taken off his glasses, cleaned them with a tissue and replaced them.

'Kenzie, you are going to be fine. When the time comes, you'll rise to the occasion. Mother Nature helps with that, too. And I'll be there, every step of the way.'

She'd nodded at the file lying on his desk, then, as she'd stood up, she'd said, 'Did you write it down? Put it in the file, in case you're on the golf course, or in a coma. The big guns?'

He'd flashed her a smile, then nodded. 'All duly noted.'

Kenzie had never been a long-term planner, per se, but that day she'd gone home and written down a schedule of events as she imagined them for the big day.

Her back-up for transport to the hospital was Colm, if she happened to go into labour in the night. He'd told her that he slept with his phone by his bed and that he'd have a little bag packed with things Nora might need, if they were to be at the hospital for a while, until Glenn could get there.

Kenzie now sat at the kitchen table, looking at the calendar on her phone. In roughly four months, she'd be a mother, and all the sacrifice, loss and heartache would be worth it when she held her baby in her arms. She could almost feel the softness of his skin, the way his minute hand would grip her finger, smell the powdery newness of him, and each time she let herself go there, she was overcome with love for the tiny being that had yet to enter the world.

As she looked at the list of events, all seeming perfectly straightforward, she was struck by the fact that despite all her planning, things could go still awry, and if they did, her legal next of kin was Arran. Despite their separation, he needed to know what she wanted, what her plan was, and if, God forbid, anything went wrong, what her instructions were.

He had texted her the night before, as he was doing more regularly since she'd passed the five-month mark, asking if she was OK. She hadn't read into the more frequent messages, but had been grateful for his concern, so now, scrolling through her phone, she opened the text thread and typed,

Can we talk? I need to make sure you are up to speed on a couple of things.

She put the phone down and went to make some tea when she heard the ping of a reply.

Lifting the phone, a flicker of anxiety sent her hand to the top of her head.

Sure. Want to do it now?

She looked around the room, as if searching for a reason not to speak to her husband, then shook her head and whispered, 'Get a grip, Kenzie. It's Arran.'

Making tea. Give me 5?

He sent a thumbs up and so Kenzie darted to the bathroom, as she did what felt like every twenty minutes now, washed her hands and dragged a comb through her hair, then went back into the kitchen.

When Arran's face materialised on the phone, she felt the familiar tug of loss seeing him always delivered.

'Hi. You look well.' He smiled, the new, short haircut making his eyes look greener and more prominent in his face.

'Thanks. So do you.' She adjusted the stand behind the phone, changing the angle and trying to minimise the new roundness to her face.

He took a drink from a large stainless-steel water bottle, then put it down. 'Are you OK?'

She nodded, another flutter of nerves making her stomach twist. 'Yes, it's just that I've been making plans, for the birth, and I realised that you're my next of kin.' She halted as his eyebrows lifted.

'Oh, right.' His jaw tightened. 'Of course.'

'I wanted you to know what I want, what my wishes are, in case I'm out of it at any point, drugged up, or under anaesthetic for instance.' She shrugged, seeing him blinking rapidly as if processing a series of images that were not easy to see.

'Probably wise.' He frowned, then took another sip of water, his eyes not leaving her face.

'So, I've written it all down and I'll email it to you, if that's OK?' She waited until he nodded again. 'And I'll copy Glenn, because he's going to be here.'

Arran looked startled. 'Is he?'

'Yes, I asked him to.' Kenzie scanned Arran's face, a flash of surprise being replaced by what looked like resignation. 'He is my brother-in-law, Arran, and I want my family with me.'

She could see his shoulders roll forwards a little.

'Of course. I'm glad he's going to be there.'

'Well, just in the building, not the room.' She pulled a face, anxious to defuse the tension her news had caused. 'That would be creepy.'

He took a moment, then laughed softly. 'Yes, it would be.'

Kenzie smiled, relieved that they had got past the momentary blip of discomfort.

'So, let me know when you've read everything and if you have any questions, or concerns.'

'Will do.' He nodded, then for a moment she thought he was going to say goodbye, but instead he leaned in closer to the camera. 'Can I ask you something?'

Caught off guard, she said, 'Um, sure.'

'Are you scared?'

Her heart making one of its monumental swoops in her chest, she took a second.

'Honestly? I'm terrified.'

Arran gave an upside-down smile, his mouth dipping at the edges.

'I'm sorry. That wasn't fair.'

'It's fine. You can ask me anything. You always could.'

He seemed to lose focus for a moment, then he sat back and rubbed both of his eyes, his fingers seeming to press brutally hard into the sockets.

'Arran?' Her throat was narrowing, so she forced a swallow.

He looked at her, his eyes shining.

'It's OK, you know. I'm going to be fine.' She smiled her bravest smile. 'You can stop beating yourself up.'

His eyes widened, recognising that he'd just been seen right through, then he exhaled so loudly she could hear it.

'You're remarkable. I'm just so proud of you.' He paused. 'I miss being there. Talking to you. Just being us.'

'Me too,' she whispered. 'But this is what's happening, and we're going to be all right.' She drew a line in the air from her chest to the phone. 'We both are.'

Arran took her in, then nodded.

'I've got to go, but send me the email, OK?'

'I will. And thanks.' She gave him a little wave. 'Talk soon?'

'Of course.' He pressed his fingers to his lips and blew her a kiss, the gesture so intimate and touching that Kenzie gasped, but before she could respond, he ended the call.

She sat still, her mind spinning through all the what ifs. What if he meant that kiss as a final goodbye? What if he was just being kind because he felt bad for her? What if he missed her as much as she missed him, but just couldn't tell her?

She stood up abruptly, sending the chair grinding away behind her on the wooden floor. Enough. She had been down this road enough times, torturing herself with questions and moments of regret, but now she would look forward to the new life that was growing inside her. Because the future was bright, with or without Arran in her life.

39

Kenzie had soaked in the bath for a while, a candle flickering on the cabinet next to the sink. She'd put her father's old radio on the bathmat and tuned it to Classic FM, as she'd been doing ever since she'd read that babies responded well to classical music.

As her mother's favourite piece, Vaughan Williams' 'The Lark Ascending', had floated around the room, the music so evocative and touching, she'd enjoyed the release of tears trickling down her face, all the while smiling, grateful for her life, the bubble of love she'd been raised inside, her sister, her home, her new friends and the baby that would soon be her focus. All the good in the world had seemed magnified, and she'd floated on the promise of what was to come.

Two hours later, she was tucked up in bed with a book about the social behaviour of seal colonies. Ten o'clock was her limit, as far as staying awake these days, and as she checked the clock on her bedside table, seeing it was 10.12 p.m., she yawned. Just as she put the book down, and switched off the lamp, there was a strange rattle coming from the hall.

Her breath catching, Kenzie sat bolt upright, straining to make out what she'd heard. After a second or two, she heard it again, this time, more of a scraping of metal on metal. Her pulse throbbing in her ears, she threw the covers off and got up, scanning the dark room for a weapon, something she could use to protect herself, and her baby, from an intruder. There was nothing.

As panic began to rise up in her throat, suddenly she remembered the old walking stick of her father's that was tucked away at the back of the wardrobe. Flying across the room, she opened the wardrobe door and dug in behind the clothes, her fingers grappling for the stick. Just as she felt the cool of the metal, and clamped her fingers around it, she heard something move behind her, so she dragged the stick out, and spun around, waving it wildly in front of her.

A tall figure, broad-shouldered and threatening, stood in the bedroom doorway, the backlighting from the nightlight in the hall turning them into a silhouette.

Kenzie's heart was about to tear through her chest, so she stood her ground and shouted at the top of her lungs. 'Get out. Get the hell out of my house.' She stabbed at the air in front of her as she heard him speak, the voice staccato, panicked.

'Kenzie, it's me. For God's sake, it's me.'

She stood still, the stick pointing at his chest, her hands shaking so much she grabbed it with her other hand, both fists now wrapped around the worn handle.

Suddenly, the bedside light came on, and as Kenzie blinked, adjusting to the brightness, the man stood next to the bed, his hands held up in front of him like he'd been put under arrest.

Recognition, and relief coursed through Kenzie like a river, but before she could appreciate either sensation, fury took their place. She dropped the stick to her side and shouted, 'What the hell are you doing here, Arran? You scared me half to death.'

Her voice was quaking, her insides following suit as her free hand instinctively went to her stomach.

'I'm sorry. I texted you hours ago. Right after we talked. I told you I was coming.' He was ashen as he turned and looked at the bedside table, where, at night, her phone usually sat on the charger. 'Where's your phone?'

Her heart still racing, Kenzie snapped, 'It's right there.' She pointed at the empty charger, then frowned. 'It *was* there.'

Arran dropped his hands to his sides, then took a step towards her. 'I'm really sorry. I didn't mean to scare you.'

She walked unsteadily across the room and looked at the charger, her face tingling as blood seemed to be coursing through the veins at her temples. 'That's weird. I always put it there when I go to bed.'

Arran moved past her and switched on the overhead light, then stepped backwards, giving her more space. 'You must've forgotten.' He met her eyes, his face still looking drawn and shocked.

She tossed the walking stick onto the bench at the bottom of the bed, trying to remember when she had last seen her phone.

She laid her palm across her forehead. 'What are you doing here, out of the blue, and so bloody late? I nearly impaled you, you idiot.'

He moved in closer to her. 'I needed to talk to you.'

Kenzie's pulse was slowly returning to normal, but something in his tone set alarm bells ringing. 'Why didn't you just phone me then?' She backed up and sat on the edge of the bed, suddenly aware that she only had a long T-shirt on, her bottom barely covered, and the deep V-neck exposing much of her newly acquired cleavage.

He stood in front of her, his pale-blue shirt loose over the top of his jeans, and his feet in canvas lace-ups that she didn't recognise.

'I needed to see you, in person. A phone call wasn't the right way to say what I have to say.' He put his hand on his heart, the evocative movement making Kenzie's own heart falter in response.

'Well, you're here now, so tell me.' She folded her arms, aware that she might need protection from whatever was coming next.

He hesitated for a moment, then, surprising her, he crouched down in front of her, made to reach for her hand, but then hesitated.

'Is this OK?' He looked at her, but when she kept her arms tightly folded, he simply nodded and sat back on his heels. 'I need you to hear me out, then we talk as much as you want. OK?'

She frowned, her mind instantly spinning through all the reasons that could have sent him to his car right after they spoke, making a five-hour drive at night to see her. Perhaps he'd read the email and didn't want to be her next of kin anymore, the responsibility too much, given their circumstances. Perhaps he was going to suggest she make Glenn the person who made those decisions for her, if she were incapacitated. Perhaps he wanted a divorce, the final nail in their marital rift. As she stared at him, ready for the hurt that was coming, his expression halted the internal dialogue.

'Can you please hear me out, Kenzie?'

She knew that look, the way his eyes became slightly distant, his jaw rippling as he suppressed something difficult to say, the way he licked his lips right before he shared whatever it was that he'd given a lot of thought to, and seeing it now, Kenzie instinctively held her breath as she gave a single nod.

'Thanks.' He exhaled, readying himself as she waited, her pulse still throbbing at her temples. 'I need you to know that these past few months have been brutal. I know I was the one who left, but it's been brutal, nonetheless. I had so much time to think about what was happening, what we both chose to do, that I became almost numb to the reality of it. It was as if I told myself it *wasn't* real. The whole going our separate ways and letting go of the future we'd planned part. I think I made it temporary, in my head, so it wouldn't hurt as much.' He took a moment, then looked as if he might reach for her hand again.

This time, her emotions on autopilot, she unfolded her arms and gave him her fingers, the contact sending a shiver of longing directly to her core.

'The more time that passed and we weren't together, the more I numbed myself to what was coming, trying to tell myself that I was OK with it, but when I read your email today, all the denial was stripped away. I remembered how I felt when I was here at Christmas, and the way you handled that crisis with such grit. It hit home that you were ready to do this, with or without me, and I'd not really taken that in until then.' He paused, shaking his head slightly. 'Then you told me about Norway, and then your words in the email drove straight to the heart of what we were doing... or about to do, and seeing it like that, in black and white, none of my reasons for leaving you alone seemed enough anymore.'

Kenzie heard him, but the words were surreal, their meaning smothered under her fear that she was misunderstanding him. Afraid to speak, to say something naive that would hack away at her new-found confidence in herself, she pressed her lips together and waited.

'Kenzie, you are my world. I was deluding myself to think that any universe without you in it was a place I'd want to live.' He swallowed hard, his eyes filling.

Kenzie's instinct was to pull him in to her arms, but there was too much still unsaid.

'If being with you means I have to face my fears, banish

demons from the past, let go of what happened to Danny and my parents, and open my heart to a child, I'm willing to do that. No. I *want* to do that, whether it's here, or in Norway, or Timbuktu.' He dipped his head to the side and wiped a stray tear onto his shoulder, a tiny damp circle appearing on the material of his shirt. 'I can't promise to be good at it, being a father, but I want to try.'

As Kenzie watched the wet patch expand on the pale-blue cotton, he put his finger under her chin and met her eyes.

'Can you give me another chance?' He blinked as another tear oozed over his lower lid. 'I will never let you down again, Kenzie. On my life, I will be a better man, and I won't ever let you down again.'

Kenzie scanned his face, the features she knew so well and that had been at the centre of her world for five years. He was really here, asking her for another chance. He wanted her. To be with her despite the trauma of his past, and seeing his parents destroy one another after Danny died. Every part of her wanted to believe that he meant this, that he was in. Really in. But he'd walked away from her when she was at her most vulnerable. What made things different now, however much she wanted them to be?

'I appreciate what you're saying, and believe me, part of me has wished for this. But how do I know that you won't change your mind again? When we're up at 3 a.m. pacing the floor, up to our ears in dirty nappies and growling at each other about whose turn it is to get some sleep. What if we do this, we try again, and you end up blaming me? Resenting me.' She swallowed over the burn in her throat. 'I love you. I've never stopped loving you. But it's not just about you and me anymore.' She covered her stomach with her palm. 'This little chap deserves everything. The best I can give him. He's the product of love, of my sister's wish, and, of my own.' She nodded to herself. 'If you come back, you're coming back to both of us, and there's no trial period. If you're in, you have to be all in, and I'm not sure I trust that you can do that.'

His eyes were locked on hers, his mouth pursing as he sucked in his lower lip. 'I understand, and I deserve that.' He nodded. 'But I know that I don't want to be that person. Someone who lets fear rob him of the best thing that has ever happened to him. I want to earn your trust again. To show you that I can be the man you deserve, that this little boy deserves.' He gestured towards her middle. 'He is you, and I want *all* of you. Everything that makes you who you are. Like I said, I can't promise to be a great dad right off the bat, but what I can promise is that I'll die trying. If you'll let me.'

Kenzie's heart was clattering in her chest, this scene one that she had played out in her mind repeatedly, her dearest wish that, as time had passed, had seemed to slip further and further from her grasp. Could she trust him again after he'd let fear get between them? Could she let him into her and Jack's lives without a trickle of worry running beneath them all that one day he'd have enough?

As she took in his face, the way his mossy eyes seemed to see directly into her soul, the answer was clear. More than anything, Kenzie wanted to rebuild her family, for herself, for her parents, for Jack, Olivia and for Glenn. No matter how much had gone before, how much pain and loss, and the separation from Arran, when she thought about family, he was an indelible part of that. Whatever risk was involved in opening her life back up to him, she had to take it, the potential reward too precious to walk away from.

She stood up slowly, tugging the T-shirt down at the sides, as Arran also stood, looking unsure of what was happening. Before he could say anything, she took a step forward, seeing his arms begin to open, and as she walked into them, he circled her back, pulling her gently in.

They stood still, Kenzie's forehead against his collarbone,

his skin warm under her cheek and his cool breath brushing her eyelids. The world was at peace, everything frozen in this perfect moment, when, inside her, Jack moved, a tiny heel pressing into Kenzie's side.

'Oh.' She gasped, as Arran started and leaned back from her.

'What's wrong?'

'It's Jack.' She took Arran's hand and laid it on her stomach. 'He's playing football in here.' She held Arran's palm still, feeling the baby move beneath their locked fingers. 'He's saying hello.'

Arran's eyes were wide as they waited for another kick, and when it came, he jumped. 'He's a striker, all right.' He looked down at her stomach, his eyes full. 'I feel you, wee man?'

Kenzie's eyes filled as she smiled up at her husband. 'He says good, but that he thinks Mum needs the loo again.' She laughed through tears, her voice catching. 'Don't go anywhere. I'll be back in a minute.'

Arran released her and watched her walk towards the door.

'I'm not going anywhere, ever again.'

Arran moved his things back in within the week and gladly paid the penalty for breaking his lease in Wick. He had surprised Kenzie with the news that he was going to apply for a consulting job in Bergen on an upcoming project at the UNESCO site, and overcome, she'd dived on him, wrapping her legs around his waist as he'd spun her around in the living room.

Having him back at the flat was wonderful, the planet back on its axis, and the easy way Arran had met and seamlessly bonded with Colm and Nora had added to Kenzie's joy.

When she and Arran had a video call with Glenn to tell

him what was happening, Glenn had leapt from his seat and punched the air.

'Thank you. That's what I've been waiting for. *Finally.*' He'd beamed at the camera. 'Honestly, the best news of the year, you two.'

Kenzie had laughed and blown him a kiss.

'Your appointment as Funcle Glenn is firmly endorsed, by the way.' Arran had given Glenn a thumbs-up. 'Just no beer or gambling until he's twenty-one.'

Glenn had laughed. 'Right-o. I think I can manage that.'

He had said he'd come back for a weekend soon, and as they'd ended the call, Kenzie had had a moment of clarity that now, a few days later, she was ready to share with Arran.

He was sitting in the living room with his back to the window reading the news on his phone. The mid-May morning was bright, and, in the distance, Ben Nevis loomed, majestic as ever.

Over the past weeks, Kenzie had found that she'd been able to look at the mountain without the customary flash of anger, her bitterness dissolving the closer she got to Jack's arrival.

As she passed behind Arran, her hand trailing over his shoulder, she stood at the window and took in the scene, a lacy stretch of cloud reaching around the summit, and the upper slopes snow-capped as they remained much of the year.

Behind her, Arran put his phone down and got up.

'You OK?' He walked over to her, then his arms circled her from behind.

'Yes, I am.' She leaned back against his chest. 'I have something I'd like you to do with me.'

'Sure. What is it?'

'I spoke to Glenn about Olivia's ashes, and he wants me to scatter them somewhere that I choose.'

'Really? He doesn't want to do it?'

'No. He said that he thinks it would have made Olivia happy if I did it.'

Arran moved to her side. 'So, where do you have in mind?'

She pointed at the mountain, her finger steady as she studied the lower slopes that she, Olivia and their parents had walked on so often, as a family. 'There. Where she was happiest.'

Arran looked over his shoulder at her, then took her hand in his.

'I think that's the perfect place.' He kissed the back of her hand. 'When do you want to do it?'

'Tomorrow. I'd like to do it before I'm the size of a barge and can't get up there.' She laughed softly.

'Can I ask, why now?'

Kenzie turned to face him. 'It's time. I need to make space in here for happiness, and the last part of doing that is forgiveness.' She patted her chest.

'Forgiveness?' He squinted at her.

'Yes. I'm ready to forgive the mountain now, because if I can't do that, then I can't live my life with pure joy.' Her eyes filled, so she looked back at the hills, finally letting their beauty back into her heart.

'Well, I think that's wise, and brave.'

'I've hated it for so long. For taking my parents, then Olivia, too, but letting that go is freeing, and, Arran, I want to be free of what's passed, all the secrets, and hurt, the lies and betrayals. From now on, we look forwards. There is so much to look forward *to*, I don't want to miss any of it.'

He turned her to face him, leaned in and pressed his lips to hers. 'I'm with you. Every step of the way.'

Kenzie cupped his face in her palms, taking in the chiselled jaw, the gentle eyes, the wide mouth, all the parts of his face that made him hers. 'I love you, Arran Ford.'

He blinked, a single tear escaping from the side of his eye.

'I love you right back, Kenzie Ford.'

She rose onto tiptoe and kissed him again, feeling the tip of his tongue touch hers. There was nothing that they couldn't do together, and the next phase of their lives was bursting with promise, little Jack bringing yet another facet of love to their relationship.

They were a family again, and more than that, neither Kenzie nor Olivia could have wished for.

EPILOGUE
DECEMBER

Kenzie settled Jack into the stroller, his puffy zip-up suit the same striking azure colour as his eyes. At three months old, his sandy hair was beginning to thicken, his full cheeks were a healthy pink, and his tiny nose turned up ever so slightly at the end, giving him an elf-like appearance.

Seeing a telltale glistening on his upper lip, she pulled a tissue out of her pocket and wiped his nose, chasing his face as he turned it from side to side.

'Keep still, you little monkey.' She laughed.

Behind her, Arran was putting on his padded ski jacket, his black woollen hat already pulled tightly over his ears.

'He's a bloke. We don't like to be fussed.' He wiggled his eyebrows at her. 'Are you ready?'

'Yes.' She tucked the fleecy blanket around Jack's thighs, then zipped the outer cover over his legs. 'All set.'

Arran edged behind her, taking a canvas shopping bag out of the hall cupboard.

'Last-minute shopping before Funcle Glenn arrives, Jack-o.' He hung the bag over one of the handles on the stroller as

Kenzie wrapped her long tartan scarf around her neck, then tucked the ends into the collar of her navy pillow coat.

Their two-bedroom flat was three streets up the hill from the harbour in Bryggen, and the long picture window in the airy living room framed the view of the waterfront that had captured Kenzie's heart the first time she'd visited. The living area was open plan, and sparsely furnished compared to the house in Inverlochy, but the natural wood furniture, tan leather sofas, scattering of thick rugs made by a local artisan and the wood-burning stove churning away in the corner, all made the space warm and homely.

They had settled in quickly when they'd arrived in November and now, having Glenn coming for Christmas, Kenzie felt their new place would feel even more like home with him in it. Their little family complete.

They all planned on travelling back to Inverlochy together, to bring in the new year with Colm and Nora. Weekly video calls had kept them connected – Nora ending each one the exact same way by counting the sleeps until their visit, then leaning in and kissing the screen as Colm laughed and waved from behind her.

'Right, you two. Let's go before the best fish and veggies are all gone.' Looking forward to the walk down the hill to browse at the weekend farmer's market on the wharf, Kenzie manoeuvred the stroller into the narrow hall, as Arran opened the front door, then stood aside to let her pass.

As they walked out into the street, the dry cold snatching at her breath, Kenzie smiled at the wreath that Arran had hung on the front door, the long lengths of golden wheat twined into a plait, with some dark-green ribbon at the base in a large bow.

They'd enjoyed buying some new tree decorations in the local shops, a selection of various-sized paper baskets called *julekurver*, that they'd hung on the small tree in the corner of the living room the night before. Kenzie had felt only momentarily sad as she'd recalled the box containing her half of the family decorations that she and Olivia had shared, now tucked under the stairs back at home in Inverlochy.

As Kenzie moved the stroller onto the pavement, Arran leaned in and pushed Jack's wool hat higher up his forehead.

'There you go, pal. Can't have you missing anything.'

Kenzie smiled at her husband, his eyes full of affection as he looked down at their son. Arran's initial nerves around Jack had eased over time and now, he was as confident with the little boy as Kenzie had been from the very first moment Doctor Kennedy had put Jack in her arms.

'So, what's on the list?' She walked along the road, waving at their neighbour, Nils Storstein, an elderly man who was filling a bird feeder that hung on the outside of his window.

'Not much. A few bits of food, a bottle of gløgg for Glenn's stocking, and some more nappies for his nibs.' Arran nodded at Jack, who was making a gurgling sound, gooey bubbles forming on his rosy mouth.

Kenzie smiled, the way Arran's hand lingered on Jack's cheek sending a shiver of happiness through her, a reminder of everything that they had together, and everything that they had overcome. 'Perfect.'

She heard the familiar, long calling of the great black-eyed gulls that inhabited the wharf, the ack ack ack of the indigenous scavengers having become as much a part of her day now as the common gulls were back home, in Fort William.

'What time does Glenn's flight get in?'

Arran moved back to her side, his right hand settling in close to hers on the handle of the stroller. 'Eleven forty-five.' He slung his left arm around her shoulder, then pulled her into his side. 'It'll be good to have him here for a few days. I've missed him.'

Kenzie leaned into her husband's side, just as Jack let out

another shrill squeal, his chubby arms batting the top of the cover over his legs.

'Someone's excited to see their Funcle Glenn.' Arran laughed, his arm tightening around Kenzie's shoulder. 'It'll be great to have the family together for Christmas, won't it?'

For a second, Kenzie felt slightly jarred, like there was something critical missing from his picture of family, then, seeing her sister's face, the gentle smile, the wide-set eyes, duplicates of her own, Kenzie swallowed over the knot of sadness gathering in her throat.

'Yes, it will.' She looked up at Arran, the weight of his arm around her an anchor that grounded her in her new life. 'Olivia would have loved it here.'

Arran's arm relaxed and he moved slightly to the side of the stroller. 'She would.' He looked down at Kenzie. 'She's here, you know. In everything we do, and see, and experience.'

Kenzie nodded, the thought comforting. 'Yes, she is. And she always will be.'

They took a second to lock eyes, then Jack squealed again, breaking the silence as they crossed the street and headed for the harbour, the winter morning bright, welcoming them to the day, and to their future, as a family, wherever that took them.

A LETTER FROM ALISON

Dear reader,

My heartfelt thanks for reading *My Sister's Only Hope*. I hope you enjoyed it. If you would like to keep up to date with all my latest releases, just sign up at the following link. Your email address will never be shared, and you can unsubscribe at any time.

www.bookouture.com/alison-ragsdale

While this is a story about loss, it is also about the unbreakable bonds of sisterhood. Kenzie and Olivia have a precious connection that was forged in their early life and made stronger by the mutual loss of their parents. As adults, their bond strengthens until it transcends the challenges of long-held secrets, betrayal and even death. In creating their close relationship, I was inspired by my connection with my own sisters, my best friends for life.

Thanks again for choosing to read *My Sister's Only Hope*. If you enjoyed it, I'd be so grateful if you would take a moment to write a review. They are a great way to introduce new readers to my books.

I love to hear from my readers, and you can connect with me through through social media or my website. I look forward to hearing from you.

All the best,

Alison Ragsdale

www.alisonragsdale.com

facebook.com/authoralisonragsdale
x.com/AlisonRagsdale
instagram.com/alisonragsdalewrites

ACKNOWLEDGEMENTS

Thank you to my stellar publisher, Bookouture. I am fortunate to work with such a talented, and professional group. Special thanks to my editor, Jess, for her guidance and flawless instincts, and for encouraging me to keep delving into the make-up of these characters, to bring even more emotional depth to their story.

Thanks also to Noelle, Mandy, Imogen, Saidah, Celine, Jade, Anne, and everyone who helped this story make its way into the world. It takes a village was never a truer statement.

Thank you also to all the friends, readers, reviewers, book bloggers, my Highlanders Club members and ARC crew who support me and my books. You are all an essential part of my writing life, and I treasure every one of you.

Finally, to my brilliant husband. There isn't a single day that passes when I'm not grateful for you.

PUBLISHING TEAM

Turning a manuscript into a book requires the efforts of many people. The publishing team at Bookouture would like to acknowledge everyone who contributed to this publication.

Commercial
Lauren Morrissette
Hannah Richmond
Imogen Allport

Cover design
Emma Graves

Data and analysis
Mark Alder
Mohamed Bussuri

Editorial
Jess Whitlum-Cooper
Imogen Allport

Copyeditor
Jade Craddock

Proofreader
Anne O'Brien

Marketing
Alex Crow
Melanie Price
Occy Carr
Cíara Rosney
Martyna Młynarska

Operations and distribution
Marina Valles
Stephanie Straub
Joe Morris

Production
Hannah Snetsinger
Mandy Kullar
Ria Clare
Nadia Michael

Publicity
Kim Nash
Noelle Holten
Jess Readett
Sarah Hardy

Rights and contracts
Peta Nightingale
Richard King
Saidah Graham

RAISING READERS
Books Build Bright Futures

Dear Reader,

We'd love your attention for one more page to tell you about the crisis in children's reading, and what we can all do.

Studies have shown that reading for fun is the **single biggest predictor of a child's future life chances** – more than family circumstance, parents' educational background or income. It improves academic results, mental health, wealth, communication skills, ambition and happiness.

The number of children reading for fun is in rapid decline. Young people have a lot of competition for their time, and a worryingly high number do not have a single book at home.

Hachette works extensively with schools, libraries and literacy charities, but here are some ways we can all raise more readers:

- Reading to children for just 10 minutes a day makes a difference
- Don't give up if children aren't regular readers – there will be books for them!

- Visit bookshops and libraries to get recommendations
- Encourage them to listen to audiobooks
- Support school libraries
- Give books as gifts

There's a lot more information about how to encourage children to read on our websites: **www.RaisingReaders.co.uk** and **www.JoinRaisingReaders.com**.

Thank you for reading.

Printed in Dunstable, United Kingdom